Horrors of the Deep

Startling Sea Stories

Edited by Franklin Ard

Rogue Owl Press

Horrors of the Deep

First edition. July 25th, 2023.

ISBN: 979-8-9873401-3-4

Edited by Franklin Ard

Contents

Introduction   1

Saitan Reef   2
by Derek B. Hoffman

The Abyss Looks Back at You   18
by Sarah Parke

The Wildwood Hog   30
by Cristina Perachio

The Thump   54
by Paul Carro

Fynn and the Infersagax vs. the Warmongers   74
by Richard Squires

The Deer Serpent   97
by Genevieve Williams

Invasive Species   110
by Karen Menzel (née Bovenmyer)

[...] at the end of a stalk   112
by John Christopher Nelson

The Keepers of Deerback Isle   126
by Joseph Carro

You Always Have a Choice 143
by Elizabeth Beechwood

Westward Wind 153
by Shane R. Collins

The Beast 168
by Rebecca McKenna

Disappearance of the Dawn Bringer 176
by Devin J. Gaither

Beauty Shimmers Before Darkness Falls 200
by Renee S. DeCamillis

Summoner 223
by Franklin Ard

Till Human Voices Wake Us 229
by Rachel Halpern

About the Authors 249

Acknowledgements 255

About the Publisher 257

Introduction

Welcome to the abyss. The ocean is a vast and mysterious place, full of secrets and terrors that we can only begin to imagine. What unites the stories in this sea-themed collection is a desire to face the unknown, an embrace of the primal and powerful emotion of fear. So come aboard, if you dare, and let us take you on a journey into the murky depths.

The sea has long been a source of mystery and trepidation for humanity. It's a place of immense beauty and wonder but also of danger and death. The sea can be cruel and unforgiving, and it can hide secrets that are better left buried. The tales herein relentlessly face what waits below, as well as the anxiety of what we cannot see or understand.

By confronting this fear of the unknown, we can discover new worlds and possibilities. This is the journey we invite you on in these dark, visceral, and emotionally resonant stories. In these pages, you'll find tales of terror that take you all the way from the stormy horizon down to the ocean floor. You'll explore the dark side of the sea and witness the horrors that it can unleash. You'll encounter creatures that defy logic and nature, as well as humans who succumb to madness and those who resist evil with all their being. From ancient sea monsters to cursed ships and haunted lighthouses, you will discover that the sea is not only a realm of water but also of blood.

And finally, we must advise you to read this book with caution—and not before bedtime. You never know what might be lurking in the dark waters...

Saitan Reef

by Derek B. Hoffman

Tayung pauses as she stands at the edge of her family's *lepa* boat. The ocean before her is uncommonly still, almost mirror-like. It is the last morning of their three days on the open sea. What little wind buffets her back is coming from the coast. It smells of burning trees. A headache will haunt her by midday, but the sunset will be worth it.

A speargun and net slung across her back, she secures a bundle of empty bottles to her waist for collecting sea cucumbers. She imagines all the fish she will catch, certainly more than her older brother.

She calls over her shoulder, "Ready Lumo?"

Instead of answering, she feels him leap off the boat. She takes a deep breath and follows.

It is cold and warm at once. Her eyes adjust to the dim light. Her body adjusts to the current. She kicks herself down to just above the reef, looking for sea cucumbers, lionfish, and urchins.

Lumo is fifty meters away, already spearing a medium-sized grouper. He kicks back up to the *lepa* to secure it before reef sharks or barracuda come to investigate.

Tayung glides above the coral, spotting a lionfish. She swims behind it and readies her net. The muscles in her chest crave a breath, but she dives after her venomous prey. The chase is short. She charges forward and nets the spiny fish. Quickly, she pivots, kicks off the rocks and exhales as she shoots up to the surface. She takes a deep breath and swims to their *lepa*.

Cahaya, her mother, opens a cooler and leans over the side, skillfully scooping up the lionfish. "Be careful, Tay. You were under for longer than usual.".

"How long?" Tayung asks, smiling.

Her mother raises an eyebrow. "Ten minutes. But you—"

Tayung dives back to the coral. She catches sight of Lumo. He holds up a sea cucumber in one hand and four fingers on the other. She taps her wrist and wags her finger, egging him on.

She spends the next few dives collecting everything on her father's list. Her family operates one of the only native boats that provide fish for the resort on Mabul. Tayung hates that the resort pays her father so little compared to what they could get on the big island, but it keeps them at sea. And her family belongs to the sea.

Her containers full, Tayung returns to the *lepa*. She passes the bottles to her mother.

"What is the nudibranch for?"

"I was going to put it back. I just thought it was pretty, like you Mama," she says with a gleaming smile.

Her mother caresses Tayung's wet hair. "I already like you best, dear one. Now, go get our dinner." She winks and shoves her daughter's head underwater.

Tayung sinks down, spinning to easily find her brother. Lumo gives her a shaka sign and waves her over.

She takes a stroke toward him when suddenly all the fish and creatures below her scatter for cover in the fields of coral. Tayung looks up at her brother as an explosive current hits, sending them barreling over the drop-off.

Bits and pieces of debris cut through the water around them. A metal shard lodges in Tayung's arm, forcing precious air from her. A large cylinder twice his size knocks into Lumo, his speargun dropping to the dark below.

She kicks to him and swims beside him to the undulating surface. There is a dark cloud blooming to the southwest.

"The *lepa* is over there!" Lumo yells and points behind her.

Their mother is already bailing water with a pot. "We need to get to Mabul. Tay—help bail. Lumo—patch."

"What about Papa and Uncle Timo? Weren't they going to meet us?" Tayung asks.

Cahaya nods.

"I can stay," Tayung says.

"Tay, you are brave, but you are bleeding. We need you alive and with us."

Obeying her mother, she pulls herself aboard. Cahaya dislodges the shard and cleans and wraps Tay's arm. Lumo surfaces from patching the bottom of the boat and starts bailing.

"I hope Papa and Uncle Timo are okay." It's a whisper. Tayung considers praying to the *jinn* like her grandfather did, but she doesn't believe and worries that would make things worse.

As Lumo raises the sail, she tries to memorize this part of the Celebes Sea so she can return. The dark cloud to the south grows across the sky, moving against the wind.

Their *lepa* limps to Mabul. There are two military boats moored close to shore.

"They look fast," Lumo says.

Their mother squints. "They aren't welcome here. They took out six of the Bajau-Dilaut *lepas* last year."

"Is that what happened to your cousins?" Tayung asks.

Lumo flicks the back of her head, making a shushing sound.

Cahaya tightens her grip on the rudder. "I will stay here. You two go to your Aunt Lena, trade the catch for what we need. Be back before sunset."

"What about—"

"I will find Papa and Timo. They know to come here."

The siblings leave with their hands and shoulders full.

The island feels anxious. Tayung and Lumo overhear other fishers and workers at the resorts talking about the explosion, the cloud, and the military. The gossip is that pirates blew up a navy vessel. The superstitious ones talk about strange waters and stranger fish in the catches.

They scamper through the maze of dive shops, tourist restaurants, and native shanties. Tayung leads them down a narrow alley. Almost to the other end, Lumo looks both ways before opening the hidden door to Lena's kitchen.

The smell of incense hits Tayung, reminding her of how much her head hurts. The smoke swirls to the chimney above several folding tables and a basin sink. A wood fire box smolders in the corner. She feels the heat in the air. Her aunt has a wrap around her and *burak* covers her face, even though Lena rarely sees the sun anymore.

"Is it true? The pirates hitting a Malay ship?" Lumo asks Aunt Lena.

"Only the sea knows. All I know is that you must have left your manners in the *lepa* with your mother," Lena says as she takes the bottles and coolers of fish from her niece and nephew.

"I'm sorry, Auntie," Lumo says. He grabs a broom and begins to sweep as an apology.

"It is true that the military is here to spread the word that they want wreckage found—two *ringgits* per piece," Lena says as she cleans and transfers their catch. "They're also looking for anyone who was in the water."

"Oh," Tayung lets slip.

"Yes. You need to both be careful," Lena eyes Tayung's freshly bandaged arm. "Even with all the changes, this is new. They rarely take interest in us or this island. But one of the diving boats and its guests is missing. And my friend at the resort said that they were asking about your father."

"What?!" Tayung says.

"I will not say you have nothing to worry about. You are too old for that lie. But your father, Qawi, is capable. He married my sister, and she would settle for nothing less." Lena separates packs of steamed rice, sliced eel, and water weed, then hands them to Tayung. "Take your list to Noah at *The Coral Ape*. He won't ask questions. Be careful. And tell my sister to come ashore next time."

Lumo disappears out the front door as Lena turns back to the basin. Tayung approaches her. Lena shivers in the heat even as sweat drips from her face. She brushes aside a lock of her black hair and peers into a small mirror at the bottom of the sink.

Tay watches her scan every speck and reflection. The shaman told Lena that she would see her children again, but she had to keep looking, so she barely ever stops. Tay touches her back. She takes a cloth to wipe Lena's forehead. She hugs her gently before following Lumo. "*Palanjal na aku.*"

The Coral Ape is bright and freshly painted. Every T-shirt folded neatly. The floor swept clean of sand. Tourists from Malaysia, Australia, and beyond congregate at the café. The chatter and sheer number of people jars Tayung after being at sea. She follows Lumo to the office door. He knocks and enters.

Noah sits in a swivel chair tapping at a TV filled with broken lines. Though he is much older, Tay still notices his thin, muscular build from freediving. He was the island's best fisherman until her father started trading on his own.

"Noah?" Lumo says.

He keeps tapping the TV. The sound of static mixes with the waves. Lumo knocks on the wood desk.

Noah spins around and smiles. "Lumo! Tay! So good to see you safe!" His hair is almost gone except for a peppered mustache. Dark glasses cover his eyes. An ancient hearing aid covers his right ear. All the old divers punctured their ear drums when they were kids, causing deafness if they lived long enough.

"We have a list from our mother. Lena said you would help."

"Ah, yes. Yes." He takes the paper from Lumo and scans it quickly. "I have all of this. I'm assuming you were out there when the big boom hit? You need root fiber and tar to fix leaks, yeah?"

Tay and Lumo nod.

"Tell no one else. It was not pirates, but pirates are here now." Noah paces his office as he gets more animated. "Hundreds of giant clams were just found in the channel north of Omadal Island. They were all over 200 kilos! They should be on the Great Barrier!" Noah throws his hands up. "Anyway, pirates raided those fishing vessels within an hour. Now they are looking for whatever the Navy seeks." He points to the marine radio in the corner. "If you ask me, it is a *saitan*. I know your family does not believe the tales of the sea demons, but the water is not right. Don't you feel it?"

Tay nods again.

"Good girl. You both are young, but you live the sea. It is not like this—not supposed to be like this. Someone has made the *jinn* angry. All of them." He shakes his head. "I'm sorry. You don't need an old man's worries! I will get these and put them in a bag by the swill can out back. Go directly to your *lepa* with purpose. Do not let the Navy or police question you."

The siblings look at each other then nod to Noah, "*Aho', magsukul.*"

After they clear the storefront, Lumo pauses. "What is going on?"

"It feels like adults being adults. They make a mistake and blame everyone but themselves," Tay says.

"Don't be sour. It may be that, but the thing that hit me in the water, it had a mark on it. I thought it was a surf mark because of the curves and points. I was wrong. I looked it up."

"On what?" Tay asks.

Lumo holds up a phone in a thick case.

"Did you *steal* that?!"

"Quiet! No! But I may have speared a few things I was not supposed to."

"*Lumo*! That could get us arrested or Papa's license revoked."

"I know. It was just one—well, two times. I had to see what all the fuss was about. And this time, it is worth it. Look…" He holds the screen to her face.

"What is it? It looks like an angry octopus," Tay says.

"A biohazard. I don't know what that means, but I think it can hurt the fish. And us. And it landed right near the reef."

"We need to tell someone!"

Lumo rests his hand on her shoulder. "Wait, sister. Let's find it, *then* tell someone and get paid."

"That is dumb. Do you think they will let us just boat off? Do you remember what they did to our fishers? We are worth nothing to them. And we don't follow their ways. We don't follow the ways of most of our people either." Tay puts the sacks of food down and squeezes her brother. "We aren't welcome here. That's why we can't leave the sea."

"I thought it was because Papa wanted to follow the old ways," Lumo says. A tear falls on Tay's shoulder.

"That is what Mama said, but Lena told me the rest of the truth last time we were here with Timo."

Noah drops the bag outside. They take it and head to the beach. The sunset does not disappoint, though the southern sky is covered in billowing black clouds. Tay knows they are not filled with rain.

They reach the end of the stilt houses and head toward the lee side of the island. Tay sees someone point them out to a Naval officer.

"Lumo, they know we are here. Take the duffel from *The Coral Ape*. Swim out then under. Hold your breath until you are on the sea-side of our *lepa*. Start repairs. I will take the rest and lead them off to the west. We will meet past the first break to the south. It may be for nothing, but I don't want them to touch us."

"*Pahala '*, sister."

Tayung turns from her brother and fast-walks up steps to a series of wooden walkways. She knows at the third turn she can sprint left and slide down the last post to the water below. She hears the heavy footfalls of both officers following her. *Good*. She picks up her pace to just short of a run. Tay controls her breath, preparing for a long dive.

She breaks left into a sprint. The footsteps behind her stumble into a run. She dodges a young mother and her baby. Tay leaps for the pole at the end and swings around, landing with her arms encircling it and feet ready to shimmy down to the sea. As soon as she touches the water, she slides in and dives deep, finding the current.

Tay hooks low and under the coral line, hoping not to be spotted. She kicks harder, knowing she must clear the ridge before hitting the open sea.

She is aware of the food she carries and what it can attract. It helps her swim faster.

Minutes pass and Tayung hasn't reached the ridge. She is tired and her lungs burn.

The seascape shifts in front of her, and she stops. An eye opens from the middle of the coral. It stares at her, holds her sight. The features around it turn reddish orange and the octopus shoots toward Tay.

She stumbles backward. The creature stretches out its arms and puffs up its head.

You shouldn't be here, big boy. You belong up north. Way up north.

The octopus is easily bigger than her father. Tay is amazed and a little frightened. At this last thought, the cephalopod pulls back, spins, and shoots off like a missile, right over the ridge.

Tay surfaces and sees her father already reaching for her. He pulls her from the water with one arm. The other is cut bad and bleeding. Uncle Timo puts a towel around her. Damp, red bandages take the place of his right hand.

"I know you have questions, but we must get to your mother and Lumo." Her father says, guiding the *lepa* as Uncle Timo adjusts the sail.

Tayung looks to the south as the last rays of light reach above the horizon. Darkness fills half the sky now. It pushes toward them as lightning silhouettes distant islands.

Lumo and Cahaya tie the boats together while Timo and Qawi set up motors for both *lepas*.

"They aren't traditional, but I'm not sure we can trust the wind anymore," Qawi says.

Tay wants to ask him what happened. She wants to ask about the clouds, anything they know. She already knows that the quiet life they led is over. She has no idea why. "I saw a giant red octopus on the reef before you found me," she blurts.

Qawi and Uncle Timo look at each other, uneasy.

"It is like the ones we saw far to the north, beyond all of our home waters."

"Cahaya?" Qawi says.

She nods to him and serves bowls of warm rice and eel.

"We are sailing around the southern tip of the Ligitan sandbar then circling back north to where you were fishing when the explosion happened," Qawi says before scooping some food to his mouth. "I know we could cut by the dive resort, but that is how Timo and I came upon trouble."

Tay notices Uncle Timo huddled in the bow, shaking. The sea breeze is hot all day and night.

"We had just pulled in our nets. A flare went up. Between the surface current and the wind funneled between the northern islands, we got to them quick." Qawi hands his bowl to Cahaya, bowing to her. "What we saw was no good."

Uncle Timo cries out.

"The crew were pulling parts of divers onto the boat. Blood was everywhere. We called out as we neared, but they waved us off. Then the orcas hit. I've never seen them over the reefs before. And these ones weren't aggressive, they were mad. They rammed that boat until it, and everyone aboard, was in the water. The screams. The sounds they—"

"That's enough, dear," Cahaya stops him. "I'm sorry for them and for you, but we must look forward. Why do you want to go where we were fishing? Shouldn't we go to land?"

"*The Eyes of Bajau*," Uncle Timo croaks out.

Cahaya throws up her hands. "Not this nonsense again."

"He will rise again, and he will need his sight!" Uncle Timo yells.

"Enough!" Qawi says. "Whatever is happening, we are but small pieces in it. We must continue to do what is right. As we went to meet you, I searched below the sea to make sure your *lepa* hadn't fallen victim to the orcas as well. I was thankful not to see you, but I did see something else. The coral had turned white."

"How?" Tay asks. "You couldn't have been but hours behind."

"Exactly. Something is there. If we can stop it, or learn more to help others, we should," Qawi says.

"What about wisdom?" Cahaya asks. "You speak of doing what is right, but what of doing what is wise? I don't doubt what you saw, or its importance, but it sounds bigger than us. It seems like we are about to pull a shark's fin without a spear."

"Always the wisest among us, my beautiful Cahaya," Qawi says. He leans in and kisses her forehead. "Thank you for your counsel. We'll spend the night on the sandbar."

Lumo and Tayung ready the boats. Tayung grabs her towel and settles in the stern of the *lepa*. Lumo slides a cooler over to sit by Tay's feet.

"What do you think we should do?" her brother asks.

"I want to do good and help people, but what can we do? What help is there to give? I held my hand overboard while we ate. The water doesn't feel right. I don't know how else to say it. It is not a feeling, but a *feeling*." Tay wraps herself further in her towel.

Lumo nods. "There are too many strange things happening in the ocean. I've never seen them this worried. And Timo is cracking."

"Not cracking, but he is scared. It is why he speaks of *Bajau*—the great giant who rose from the sea, pouring fish into the empty nets of those who would be known as his people. Why wouldn't he want to believe in that? I want to. But whatever is happening with the sea and sky, I don't think even *Bajau* could save us this time."

They sit in silence, eyes and hearts heavy with exhaustion. Lumo flashes a shaka. Tay signs one back.

The boat sways in the blue-gray light of dawn stars and the growing storm.

"You were born at sea. On this very *lepa*. I held you above the ocean like you were its queen. But we know the sea. We know that even at its most calm, she will never be ruled by, or even have need of us," Qawi whispers as he gently touches his daughter's feet. "Though Lumo was first, you made me realize that it was not a risk, a weakness, to have children in these times. It was not an honor either. It was not even a gift. It was simply what was meant to be. From the beginning of time to this moment. There may have been choices, but this was always the path we would take."

Qawi looks up at the stars. Over half the sky is missing now. The clouds seem emboldened by the lack of sunlight and fire lightning bolt after lightning bolt from heaven to sea.

"I have never seen the waters like this. The fish act without wisdom or sense. Some are not supposed to be here, and so many are angry. We could go to land. We could flee to the north. Yet there is something in me that believes we were meant to be here, now, on our way to a dying reef..."

"But you are asleep, and I am feeling old and at an end that may not be an end. Just know, I love you, Tayung."

"I love you, too, Papa," she reaches for his hand and sits up. "I will always go with you. My world is this family. If it is the end, then why wouldn't I want to be with you all?"

He presses her hand between both of his. "Thank you, daughter."

Qawi awakens everyone with a flute song. Tayung lays back, breathing in the heavy morning air tinged with smoke. She twists to drape her arm over the stern to feel the water. The flat of a spear slaps her hand. Uncle Timo stands by the cooler at her feet. He shakes his head, then leans over and pierces the water. A three-meter-long box jelly writhes on the tip.

"*Saitan lagtaw*," he whispers.

Tay wonders why her uncle speaks of the large demon known for tearing people in half. She peers over the rim and sees thousands of box jellies surrounding the *lepas*. Each ripple carries stingers that can stop a heart. *Perhaps he is not as off as Lumo thought.*

She takes a deep breath and realizes the smoke has changed. There is something metallic about it now. She closes her eyes and refocuses on the sound of the flute. Her father is good, but the notes can't quite carry away what eats at the air to the south. *It's not far now.*

They sail north, passing out of the jellyfish bloom. Everyone busies themselves in a quiet routine, preparing the *lepas* for what they all know may be their last dive. They pause on their approach to the last sandbar and count five beached great whites, caught by the low tide and shredding their scales as they writhe on the reef. Their deadly mouths remain open, as if they are trying to breathe without gills. Seagulls circle above the grand hunters, waiting to feast.

Qawi holds Cahaya, gently moves the hair away from her ear and whispers. She kisses him. Tay thinks it is a goodbye. It hurts her heart. She pushes a breath out with the thought of her parents gone...or worse.

"Do we have a plan?" Timo asks.

"Not one known to us, but there is a plan," Qawi says.

"Papa, Lumo and I think that there is something in the drop-off, just past the southeastern reef. It knocked into him. It was big. We think it had something in it. Something like poison. But maybe much worse."

"Then that is where we start. Are you ready for that kind of dive? You know what happened last time. We can't afford that now," Qawi says.

Tay nods. "I'm ready, Papa."

He nods to his daughter, turns to Lumo. "I love you both. All of you. Thank you for sharing in this life."

"To the end!" They all yell.

Tay and Lumo strap diving knives to their legs. Uncle Timo hands Lumo his hand-carved, driftwood spear. "It is no gun, but it will still do the work."

Lumo taps it on the side of the *lepa's* hull. "Thank you, Uncle." He dives in.

Tay straps a second knife around her waist. "To the end," she whispers, tossing herself backward into the water.

The sea feels electrified and anxious again. They swim silently to the reef. The currents pull and push them differently than yesterday. It is harder to kick. She feels sluggish, no longer gliding and free.

They take deep breaths and dive. An underwater current knocks into her as soon as she hits ten meters. It stings her skin. She looks for more jellies as pink blisters bloom across her arms, belly, and legs. There is nothing around them.

As they crest the last ridge before the reef, Lumo catches her eye and points down. The coral is dead as far as the eye can see. There is nothing alive. Not a single carcass, no bones, not even the base of an anemone, not a thing that proves this was alive and thriving the day before. It was as if every ounce of life had been sucked off the reef.

Tay and Lumo return to the surface as Qawi joins them.

"How bad?" he asks.

Tay shakes her head. "The entire reef is gone."

"Then we must dive. Take these." Qawi throws them lights to strap to their heads. "Check the ledges first. Conserve your strength. Stay close." He flashes a shaka and sinks beneath the waves.

The three of them ride a surging current over the edge and begin searching for a cause for the bleaching. They fan across the drop-off.

Tay hadn't seen it from above the reef, but she notices bright lines of silver cutting across and into the rockface. She traces the cracks to a ledge jutting out from the shelf thirty meters below.

Lumo gets there first. He tinks the end of Timo's spear against a large metal object embedded in the cliff, a dark cylinder that's been torn open. He points to the biohazard symbol. It's part of the canister that hit him. Tay and Qawi swim closer.

As they near the ledge, Tayung hears something below the ocean noise. She signals her family, tapping her ear and pointing to the container. She hones in on the sound. Grinding like a parrotfish eating coral, it begins to grow louder.

She kicks herself closer. Her mind feels like it is vibrating.

Another determined kick.

A rattle starts at the base of her skull. Thrumming waves press into her, squeezing her mind and lungs.

She hovers just above the ledge. Her brother seems unfazed by the sound. She studies the canister. It has an American flag on it and writing in their alphabet. She was wrong about it being torn open. It looks like whatever was inside exploded. All that's left is a strange silver liquid that drips to the rock and flows into a cave in the shelf break.

A pool of the silver liquid shimmers at the cave entrance. She turns on her light. It reflects from inside the cave—mirrored walls...and something else.

Lumo pokes the pool with the spear. It begins to spin, and the shiny liquid runs up the blade, then the wood. Lumo lets go, but the spear remains upright. The shimmer envelopes it and quickly sucks it into the mirror.

The grinding in Tay's head stops.

With a sudden wailing, the spear explodes from the mirror, shooting to the surface.

Before she can look up, a giant tentacle wraps around Lumo. The mirror comes alive. Quicksilver swarms out of it and over his face. Tayung grabs the tentacle holding him and plunges in her knife. The tentacle releases, spinning its focus toward her, emerging and rising over the ledge. Another arm grabs Lumo as he pulls at the material covering his mouth, nose, and eyes. A shadow covers them all as a giant squid, easily the size of ten men, crawls above the ledge. The second tentacle squeezes. She watches Lumo's breath get pushed out. His face freezes, then the silver disappears into his mouth. Another squeeze. He tries to spit out the silver.

The creature's eyes turn to her as she reaches for her speargun. Its beak clicks as it snaps shut. It pulls Lumo's body closer to its mouth. He doesn't struggle anymore.

Tay aims for its left eye and fires. The spear hits its target. But instead of letting go of Lumo, the squid rips him in half and sucks him inside.

In a moment, Tay's world freezes. She holds back her cry, struggling to keep the air in her lungs. Part of her doesn't want to.

Another spear glides past her head, piercing the other eye of the huge squid. A jet of ink begins to darken the waters. Qawi swims to his daughter. He grabs for her, but the quicksilver begins to swirl like a death cloud. The tips of his fingers catch Tay as the ink blinds them. Qawi pulls Tay close, wrapping her in his big frame as the darkness envelops them. She hears and feels the bits of silver ripping at his skin.

The ink clears the maelstrom, and she helplessly watches her father get picked apart and consumed by this horrible—*saitan.*

In seconds, the toxic cloud extends for as far as she can see, consuming all life. It even destroys the giant squid. There is no trace of Lumo or her father. Tayung simply floats. Heartbroken. Shocked. Is she all that is left alive?

Click. Click. Click.

A new sound grows, punching back against the cloud.

At the edges of light, dark masses line up vertically—a circle of sperm whales. They groan angry and wild, fighting back against the demon.

Their sonic waves pound and pound, until blood trickles from Tay's eardrums.

She squints from the pain and hears the cave and ledge begin to crack. Streams of bubbles release, following a great line in the rock. The ocean floor splits, from the deep up to the reef, into a giant crevasse, sucking in an avalanche of sand, bits, and swirling water. The silver reabsorbs into a shivering, stuttering mass, grabbing for the ridge. Trying to survive. But the abyss is too powerful.

Tay feels her eyes closing as the current pulls her down as well. Her mind spins and her lungs let go.

Da'a busung.

The Abyss Looks Back at You

by Sarah Parke

Off the coast of southern Spain, October 1805

T he sky was still bruise-colored when Archibald Gilchrist woke to find Lieutenant Commander Rochefort peering down at him at the bottom of the ship's dinghy.

"Gilchrist, the Vice Admiral requests your presence in his quarters." Rochefort eyed Archibald's slovenly appearance with distaste. Archibald knew what he saw: two days' worth of stubble above a standard Navy-issued wool coat flecked with vomit and a film of salt from a night spent on deck. By contrast, Rochefort's uniform and hair (or what was left of it) was impeccably brushed without a speck of lint.

Archibald cared little for winning the approval of the French or Spanish officers in the fleet. He had little regard for the navy in general. It didn't matter that the men distrusted him, calling him traitor. Turncoat. Napoleon Bonaparte had chosen Archibald for this campaign because of his magic-wielding ability and his familiarity with British naval vessels. The only man in the whole damned ocean that Archibald had to answer to was the Vice Admiral, which was the sole reason he summoned the energy to sit up in his make-shift bunk. The liquid contents of his stomach sloshed like the sea in a storm. His head was also spinning, but it helped counterbalance the rocking of the ship beneath him. His foot kicked a pyramid of empty bottles as he climbed out of the dinghy. Slowly, he straightened his spine until his head brushed the rigging. Rochefort had already spun on his booted heel and was striding across the deck, assuming Archibald would follow.

All around the *Bucentaure* dozens of square-rigged warships were anchored bow-to-stern, forming a blockade for as far as the eye could see off the coast of Trafalgar. Vice Admiral Villenueve commanded a combined French and Spanish fleet of more than thirty ships, five frigates, and two brigs. Gulls cried and shouts carried from one deck to another across the floating wall. Thirty-thousand men awaited orders to decimate the British fleet.

Crew members emerged from their quarters below-deck to begin their duties. No one raised their eyes to meet Archibald's gaze. Even after weeks together aboard the *Bucentaure*, most of the crew still crossed themselves or spat into the sea whenever Archibald came upon them. As if their silly superstitions were any defense against his magic.

He itched for a change of clothes and a shave, but before he could duck into his private cabin, he saw the men—all senior officers—gathered in the Vice Admiral's quarters down the hall. Something was wrong. An unexpected setback for the campaign was the only plausible reason for summoning the men together at such an hour. Archibald sighed. His daily ablutions would have to wait.

Archibald was the last to file into the Vice Admiral's dim cabin. The door closed behind him. The cabinet bed had been folded away to make space for the men who gathered around the table at the center of the room. The bronze and brass chandelier suspended over the table threw Vice Admiral Villenueve's face into harsh relief as he studied the wooden miniatures of the French and Spanish fleets that had been positioned on a map across from the British Royal

Navy ships like pieces on a chessboard. The officers flanking him were already speaking in low, urgent voices, gesturing to the British line.

The room was warm, a fire crackling in the hearth made the wood-paneled cabin smell like linseed oil. Archibald's mouth tasted sour.

"Admiral Gravina, what news?" Villeneuve asked.

"Nelson directs his ships toward our flank," the Sicillian replied.

Angry murmurs rose in response.

Sweat dripped down Archibald's spine. He drifted toward the gallery of windows at the far end of the cabin and opened the glass. The black shapes dotting the horizon off the stern were larger than the day before. If he squinted, he could make out individual ships forming three separate columns.

A gust of cool, salted air dried the perspiration on his face. He detested enclosed spaces. It was why he preferred sleeping out on the deck instead of in the private cabin that had been provided for him. He had been at sea too many weeks. This journey marked the longest time he had spent aboard a ship since...

Months in the ship's brig, his feet festering in ankle-deep bilge water, his body growing weaker from moldy rations. The crack of thunder and the ship run aground. Trapped in the dark as water flooded through the holes in the hull...

Archibald still had nightmares about that night.

If the forthcoming battle was won and Archibald proved himself indispensable to Bonaparte's new empire, then he'd never have to live onboard a ship ever again.

"Let Nelson break his ships against our blockade," said Villeneuve. "Ready the guns to fire upon them when they get within range."

"With respect, Vice Admiral," Admiral Gravina replied. "The ships themselves will cause more damage than our guns. We can pick them off at a distance, but if they manage to break through the line and surround us, we'll lose the tactical advantage."

Silence fell around the cabin.

"Thankfully, we have in our possession a weapon that Lord Nelson does not," Villenueve said.

Archibald felt rather than saw the moment all eyes landed upon him. His shoulders tensed as he turned to face the room. His fear still felt fresh. He couldn't let the other men see.

"Well, War-Lock," the Vice Admiral said, "The time has come for you to justify the Emperor's faith in you. What is your plan?" The words were spoken with such irreverence, as if Archibald was being asked to perform a parlor trick. The other men around the table smirked at one another.

Their insouciance angered Archibald. He ignored the pounding in his head and the nausea that always plagued him at sea. He turned his focus inward, to the source of power coiled in his gut, and he slowly let it unfurl. Energy flooded his veins, arcing from the joints of his body with crackling light. He let it burn in his eyes as he glowered at the officers around the table and he took a small pleasure at their horrified expressions. Rochefort whimpered.

The Emperor had given Archibald carte blanche to use his magic as he saw fit. But before today he had not seen the point in demonstrating his full ability for the crew. These men knew nothing about Dark Magic, but they were about to bear witness to its terrible power.

"I will summon a great beast from the depths of the sea to destroy the enemy's fleet."

Villeneuve swallowed hard. "H-how do you intend to control the creature once you have summoned it?"

Archibald had summoned creatures before, but never one as big as what they required to rout the British. Magic was complex—Dark magic doubly so. Spells required focus, physical and mental strength. He was kicking himself for having drank so heavily the night before.

"The spell will bind the creature to me. It must answer to my will," he replied, his voice deepened with the timbre of magic.

"And if it doesn't?" This from Rochefort, who eyed Archibald with fear and suspicion. "What if you lose control and the beast turns on the fleet?"

Then we're all dead men, Archibald thought. Aloud he said, "Tell your men to prepare the guns."

The officers murmured among themselves, but Archibald was already striding toward the cabin door, casting about his mind for the largest, most destructive monster in his memory.

One of the first things the African shaman had taught Archibald about magic when he washed ashore was that it was impossible to create something from nothing. However, one didn't need to create a monster from scratch when so many horrifying creatures already existed in the myths and nightmares of men. Fear gave them life and power.

Fifteen minutes later, Archibald had forced down enough food to make his stomach uncomfortably full and soak up the remaining alcohol. He didn't bother changing his clothes for the spell; blood would likely ruin them anyway. His ceremonial knife bit into the flesh of his palm and blood welled up along his life line. Possession spells, like the one that would link the beast's mind and body to Archibald's, required blood to bind them. The bigger the creature, the more blood required. The War-Lock would have to act swiftly before he lost consciousness and bled out on the deck.

Magic pulsed in his veins, seeking a release. Archibald used his blood to mark out a spell circle on the wooden planks of the top deck. Villenueve, Rochefort, and a handful of other sailors stationed on the *Bucentaure* stood against the taffrail and watched in silence. The sun was nearly at its apex in the autumn sky. The air was still, as if the sea itself held its breath.

"Do not cross the circle," Archibald ordered the onlookers. To break the circle would cause his magic to flow from him unchecked. He had witnessed men burn themselves up from the inside due to carelessness. He knelt within the boundary, his power flaring just beneath his skin as his knees protested the deck's hard surface. The pain anchored him in that moment, in that body. He would need the pain to return his mind to his mortal form—assuming the spell worked.

Ignoring the pain for now, he slowed his breathing. The sound of blood dripping onto the deck was steady as a metronome.

He reached out with his power, sending it down, down, down, through the decks of the ship and the hull, deeper, into the roiling waters of the sea, and deeper still until the darkness chilled his body and the pressure squeezed a gasp of air from his lungs.

A memory surfaced, pulling at his focus.

His limbs grew weak, and he swallowed more saltwater with each gasping breath. The shore never grew any closer and the weight of his clothes, his tired limbs, were sucking him under the surface. His lungs burned for clean air...

Archibald shoved the memory aside. Focused again on his heartbeat. Gripped the tendril of magic and propelled his power deeper, blindly seeking out the beast below.

It was minutes or hours later when his power brushed against something ancient, something that the magic recognized from before the world was made.

Found, his magic whispered.

Yessss, the sea serpent replied.

The world shifted as Archibald's consciousness joined that of the ancient serpent.

They stirred against the ocean floor, their great scaled tail dislodging rock and reef. The current shifted around them as smaller, weaker creatures fled. They felt ravenous. They did not need to open their eyes to know the way to the surface. Their massive body propelled them up from the abyss until the fractured sunlight warmed the water around them, stroking their face for the first time in millennia.

Hunger.

Eyes opened to find the seas clogged with wooden vessels that reeked of sweat and shit. They slithered through the water at a speed that outpaced the fastest ships in the fleet, bearing down on a column of ships under full sail. There was a new scent in the air now, primordial and intoxicating.

Fear.

They reared out of the waves and roared, the sound shaking the sun itself. The nearest ship tried to slow, to turn off course, but it was already trapped within their massive coil. The vessel was broken to pieces before the men stopped screaming. Some clung to bits of debris or tried to swim to safety, while other men stabbed their scaled hide with rigging knives and cutlasses.

Pain.

One-by-one the men's bones snapped between their jaws. Hot, terror-spiked blood coated their throat and pooled in their belly.

More.

The metallic taste of blood made Archibald recoil against the magic tether. Memories came unbidden.

The captain's eyes lit with bloodlust as he brought the whip down upon naked backs, again and again, its sharp crack echoing off the walls of the hold.

The serpent flicked its tail against the masts of the nearest ship. The timbers splintered and fell, crushing men beneath them. The tail lashed out again, swiping men off the deck into the sea.

Like a whip, Archibald realized. He hadn't issued the beast any orders, but it acted on his memories as if it could see his innermost thoughts. The link between their consciousnesses worked both ways. He felt exhilarated by the evidence of his power; perhaps no mortal man had ever controlled such a beast before! The emotion excited the serpent, and the beast roared again, rolling itself among the waves and causing the British ships to nearly capsize.

Nelson's *HMS Victory* led the nearest column of ships. He had led the charge and would not abandon his men at the final hour. Archibald could not let him escape if it might mean the British would rally again under his flag. He had an idea.

Submerge, Archibald commanded. The beast did so willingly. Archibald counted the yards until they swam directly beneath the *Victory*. The serpent had crushed the other vessels with its powerful tail and massive jaws. But drowned men told no tales. He wanted men to bear witness, to tell stories decades from this day of the horrible monster controlled by a great War-Lock.

Rise! The serpent acted instantly, as if Archibald's wishes were its own. The War-Lock was dizzied by the speed at which the serpent shot toward the surface, hardly disturbing the waves. Archibald searched the pale, terrified expressions of the sailors cowering on deck. He spotted Nelson on the middle deck, crouched in a defensive stance with a harpoon-gun aimed at the serpent. Now, how to direct the serpent to kill the admiral?

A spear lodged itself in the serpent's exposed chest. It roared again, thrashing its body beneath the waves and making the boat pitch violently from side to side.

Pain!

Archibald felt the pain searing his own chest. Then he was thrown back into his body again, kneeling on the deck. He kept his eyes squeezed closed, but men shouted all around him. He followed the thread of power back to the serpent.

The deck of the *HMS Victory* was a hundred feet below. They heard Nelson shouting orders to his men while positioning another harpoon in his gun.

Feed, Archibald ordered the beast, picturing Nelson's torso impaled by the serpent's massive jaws.

They struck fast and bit down hard, breaking the man's spine before flinging him back down their gullet. Archibald recognized the terror in Nelson's eyes, then a moment of disbelief before his life ended. He had seen that look on men's faces before.

His friends—his co-conspirators—hung from the ship's rigging, their bodies convulsing until the light blinked out of their eyes.

No. Archibald shoved the memory aside. These men were enemy soldiers. They deserved their fate.

But the dull pain radiating in his chest had nothing to do with the head of the harpoon lodged between the serpent's plate-sized scales.

The British fleet was falling back, hoisting their sails into the wind and fleeing the scene of the massacre. The serpent had destroyed at least a dozen ships.

The beast's hunger was satiated for now, but still it toyed with the men. Archibald sensed something akin to pleasure in the beast as it batted them around in the waves and tossed them against ship debris with its tail. The drowning men stared up at the serpent, clinging to one another and crying in terror.

Dark faces crowded together in the bowels of the ship, the whites of their eyes pleading with him. The smell of blood, shit, and human suffering choked him. Men, women, and children weeping and moaning in a hopeless, haunting dirge that woke the sailors in their bunks.

Enough, Archibald commanded. *Stop!*

But the beast ignored him.

They struck at a drowning man, grasping him in their jaws and diving deep until the man's fists stopped beating their snout and fell still.

The great serpent spat out the corpse and launched itself out of the water. It shot through the waves toward the French and Spanish fleet.

Turn back, the War-Lock commanded, wrestling against the magic tether that bound him to the serpent. It was frayed, slipping through his fingers as his mortal body weakened.

Archibald slammed back into his own body, where he slumped over onto the deck of the *Bucentaure.* Men crowded the rail, watching the sea serpent bearing down on the blockade.

Someone screamed, "Ready the cannons!"

Shooting at the beast would only anger it more. He needed time, he needed the men to stand down. He braced his hands on the deck and tried to lever himself up, but his blood-slick palms slipped out from under him. One of the sailors saw him struggling and approached with an outstretched hand.

"Stay back!" Archibald roared, sounding like a beast himself. The man halted just shy of scuffing his boot across the power circle.

Screams sounded close by. Too close. Cannons fired and filled the air with smoke. The beast was attacking the French fleet.

He had to focus. To regain control of the beast.

Rochefort came into Archibald's line of sight. He carried a flintlock pistol, cocked and ready.

"I may not know how magic works, but I suspect that if I kill the man who made that beast, it will die, too." He aimed the pistol at Archibald's head.

"Do that and you'll damn us all," Archibald said through gritted teeth. "I am the only one who can command the beast."

"Command it to do what? Destroy the fleet to win yourself a pardon from your king?" Rochefort sneered. "I know all about your past, Gilchrist. You started a mutiny and tried to murder your captain. Killing you would make us all a lot better off."

Something moved in Archibald's periphery. It struck out toward Rochefort, slamming the butt of a rifle against the man's head. He collapsed onto the deck with a groan.

Archibald glanced up and saw Admiral Gravina lowering the weapon to his side.

"Whatever you've got to do, do it fast," the man said. "I can't fight them all off."

Adrenaline flooded Archibald's body and heightened his focus. He squeezed his eyes shut and reached out for the tether of magic connecting him to the beast, tugging it hand-over-hand until he had its mind in his grip again.

Sleep, he ordered the beast. He held an image of the dark, quiet oblivion at the bottom of the sea fast in his mind. But the serpent roared, its body rolling in the waves as if it thought it could buck the War-Lock from its mind. The ships knocked into each other but did not capsize.

He had to get the beast away from the fleet. Away from the bodies floating in the waves that provoked its hunger and violence.

Dive deep, he commanded.

They plunged beneath the surface, slicing through the current. The pressure built, crushing their scaled body like a fist. The air in their lungs grew stale, but still their great tail propelled them deeper into the dark abyss until no trace of sunlight remained and it was impossible to tell how far they had traveled or if their eyes were still open.

There was no sound. The cold pressure slowed their heart, stiffened their muscles.

Like a dark, locked cell, Archibald was trapped inside the beast at the bottom of the sea. He had never experienced such emptiness, such loneliness. Even the serpent's mind was silent. He would die here and spend eternity in the dark. This time there would be no rescue from the abyss.

The man with the pitch-black skin swam up to his cell as silent as a shadow. He was emaciated from weeks in the hold, but strong enough to shift the beam that had fallen against Archibald's cell door. And he did. His eyes and teeth shone bright as stars when they reached the deck. He never spoke a word or made a sound. Not even when the shackles on his ankles dragged him beneath the sea. Archibald's limbs were too weak to save him...

Archibald thrust against the memory, and the motion fractured his frozen grip on the magical tether. He sensed himself rising fast, dizziness accompanied by burning nausea until he heaved the contents of his stomach onto the wooden deck. He opened his eyes to find himself back in his body, curled on his side and lying in a puddle of his own sickness within the power circle. Boots filled his line of vision.

He groaned, and the sailors gathered around him sighed in relief. Some cursed in multiple languages.

"Is it gone?" A hoarse voice he recognized as Villeneuve's demanded.

Archibald's mouth was sour for the second time that day. "Yes," he said, rolling to sit up on his backside. He glanced down at himself, as if to confirm he was whole once again. Blood had crusted in the palms of his hands; red-brown smears stained his sleeves and pants. New vomit flecked his boots. So, all in all, things were back to normal.

"Help the War-Lock to his cabin, and someone clean this mess up!" Villeneuve ordered, gesturing to the blood and the vomit.

Archibald was too tired to protest as a pair of deckhands pulled him to his feet and half-carried, half-dragged him to his private quarters. He was too spent to brush aside their rough hands as they stripped the soiled, bloody garments from his body and laid him in his bunk.

Despite the soul-numbing exhaustion that would likely leave him too weak to leave bed for a week, Archibald did not sleep.

He had proven himself powerful beyond reckoning and indispensable. When they returned to Paris, no doubt the Emperor would shower him with praise, titles, land, and riches.

But Archibald was afraid. Not of the serpent. Or of the British fleet seeking revenge against him. He wasn't even concerned about Rochefort's murder attempt.

He feared the darkness and the emptiness he had experienced at the bottom of the sea. Somehow, he had taken a piece of that darkness back to the surface with him. *Inside* him. It lurked in his mind, whispering to him in quiet moments. He feared that he would never again know peace because he had sought to wield a power he didn't fully understand. He had let his quest for vengeance make him monstrous.

When he closed his eyes to shut out the world around him, he stared into the abyss, and the abyss looked back at him.

The Wildwood Hog

by Cristina Perachio

A feral hog can crush and devour bone, leaving no trace of the species it had once occupied. Wild hogs are considered an invasive species, not native to North America. They are powerful, solitary creatures that can become hostile and territorial in a flash. They are driven by an endless hunger and reproduce to pass on that hunger. All the cells in their body demand it: to pass on the knowledge of that hunger and how to feed it.

One of my customers at the diner had told me this. It was the end of the season and I'd been serving Teddy for two months. He's dry wheat with hard scrambled eggs, scrapple, coffee black, side of maple. Teddy was angry his off season was all screwed up. Over summer, he claimed a wild hog got into his farm, somewhere near West Cape May, destroying his blueberries. He called it the Wildwood Hog, even though, as far as he was concerned, the thing could have been dropped here from outer space.

Teddy said he heard of them multiplying like bunnies down in Texas, which might as well be outer space if you're a farmer in South Jersey. It'd eaten the bushes whole and even some of his fencing meant to keep out deer. I remember that much, but I didn't think it was so odd. Didn't farmers have pigs? Maybe it'd escaped somehow from a neighboring farm. He just shook his head, said maybe my ponytail was too tight, and waved me off, disgusted like someone had spit in his scrapple.

It was autumn, the early morning sand cold and crunchy, the first time I saw one. I was sitting near the dunes of the bird preserve where the bay flows into the ocean. "Sitting" is maybe too cool a term. I'd practically collapsed there. Trying to catch my breath, huffing and puffing. Pathetic. I was not a runner, an athlete in no sense of the word, but had taken it up after moving down here. Jannis Zippoli, who everyone but me calls Zip, was the one who suggested it. We work together at the Doo-Wop, a converted train car set-down lopsided beside the two-lane highway that brings tourists to Exit 0.

"You're still young. Move your body," she said, scolding me. "You can't lie around feeling sorry for yourself on your days off and expect anything to get any better."

There I was, shivering and sweating at the same time. The grass around me swooshing and the blood in my ears loud as the ocean. The ocean ahead of me was angry, churned-up and the smell of the marsh was pungent, even on a cold morning. Later, I thought maybe what I had been smelling was her. That stink. From out of the estuary came this lumbering beast. She looked like a massive, walking boulder. Something out of a children's book where inanimate objects suddenly stand up and start talking to you. Had to be 300 pounds, covered in fur. She seemed prehistoric, ancient. I watched her frozen. Afraid to even breathe. The bottom third of her was caked in black marsh mud that still twinkled with whatever little sucking critters had hitched a ride.

She was so close to me that I could just about feel the heat coming off her. There, she turned to look at me. She opened her large snout, slow, showing teeth. That massive jaw that could crack a cow's femur like sea reeds. From her open mouth emanated a sound unlike anything I've ever heard, filling the brackish air around us. A low bellow. Maybe she wanted me to turn tail. I couldn't. I couldn't move. She gave a roar followed by the most violent retching.

What looked to me like black bile spilled from the hog's mouth, foamy. Now dripping sweat, I was paralyzed with fear. The smell was horrific. In the frothing pool of sludge was an undigested toad, pale belly up, limbs splayed.

I watched the toad's leg twitch, and then a flutter in its abdomen. It croaked, flipped itself over and crawled from the goo to burrow in a large nest of seaweed washed up in a recent storm. The beast seemed to be listening then. When the toad began its throaty rhythmic chanting, she turned a wet, shining eye to me and then slunk back into the mud. I watched her swim through the narrow channel of the estuary. Her massive head bobbing above the grasses. When she reached the place where the tide of the ocean and the bay meet in little gray peaks, she turned toward the sea and went under.

There was no one around, so I just sort of sat there stunned for a while. Where had she gone? I squinted out to sea. The waves were unusually large. White foam covered the shallows, churned up from the force. Even having just watched her sink beneath the green-brown waters with my own eyes, I almost started to wonder if I'd made the whole thing up. Maybe I was losing my mind. I'd heard if you weren't well-fed, your brain starts to eat itself. I was on a diner waitress budget after all. My stomach turned. If it weren't for that lingering smell, I might have convinced myself I really was cracking up.

Later, talking about it, I don't know why I didn't run like hell out of there. "You're lucky she didn't charge you," Jannis had said when I told her.

"Do you think she was rabid? Something wrong with her to go out in the ocean like that?"

She just shrugged. Though I don't think she really believed me when I said how large the hog had been. I could hardly believe myself, so I don't blame her thinking I'd been exaggerating for the sake of the story.

Jannis doesn't hesitate to exaggerate for the sake of a good story. And it's why the regulars like her so much. She keeps them entertained. It is a long, lonely winter here on the island and entertainment of any sort is limited. The people who live here year-round are mostly elderly, or grew up here and so poor they can't help but stay put, or running from something even worse than the isolation of the off-season. I fall into the last category.

Ronnie was a junkman. No punchline there, just the truth. It was how he made his extra cash in the off-season. He made minimum wage as a sanitarian at the Bumble Bee Tuna plant, which was a nice way of saying he wore a helmet and beard net to spray fish guts off the floor with a hose full of chemicals. So junking was how he made the extra he needed to keep me home. And if I was home, he didn't need to pay for daycare on the days we had his kid.

With mostly metal scraps, he'd taken to making these great big ugly sculptures in our front yard that overlooked the shortcut traffic on route 52. Sometimes during the season, tourists would stop to look but no one ever bought anything except bottles of water I sold in an old cooler for a buck fifty. The only thing artistic about Ronnie was his temper and inflated head size.

The morning I spiked his coffee with the good blow, he thought we'd be going junking first thing, bright and early before he had to be down at the plant. He said I had an eye for it. An eye for junking. Ronnie could dole out a compliment so weird, you couldn't help being flattered. Even if the flattery wasn't something you were so sure was a good thing at all.

His coffee was hot and waiting for him in the big thermos he had down in his truck before his shift like always. The lying wasn't hard—I really *had* made myself sick with worry. Worry could kill you, that's what my mother always said. Instead, I said I couldn't go—cramps—and made a big show of grabbing the floppy, liver-colored hot water bottle from under the sink before getting back into bed. I actually thought I'd made too big a show of it, but he didn't ask any questions. Squeamish that way, as most of them are.

By the time I made it out past the Pine Barrens, I knew he'd pissed hot, not his first parole violation, and was likely on his way to county lock-up. If he got one call, the avocado green phone hanging on the wall just rang and rang in the empty kitchen. And I have to admit, that made even me feel a little sorry for him.

At first, that had all seemed like the hard part. I thought the leaving would be the part I might not make it through. It took me years to do it, and I try not to regret that because, as Jannis likes to say, "It's just part of the movie of your life, hon." But it must have all shown itself on my face, something just gone rotten still coming out of my pores, and that's how Tana found me. She could sense it, or smell it, on me.

After I first saw the pig, I went running at the same time on my days off. I even took the same route, half-dreading, half-hoping I'd see her again. I started walking the same route to the diner, on the old boardwalk that turned into a sugar sand path, closed in on all sides by pygmy pitch pines, to double-up on my chances of a sighting. But it had been over a week and the only creatures I saw on my walk were big grandpop gulls still as statues and dead horseshoe crabs.

If it weren't for the smell of her, which seemed to embed in my sinuses, I wouldn't have trusted myself that it had happened. This was off-putting but something I'd gotten used to. Questioning the memories, the photographs of events, that played in your own brain. By the time I got to the diner at half past six, I'd have needles in my hair and pitch sticking my sneakers to the black and white checkered floor. Coffee would be brewing, the grill being scrubbed and smoked as clean as it'd get for the day—but I'd swear all I could smell was her: the Wildwood Hog.

Tana was oatmeal with cinnamon and "whatever's fresh," which was usually nothing, two Lipton tea bags in her cup with lemon.

"She's a batty old broad," Jannis said.

I learned from her that Tana was a widow twice over. Jannis gave her a wide berth, as if she had something catching, though Tana didn't seem to be bothered by that. The woman had lived alone on Leeds Way on the other side of the preserve: a place locals called Dog Shit Beach because it was the only dog beach for tourists during the season. And as the summers became unusually hot and wet, the pine woods flanking the beach were overtaken with wild mushrooms, which only added to the musk of marsh and feces.

"Why do you go down there?" Jannis asked, as we worked side-by-side at the griddle. "I don't even like to drive down Leeds Way, let alone *walk* that side of the dunes to get here." She tossed a disgusted look my way. "Go air out. You stink like an oyster's asshole."

Leeds Way had become a desolate place, even during the season. This was the old part of the island. It was overgrown and still wild. Some called it haunted but that was just small-town silliness. The only thing it was good for, other than a fertile land for fungi, was for teenagers to park and make out. And, despite the precious privacy provided, even the kids on the island didn't like hanging out down there anymore. Not since one of their classmates had gotten drunk at the end of the summer and drowned in the cedar swamp less than three feet deep. When found, she was missing her left hand at the wrist, which was assumed to have been eaten by the large turkey vultures that scour the Pine Barrens.

She was named Shelly—coffee to go with four creams, three sugars.

There was rumor she'd ingested a poisonous mushroom called "destroying angel" that spread as fast as dandelion, all over the woods there. Or that something more sinister had occurred but maybe only to cover up the fact the truth was just too sad to accept. Whenever a young one went before them, the eldest of Doo-Wop diners were prone to talk of the Jersey Devil, a goat-faced, hoofed demon creature with bat wings and red eyes born, the thirteenth child, to Mother Leeds of Leeds Way in the 18th century. Born feels too precious a word, as the story goes, the thing burst from Mother Leeds' womb and flew, screeching into the woods, into the night.

None of it seemed to bother Tana who'd lived on Leeds Way for longer than I'd been alive. Out of her little wooden bungalow, she sold hippy-dippy creams and salves and medicinal teas with things like calendula, hyssop, horehound and whatever else she managed to grow herself on her marshy plot of land, hidden from the road in the pines.

In a whispered voice, flipping a pork roll on the griddle that screeched with the heat, Jannis claimed she was selling more than tie-dye soaps and sandal-wood-scented lotion. She'd helped teenage girls who bled so much that they'd miss school, or once-hopeful mothers who didn't want any more babies born ill-formed or perfectly formed blue and still, and their grandmothers who's burning night sweats and restless legs bred insomnia, leaving chunks of hair on the pillow. What people called "women's troubles" to avoid any talk of blood or pain or female bodies that could cause such destruction. "Everything else you hear about is just rumors," Jannis said.

She was baiting me to ask more but I didn't want to gossip about her while she sat in a booth minding her own business. Tana was always reading, and she must have read fast because it was always something different—my mother was like that with her detective stories, sand in the binding—often in Italian, with pages falling out, tattered covers. These were books you'd want to sniff. Tana always stayed longer than Jannis would have liked, taking up a seat for who I didn't know. But she also tipped well, crinkled bills scented with the perfume of her pockets—something between Sunday mass and a wet garden—and didn't bother us like some of the regulars would.

There was a sturdiness to her I admired. Tana was block-shaped, heavy-breasted, and it suited her. Her face was round, making her appear younger, and reminded me of the Russian nesting dolls I had as a girl: pink faded cheeks and cupid's bow. One of her hands, she kept tucked at her side, was malformed into a fist. She wore oversized tarnished silver jewelry that made a satisfying clinking with her gait. She was like a walking windchime. Her long hair, never pulled back, was the color of winter sand: pale and sparkling.

Perhaps because she'd been a young widow, and my mother had been a young widow, I couldn't help but treat her with extra care. Even though compared to her peers, sitting at the counter on any given day, she was definitely the sturdiest of the bunch. Canes and walkers lined up by the door like we were running a medical supply shop, and those wet, rattling coughs in dirty handkerchiefs.

On slow mornings, which was most mornings, Tana didn't say much but she asked me a lot of questions. I'd told her about where I came from, about Ronnie, and how I'd ended up here. I'd lost touch with most of my friends since Ronnie. And it felt good to talk about it with someone other than Jannis, who scooped up other people's stories to be doled out later for her own amusement. I'd seen her do it enough. The door wouldn't even be closed behind you before you were the main character in her not-so-funny story. That's how a lot of people can be. You can see it in their eyes when you're talking to them. How they're going to turn it around, twist it when it gets retold. But when I spoke to Tana those first few weeks of early winter mornings, she just listened.

Two weeks to Thanksgiving, Tana hadn't been into the diner, and I worried something had happened to her, all alone in that house the way she was. No family to check on her. My grandmother had gone that way, falling down the basement steps with a glass of Carlo Rossi on ice tucked into a full laundry basket and no one finding her for days.

I'd walked by Tana's little shack plenty of times on my pig hunts. She didn't own a phone, so I just went and knocked up for her after my shift. I had barely got my hand off the knocker—a big brass X, the shape of an open pair of ornate scissors—and she was already opening the door and inviting me in.

The house smelled of pine and some type of evergreen garland that was pinned over the doorways. A fat gray and white striped cat eyed me from its perch on top of a stuffed bookcase that took up the whole back wall of the cottage. Its tail ticked back and forth like a metronome. Books and brown glass jars, dried herbs and flowers hanging upside down or bundled in vases, a dusting of amber-colored pollen covered the otherwise organized shelves. In fact, it seemed to hover in the air in an orange haze, the low late-autumn light illuminating flying motes of it.

Tana did not seem surprised in the least to see me. She was recovering from pneumonia. She said this with an eye roll like it was as unlikely as it was absurd, but she claimed to be doing much better. Though she was moving slower and had a terrible cough that made me wince.

She drank tea, things she made up herself in little ribbon-tied sachets, so that's what we had. It smelled of lavender and tasted of licorice and peppermint. "Good for your nature," she said, carrying a tray and setting it on the heavy wooden coffee table. There was an old-fashioned quality to it all. She had a real tea service, which I'd only ever seen in old black and white movies. The teacups and saucers were mismatched, ornate things, each with a mother of pearl well and shining silver trim, painted in solid teal, violet, black, or yellow.

While the steam from the tea swirled above us, Tana told me that she had been ill as a small girl, and sometimes bedridden. From childhood, she had suffered what she called "imbalance of humors," whatever that was, that stunted her growth and caused severe nearsightedness. She told me that she had been born in a small village by the sea in Sicily where her ancestors had lived for hundreds of years.

"What did they do over there?" I asked.

Tana had this way of smiling that made it look like one side of her face was pinned still. "Before *I* was born, they farmed rocks," she said and laughed. I really didn't know what was funny about that, but I laughed just the same. "In reality, they were very unfortunate farmers for generations. And then my family grew and foraged mushrooms. It can be very profitable if you have someone like me to work the woods."

I told Tana that my mother had grown up on a farm and worked from a very young age too. I finished my tea and poured myself more. Tana watched me. She didn't seem to mind that I was in no rush. Maybe she did get lonely out on Leeds Way after all.

"Did you like it there?" I asked, finishing the pot of tea.

"Ah, Sicilia? I did as a girl. But then I grew up and was made to be like a slave. I had to escape so I could make a life for myself."

We had that in common.

That afternoon, for the first time I was able to get a close look at her fist-hand. She always wore this long cape-like sweater at the diner that swallowed her up, or she kept the hand in her lap. Tana said she had been born that way, though some botched treatments when she was a teenager had made the thing worse, almost calcified it in place. "This is just the body I've been given for now." She told me she believed we were reborn after death, that we came back stronger and with all the knowledge of our past selves.

"You're not a Catholic?" I know this was stupid, but I really didn't know many people who weren't.

She shook her head, no and told me what she believed in pre-dated Catholicism. I never heard of such a thing. It had been passed to her by her mother, who learned it from her own mother, and so on. And that didn't seem too different from how it always went.

"La Vecchia. The Old Way," Tana said, "It's not like how you think of it here. Christmas and Easter and that's it." She snorted, a mean laugh. "It's everything. It's how we make sense of the world and how we cure what ails us while we're here." Then she shook her little, knobbed index finger at me as she said, "We are only here for such a short time, and it is a myth there should be so much suffering."

That certainly *did* sound different from my own grandmother's Catholicism that—at least how it was in her home—seemed to me mostly about suffering. I told Tana this and she laughed.

There was the ticking sound of nails on wood and a heavy padding on the porch. A lumpy white mutt nosed its way into the screen door. She waddled over to us and crawled under our legs to put her head in Tana's lap. "Borchi, come va, eh? Come va, il mio porcellino?"

Tana went to the kitchen and retrieved an anise cookie for the dog. My mouth watered. I had the sudden and overwhelming desire to be her third pet.

Tana asked how I was liking living on the island. "You know, not many young people move here this time of year," she said, a silver eyebrow raised.

I told her the truth: not much. It was lonely and all I did was work and go home to eat frozen pizzas or sometimes canned wedding soup. Is there anything sadder than canned wedding soup? I told her that even though I was the one who got Ronnie locked up, I missed him. And that all made me feel rotten.

"It's very hard to leave a man who cannot help himself. Most women will go back."

"Not me," I said, through bites of cookie.

Neither of us were convinced.

"Don't you have anyone to look after you? You are like an addict who has just quit cold turkey."

I said no, and that I was probably too old to need looking after. Most girls I'd gone to school with were married, some even divorced and remarried, and on their second or their third babies by now. Here I was back at the beginning again. She said that we all needed some looking after.

It was then that in the center of my forehead, there seemed to be a knot, a pulsing that I couldn't get rid of. I was so thirsty too. Almost dizzy with it. I told her so and she poured me more tea from the teapot, even though I was sure we'd already finished it.

Excusing myself, I went to the restroom. There was a clawfoot tub stuffed to the rim with books. The kind of books she'd come into the diner with. Old, dusty looking things, many handwritten, with ink-stained pages and illustrations carved into the paper, so that the backs of each were bumpy with a negative image of the front. There wasn't a medicine cabinet but an old wooden milk crate with homemade jars and bottle droppers, all in different colored glass, with names I couldn't pronounce. With careful hands, I picked one up and unscrewed the cap to take a whiff of what smelled to me like almonds. Stuck in the bottom of the milk crate, something twinkled in the light and caught my eye. It was a delicate silver chain, something to go around a child's wrist or ankle. In a fine script on a small silver plate was the name SHELLY.

I closed it in my hand and a prickle of sweat stung my underarms. Coffee to go, four creams, three sugars.

The pain in my head throbbed to new levels of destruction. I held onto the sink basin for a moment while it passed. I splashed cold water on my face and wished there was a mirror to practice normal facial expressions. But there was only a faded rectangular outline in the antique rose printed wallpaper where a mirror used to have been.

"You're white as a sheet. Are you not well?" She punctuated her question with a long bout of coughing.

"I'm sure it's hormonal," I said. To complain about a headache while she was coughing up her lungs felt ridiculous.

Shelly's jewelry was still pressed into my palm. I could feel her gaze landing on my closed fist that mirrored hers, both held at our sides. "I'm sorry," I said, sounding like a child. "I, uh, I found this in the bathroom. Maybe someone wants it back."

With careful fingers, she reached for the charm. She tsk-ed and inspected it with a closer eye. "She won't be needing it back. I will give it to the mother. Poor thing."

"You knew her?"

"She worked with me for a time, in the garden this summer. She was a very bright girl." She put the charm into her pocket and sighed. "A true waste of youth."

Before I set out for home, Tana walked with me out to the beach. She liked to feed the birds, fatten them up for winter, she said. They flocked to her like she was their leader. We took turns throwing crusty bread into the sand. Watching them dive and carry bits away above the glass-topped sea.

"Shelly," she said. There was a sadness, but also maybe a defensiveness, to her voice as she spoke. "I was, perhaps, too much of a shock to her system."

Tana went on to explain that it was part of her duty to pass on "the way" as she called it, to at least one other person. She had no children. She had no family here. Tana said she felt her body preparing for the next world and she feared what would become of her future selves without passing on her knowledge of the way. The wind shifted and, just for a moment, I got a whiff of what I thought of now as sea hog.

It was me and Ronnie's anniversary. I woke up reaching for him and didn't know where I was. Every day since I'd left, I woke up like this. I fell asleep in the creaky pullout bed thinking about Ronnie trying to fall asleep in his cell, and then I woke up having forgotten I left him. It was horrible. I had been lovesick before, but this was something worse. There was a cord cut between my waking self and my sleeping self. This was love amnesia. It had been raining for three days straight. It was mud and more mud. I thought about calling in sick but knew Jannis would never buy it and she'd probably fire me out of spite.

When it stormed here, salt and sand got carried with the wind and stuck to your face and matted your hair. By the time I got to the diner, I was a mess. Jannis made me wash up in the sink before any customers arrived. We had to close when we lost power—even though we'd been dodging buckets of murky water placed under half a dozen leaks for two days. As bad as I needed the tips, I was grateful. My head was still pounding like a hangover, but I hadn't had a drop. Jannis offered me a ride home, but I told her no. I'd walk.

"You're going to see that old bat again, aren't you?" She shook her head. "You're young! Don't waste your days here and with that old woman. Go into town. Meet someone so you can start your life for crap's sake."

Despite the pain in my head, which shifted from all over pounding to the feeling of a small, hard marble lodged between the eyes, I was enjoying sitting with Tana in her dark cave of a home, listening to the storm. We were eating these hard little lacquered nubs of anise-flavored biscuits she made. They reminded me of Tana's twisted up fingers. A pot boiled on the stove, filling the house with the smell of tomato, garlic, basil, cheese, and a spice that warmed the air. Tana called it peasant food. Whenever I ate at Tana's house, I noticed I'd become ravenous. I figured it was because I'd been eating so crappy on my own and it'd been so long since anyone had cooked me anything, except for Jannis who used that ancient griddle, smelling like decades of turned grease.

Ronnie liked to cook. His Dad had been a cook in the Navy. My favorite thing Ronnie made was breakfast for dinner which was always shit-on-a-shingle. Lots of thick toasted white bread was his secret, pancakes, real maple syrup, and sausage. Working at the diner had ruined breakfast for dinner.

Everyone keeps telling me I'm young, but I don't feel it. Plenty of fish in the sea, and all that. And after Ronnie, I wasn't so keen on waiting to meet the next one, whoever he was. I told this all to Tana, who had her fist-hand in a cold bath of ice water in her plugged-up sink. She said it helped with the pain. When she was more able, as she put it, she used to take ice baths every day, stark nude, in a big, galvanized tub that still sat in the yard. And before that, she would swim in the ocean, year-round.

"You don't need anyone to start your life. Man or otherwise. You've been here much longer than you think," she said. "You understand?"

I didn't, but I nodded. I tried to explain the love amnesia and to my embarrassment I had to quit talking to keep from bursting into tears. It really wasn't all about Ronnie, I told her. There were these persistent headaches that made it hard to rest. All day my head felt so heavy, like it was filled with sand.

"Right here," I said, rubbing the spot between my eyes that radiated with pain.

"Ah," Tana patted my knee. "This we can fix," she said.

Tana drained the sink and wrapped her reddened fist in a warm towel that smelled of rose. She sat with me then, which was something she rarely did. There was this real nervous energy to her. She was always moving around the house. Usually she was up at the kitchen counter like a mad scientist or pacing back and forth from room to room, carrying a little footstool, gathering dried herbs and things that hung from the low wooden rafters all over the house.

It felt too intimate, her sitting almost touching me, and I found I couldn't look right at her. Close up, the expression on her face reminded me of this fox that used to live in the woods behind our house as a kid—the long nose, deep-set and determined eyes. My mom and I used to feed the fox until she snuck through a hole in our porch window and carried off one of our pet turtles, for which neither of us forgave her.

First, Tana said, we had to test whether the pain was natural or because of the malocchio. The evil eye. She used a glass dropper to put three drops of olive oil into a bowl of sea water held in her lap. The drops separated and smeared across the water like three synchronized swimmers backstroking.

"Does your Ronnie have reason to wish you harm? Is he the type to wish you ill if he thinks you truly deserved it?"

Tana knew Ronnie was locked up, but I hadn't told her why. I tried to think of a way to answer honestly without outing myself as the person I was. There was a desire to give her the best version of me, like we were on a good date, and I didn't want to ruin it with the truth. Another wave of pain, this time it came with a squiggling amber light at the corner of my vision. I told her yes, yes, he might have a reason.

"He's sent you the overlook from behind bars, then," she said, pointing to the bowl with the oil, shimmering in her lap. From a small velvet pincushion the color of dried blood, she pulled two sewing needles. With care, she inserted the tip of one into the eye of the other.

"Eyes against eyes and the holes of the eyes, envy cracks and eyes burst." Tana dropped the needles into each oil drop and sprinkled three pinches of salt into the water. With a pair of tarnished golden sewing scissors, she jabbed at the sparkling oil three times, once through each drop. Then she used the wetted scissors to cut the air above the bowl three times.

I watched, amused and a little embarrassed, waiting for something to happen. The striped cat called Segesta rubbed against my legs, her big belly dragging on the ground. I scratched her behind her ear and she purred. My stomach growled.

I'd eaten almost the whole tin of anise cookies and yet I was still hungry. I was hungry a lot these days.

"It is broken," she said. She brushed her good hand through her tangle of hair. And waved at the air like swiping a gnat. "You will start to feel yourself again. Come on," she said as if nothing unusual had just taken place, "let's eat."

I woke up with a start. Segesta was kneading into my belly. I'd fallen asleep on the couch. Tana's velvet throw imprinted into the side of my face. How long had I been asleep? I was wobbly on my feet like a newborn deer as I made my way in the dark towards the kitchen. There was no sign of Tana. Hello? I whispered into the room, lit only by the moon that was almost full and dripping with light. There was the sound of mourning doves, the sea, but nothing else.

At the sink, I turned on the cold water. The faucet trembled and groaned before a slow trickle of water began to flow. I drank straight from the sink as if I hadn't had water in a long time. It didn't have the sulfuric smell that came out of my sink. It was almost sweet. I closed my eyes and drank without stopping for breath. There was that pounding in my ears, and a light-headed, watery moment like vertigo as I came up for air. I held my head with both hands and there was a distinct popping in the ears as if I'd surfaced from deep water.

That night, I walked home through sugar sand and felt light as air. I slept until the sun came up and woke without the familiar pang of confusion. The headache was still there, but it dulled to the back of the head and tingled down my neck like sand draining from somewhere inside my skull.

Back at the diner, I told Jannis about the cure as we married ketchup bottles and yawned and brewed the first pots of coffee before the regulars came in.

"You're out of your damn mind," Jannis said.

"I'm telling you. Whatever she did, it worked." My good mood was an annoyance to Jannis. I stifled a smile, humming along to whatever was on the radio. A song filled with sweet harmonies on the oldies station.

"What are you so jazzed up about?" Teddy walked in, not 30 seconds after we officially opened, still sucking on the last of his morning's pipe. I didn't mind the pipe smoke but Jannis always made a big thing of it, waving a wet towel around as if the whole place already didn't stink to high heaven of smoke and grease and caustic grill chemicals.

"Not a whole lot, Teddy sir," I said. "Just woke up on the right side of the bed for a change." I set down his coffee and side of maple, then wrote out his ticket for Jannis. "Ah, shit, we're outta scrapple. I'm sorry about that. Some kind of mix-up with the delivery this week." I tapped my pen on the counter to the music and Jannis slapped at me with the spatula.

Teddy leaned in. "What's up her rear?"

I shrugged.

Teddy was a bit of a busy body, and I'd learned not to reveal too much of Jannis' personal life to him the hard way. The unsuspecting town gossip in coveralls and a brown mesh ball cap with the stitching coming undone. "Well, then tell me what's the word with you, hummingbird? You still got that beau in the can?"

"Former beau. Fully former."

"I heard that before. Fine, if you've got nothing doin', let me tell you what I got in the hopper."

I planted myself half-on, half-off the stool next to him, one foot firmly on the ground so I wouldn't take any shit from Jannis for sitting while I rolled silverware. "Go 'head," I said.

He went on about how he'd set up a hunting blind in his fields in anticipation of the full moon. He was certain that the Wildwood Hog was driven by the moon to cause destruction. "I know it sounds kooky," he said, almost bashful, "but look here." Out of his back pocket he pulled out a bent notebook imprinted with the bony curve of the old timer's butt, and wrinkled pages like he'd been sweating all over it or bathing with it. He flipped the pages. "I keep records. I write it all down in here. Thomas Jefferson did that, ya know? And goddamn it if my shit don't get eat up by that monster every new moon and every full moon since summer."

Tana walked in and waved over her head to no one in particular. Before taking her usual booth by the window, she joined Teddy at the bar. "Zip, I see you wrecked that car of yours." To my surprise, Tana asked for her tea at the counter. She hopped up on a stool next to Teddy with some effort, short legs dangling below her childlike.

"I don't want to talk about it!" Jannis hollered, whacking the grill with the metal spatula for emphasis.

"I told her," Tana said. "I told you not to let that stunad drive home in his condition."

Jannis whipped around and pointed the spatula at Tana, looking like a mean school teacher. "You put the maloik on us. I know you did. Don't get involved in my business."

Tana scoffed. "Cocciuta."

"Did she just call me? What did she just call me?"

"You're a stubborn girl. Go on. Keep up with that man and see what happens to you."

Jannis growled and went back to her work. Teddy and I stole a glance at each other. *Yikes*, he mouthed.

Teddy detailed his plan to trap the beast and prove to his buddies that she was real. Apparently, there'd been some skepticism that Teddy, who liked maybe too much of his drink, was exaggerating his claims to account for his poor crop. The destruction had continued on through autumn and the thing had even rooted up wild mushrooms growing so deep underground that Teddy's elderly pointer had fallen in a hole and got herself stuck overnight in the frost.

He hammered the notebook with a finger. "It stops tonight." He sipped from his coffee mug and made a face. "This has gone terribly bitter, hon. Can I get a refill?"

"There's half a bottle of syrup in there," I said. I topped him off with a fresh pot anyway. Tana smiled at me, her crooked incisor flashing white like a pearl, and went back to her usual booth to read. There'd be no more quarreling for the morning.

Teddy took another gulp of coffee and made his bitter face. "It stops tonight, I'm tellin' ya'!" he said, triumph in his voice.

It had become somewhat of a tradition to eat dinner with Tana on Sundays. I'd been in a good mood all day and even had the energy to bake an olive oil cake as a thank you after my shift. It was something my mother used to make with orange syrup. I pulled a sprig of rosemary from the massive bush outside Tana's house and set it on top of the loaf. I knocked on the door and it opened without my turning the handle. Letting myself in, I shooed Segesta away, who was tangling herself in my steps.

"Tana?" I said. "Whatever you did, the headache's completely gone."

The cat meowed repeatedly and pushed its head against my calf. There was no call from Tana from the backroom. Then I heard a terrible yowling from Borchi. A noise I'd never heard her make.

I ran out the back door, my boots slipping in the sugar sand that led down past the marsh and out onto the beach. Borchi was pacing at the edge of the surf, howling and howling. The sun had dipped low enough in the sky that a wash of deep orange covered the dark waters. But I could make out Tana's hair, pale and blowing in the wind, just above the foam of a passing wave. I grabbed up Borchi who had been splashing in the surf and howling in desperation. I called out to Tana, but she didn't seem to hear me. She wouldn't turn around. I could feel myself panicking and realized there was no phone. I'd have to run to get help. And by the time I got back.

That's when I saw her go under.

I put the dog back on the sand and yelled at her to stay. The water was freezing but I took off my boots and ran in. My heart pounded and my legs went numb fast. I made my way to where I had last seen Tana's head go under, but the waves were too strong for me to stay on my feet. I checked to make sure Borchi wasn't following me into the water, and when I turned back, I was staring at the large snout of the Wildwood Hog bobbing above the water directly toward me.

If I hollered, it was drowned out by the ocean. I turned to run as fast as I could in my wet clothes with my legs gone numb from the cold. I was not a strong swimmer and the beast was gaining on me. I could smell its marshy odor and the water seemed to take it on as well. I was trying not to gag and choke on the now rancid-smelling sea as I pulled myself back to my feet and crawled onto the sand and out of the surf. I screamed at Borchi to come here, come back, as she zipped up and down the shoreline in terror.

The hog had easily made its way to the channel in the time it took me to run back to shore, and I spotted its giant head weaving through marsh grass. I grabbed the dog again and pulled her to me, trying to get my breath back.

It was then Tana appeared, almost as if she'd been there all along, sitting soaking wet on a driftwood log. "My God, Tana. I thought you'd drowned." I went to her and Borchi jumped from my grasp, whining and fussing at Tana's feet. "Did you see? Did you see the hog? I thought it was going to eat you."

"I'm sorry," she said. She wiped at her face, her eyes swollen and red from crying. "I've had a terrible vision." She dreamt of walking on the bottom of the ocean, where there was no light, no sound. She knew she was dead or was dying in the dream, and she knew there was nothing beyond. She started weeping then. "I know you must think I'm a crazy, old woman. But there is no point to this life if this is all there is. There will be no future for me. No spiritual evolution. This is it."

"It's not true," I said, not really knowing what I was meaning.

"There's no one to carry on the tradition. My life has been a waste. No way for me to come back." She stood suddenly like she might try to throw herself in the ocean again, but instead she howled and doubled over, pounding at the cold sand.

"I could do it," I said, through chattering teeth. "I'll do it. You could teach me." Her despair was making me feel ill. I wanted to help her. Without speaking, I pulled her to her feet and we made our way inside. Borchi followed at our heels.

We stripped out of our wet clothes in the house, and I started a fire. We sat on the floor together, wrapped in blankets.

Looking into the flame, Tana told me how her family had thought she was the devil when she was born because of her hand. The devil's hoof, they called it. The women tried to cure her over the years, but it only got worse. And when they stopped trying to fix her, that's when Tana realized her true gifts. She could smell wild truffles buried beneath their land. She made her family a fortune for a short time, but they kept her to themselves. Never allowing her to attend school, or make friends, or marry.

When she escaped, she did so alone and at night, before her sixteenth birthday with an American man who wanted to marry her. But when they got here, and he realized she would never be able to give him children, he abandoned her. I asked her about the young widow story. "I wear black, I'm Sicilian. People make assumptions."

I laughed at this and it seemed to soften her mood.

She admitted she liked the dead husband story better than the real story. And with that, she committed herself to a solitary life. "Getting old is a funny thing," she said. "You think it won't bother you. That you'll be ready when it happens. But you never are."

That night, the full moon lit up the sugar sand beach a brilliant, sparkling white. The ocean was calmer than I'd seen it all winter. Tana had painted my whole body, my hair, with a white chalky mud. The ritual needed me to become like the moon, she said. We stood out on the beach and I didn't feel cold. There was a warmth coming off me. I couldn't understand most of what she was saying, but she traced a large circle around me while she chanted. Della luna, nella luna. Of the moon, in the moon. She kneeled in the sand, poured a clear liquid into a small metal bowl and lit it on fire. The smell of sulfur lingered. I stood completely still, as instructed, and we both watched the flame flicker.

"Don't step out of the circle, no matter what," she said. She closed her eyes and raised her hands in the shape of a triangle to the sky. Della luna, nella luna. Of the moon, in the moon.

Tana shivered and then gave a screeching yell. She doubled over as if snapped in half. Her face flopped into the sand at an odd angle. A scream jumped from me then, so otherworldly and full of terror I didn't know it as my own voice, couldn't feel it in my throat. Her head expanded like an allergic reaction to twice its normal size, and a horrific ripping sound rippled through the air as her skull opened, her hair fell away like petals blooming, and transformed into the massive head of the hog.

Tana's small, blockish body flailed frantically behind the hog head that sat snorting in the sand unable to move in its current state. Each limb, as if working independently, then broke in half—a shattering *snap, snap, snap, snap*—and rooted itself into the sand. I wanted to retch. My chest had that hot, swimming feeling. My whole body wanted me to run, but I stood shaking and rooted in place. A thick brown and black fur crawled its way like mold across the great expanse of the animal's back. With some effort, the beast pushed itself up on her newly formed hooves, her head the last to rise to meet my eyeline. Small black eyes shined. She took a slow breath in and let out a hot stream of brackish air. It was as if she'd taken on her true form and was finally able to exhale.

Even if I had wanted to run, which a part of me did, I wasn't sure if I could. My body did not seem as if it were my own. I thought of Shelly. Had she seen this? Did she try to run? Had the sight of this creature's violent transformation been what drove her to drink herself to death, her last breaths watery, face down in the marsh?

It was then three loud blasts shattered the hum of the ritual. A strange whooping I didn't recognize as night sounds on this beach. Borchi howled from the porch. The hog and I both looked to the tree line. A figure came crashing out, rifle in hand. He was dazed and stumbled, didn't see us right away. His head was down, and he was following tracks, hog tracks, and had made his way around the dunes. The full moon shone bright, though the wind had picked up and threw wisps of passing clouds past the light. It was Teddy. I crouched down, hidden behind the hog's wall of fur. Teddy mumbled to himself. The hog let out a low rumble.

"Come on,' Teddy called into the stillness of the beach. "Come on, ya'ugly monster." He shot into the air again, whooping like a much younger man.

The hog growled, louder this time. That's when Teddy saw her. He knelt and took aim.

After letting out a roar that made me clap my hands over my ears, the hog began to charge. She was fast. Teddy barely had the time to decide to turn and run for it before she was on him. The sound of her biting into his legs will never leave me. It was loud and crisp, cutting through the night air. His cries were carried away with the wind off the ocean. But the sound of those bones splitting crackled in the air like fireworks. The echo just kept on. She looked back at me once and then grabbed Teddy by an arm with her huge mouth, dragging the top of him into the ocean. He floated behind her for a time. A cloud of bright red oozed behind the hog like a long, rippling cape.

Still covered in the white moon mud, my body seemed to know what to do. I cleaned myself in the ocean and emerged as something new. The sea was charged with the moon and with life. I could feel it like electricity moving through me. Whatever rot had been seeping out of me these months was gone. It was like being baptized, reborn in the same skin. Any fear or guilt or shame was pulled from me and swept out to sea. I had the urge to drink the water then, and so I did. When I vomited into the sand, a small frog came up with the bile. It flipped itself over and followed the sugar sand path back to Tana's front steps where it sat, croaking, for the rest of the night.

The top half of Teddy was never seen again. His legs were discovered on the beach, still in his boots, untied, as if he'd slipped them on as an afterthought before tromping through the sugar sand path, following hoof prints, real or hallucinated. The Jersey Devil of course would be to blame for Teddy's death by his set. Everyone else put together a more digestible horror: he drank too much and went into the water where he was mauled by resident great white, Mary Lee, a notorious 17-foot, 3,500 pound she-monster. This was the story that Jannis herself would tell over and over and over again. Mary Lee grew larger with each telling, of course.

Tana's absence, however, went unnoticed for a time. This disturbed and surprised me maybe more than it should have. I'd been living in the home on Leeds Way for almost a whole season before someone—a tired-looking young woman, hunched with middle pain, with skin the pale yellow-gray color of a sea snail's shell—came knocking, asking for her.

We stood on the porch where we could smell the churning summer ocean, tree sap heavy on the warm air. The rash of destroying angels continued to choke these woods and you could still smell the marshy musk, though somehow gone sweeter in the heat of August. The sky lit up with oranges and lavenders, casting long pygmy pine shadows across the sugar sand like bony fingers, reaching.

I told the girl that Tana was gone on a long trip, but I'd do what I could to cure what ailed her while she was here.

The Thump

by Paul Carro

"**T**he supernatural is hogwash!" Wilbur Mussel protested.

The heavyset man in his early sixties (even his mustache wore a little extra weight) worked himself up to where he breathed noisily through blocked nostrils while crossing arms across his girthy chest and abdomen. Finding his arms too short for the task, he released the pose, leaned on his editor's desk. He wanted a sit, but he had only just now stood to signal his displeasure over his boss's request. His bum knee hated him for standing. The throbbing joint signaled his brain. *Can't you go along to get along?*

"The supernatural sells magazines," Peter Billings shot back, with a counter annoyance in his voice.

"My restaurant reviews sell magazines. They voted me top food critic in physical media last year."

"Because no one reads paper anymore! The numbers for online far exceed the numbers you are trying to brag about. Get with the times. Look around you."

Wilbur looked through the large glass window fronting his boss' office. A sea of cubicles stretched out, with only one person seated. Tabitha, old reliable. A twenty-something unpaid intern. A go-getter. Wilbur hated go-getters. They were after his job.

"Everyone reads online, and everyone works from home now. We'd all be out of the offices were we not locked into a lease and did not need the storage space for our archives. As soon as they digitize it all, we're out of here. Of that, I am certain. Even Tabitha knows it. She is here for one reason and one reason only."

"To show me up?" Wilbur asked.

"Hell no. She did that week one." Peter rose from behind his mahogany desk and opened his office door. Peter yelled out. "Tabitha, why do you come to the office?"

"My internet at home sucks. Way bettah' heah'," she said through her DNA-infused Boston accent. It stood out in sunny San Diego, California.

Peter wasn't done. "Tabitha, what do you know about the Queen Mary?" Peter walked over to the woman with Wilbur in tow.

Tabitha bolted upright with excitement. "It's wicked cool! Place is one of the most haunted ships in the world. They have an elevator with mirrored doors where people see an old woman over theah' shoulder in the reflection. Happens all the time! Then theah' is a pool where some poor girl who drowned plays for all eternity. Are we doing a story? If so, I am in like gin."

"Is she doing the story, Wilbur?" Peter asked, already knowing the answer.

Another deep breath through blocked nostrils as Wilbur shook his head. "No. It is a restaurant review. They have a new chef. As background, per your request, I will also investigate some of the hobblepop ghost garbage while there."

"Wicked, super cool," Tabitha said.

Wilbur straightened as much as his sore back allowed. Never would he look at such a young woman sexually, but her response excited him. He enjoyed how the intern looked at the man with fresh eyes and respect. Fine. Week on the ocean in a ghost boat it was.

Confirmation bias was something reporters needed to be conscious of when drafting a story, but Wilbur tossed those thoughts aside. In this one case, he knew himself to be correct. No ghosts, no supernatural, no muckity-muck haunted stuff existed. The additional reporting his boss asked for meant little work because there was nothing to report.

All he had to do was his normal restaurant review and then he would cobble together something about his forced assignment, all while using that same article to dispel many myths about the ghostly shenanigans on board. There was one other advantage to a ship-based restaurant. It would lean toward seafood. Seafood was healthier than much of what he ate for the paper. That was a welcome change because of some recent health issues.

One of the many things Wilbur kept from his boss was *the thump*. He experienced it recently after dining out for a review. His chest seized, causing immense pain, and landed him in the E.R. They diagnosed him with heartburn and warned Wilbur to stay away from spicy and rich foods. If he reported the diagnosis to the paper, he feared they might take him off the beat. Wilbur hoped seafood would give his digestive track and waistline a break. Ghosts and fish, a hell of a combination.

"Book the room," Wilbur said.

Peter patted Wilbur on the back. "Wise choice. Major clicks if you do this right. Take a few pics. We don't need professional photographers on every story any longer. The world is used to selfies and foodie pics from people's phones. I still expect due diligence. Research the ship before you go. Do you want the intern's help?"

"What? No. I can Google, thank you," Wilbur protested and marched off to a cubicle.

He took a seat and fired up the desktop. The history of the ship proved fascinating. It had a long history of transporting soldiers and cruise passengers alike. The many actual deaths on the ship engaged him more than the preposterous ghost stories that popped up with every search.

Eventually he encountered a link that read: *have you seen the crooked smile man*? Wilbur felt dirty taking the clickbait but click away he did before discovering what going down a rabbit hole meant. The link brought him to a series of pictures taken onboard the ship.

The site listed dates on each picture in two ways: upload dates and the dates the photographs were taken. The photos went back as far as the 30s, while the uploads obviously happened much later. At first, Wilbur was uncertain what he was looking at, but found another link offering the pics in chronological order of origin.

"Someone do the work for me? Sure," Wilbur said and clicked through.

The pics lined up for a scroll with the first identified as from 1939 but posted roughly five years ago. The image showed three people on the deck of a ship. A couple dressed to the nines and beaming, happy to be on board. They were Hollywood good looking and dressed formally. Standing alongside them was a man of ordinary build and features in military style clothing, which suggested he worked as a crew member.

The man stood rigid but relaxed, as if accustomed to formality on the job. Though relatively young, maybe thirty, the man's head appeared bald. The bare dome was natural or shaved clean, though it might also have been so tightly cropped that the hair vanished in the inkiness of the black-and-white photos. The man had a relatively strong nose that could have leapt off a Roman statue. But it was the man's smile that connected to the link's title.

Most notably, the man had a crooked smile. The right side of his mouth arced into a smirk, while the left side remained flatlined. It appeared he attempted to smile for the camera, as was custom, but was too serious an individual to partake in such frivolity.

Next was an image of three crewmen below deck acting goofy, celebratory. Standing behind them was the crooked smile man. That picture was also from 1939 but uploaded years later than the previous picture by a different user than the first.

What interest did people have in posting pictures of a random guy from the ship? There was nothing out of the ordinary about the man beyond the tortured smile. Something about the man unnerved Wilbur. How was it the smile was the same in each picture?

Maybe the poor guy could not move his mouth because of a stroke. The idea of a stroke made Wilbur break out into a sweat. He felt the thump coming on simply by thinking about medical emergencies. Wilbur remembered his own E.R. trip and how worried he was that his time was up.

That explained his unease. Pure muscle memory of a sudden heart issue and throngs of doctors and nurses circling him only to appear disappointed when one finally announced it was nothing more than heartburn. Thinking the man in the pictures was a stroke victim brought on his own memories.

Foolish. Why work himself up? And why research further? He had enough history on the ship already; he did not need to investigate a man people had a fixation on. Wilbur cut to the chase and scrolled to the last picture chronologically.

And blinked.

The date read 2019. Impossible. Not the upload date, but the picture's date. The upload date was 2020. The image was of a ballroom in the ship. A throng of Asian tourists stood assembled, posing for a photo. The group was all smiles. But standing in the background, hovering over a short man near the back in the image, was none other than the crooked smile man!

Such an oddity made Wilbur scroll quickly through the rest, moving backward in time. The man appeared alongside various people from different generations. Color photos gave way back to black and white. But the crooked smile man was there in each, usually standing alongside one person in each photo. The man looked the same in each and even wore...

"The same clothes!" Wilbur shouted, startling the intern. He laughed but continued, proud of himself for spotting the scam. "He wears the same clothes and sports the same smile in every photo. Hogwash Photoshop AI stuff."

Merely trick images. Paranormal claptrap was just that, claptrap. Still, he had his angle for his boss, his clickbait. *Have you seen this man?* would serve as a decent title for the required paranormal portion of the article. Uncertain how to download images onto his phone, he used his crappy camera to take shots of the computer screen in order to store a few pictures of the crooked smile man. He planned to ask the ship's staff where the whole meme thing about the guy originated from.

Never one to suffer fools, Wilbur refused to read any further about the man with the crooked smile. Besides, he had to go home and pack.

Once nicknamed the gray ghost after the color they painted it during wartime while transporting troops, the ship was back to a mix of crisp black and white.

Legend had it many "ghosts" on board were soldiers who did not make it home during the ship's years as a troop transporter. Wilbur scoffed at the idea of multiple ghosts occupying the same ship, no matter how grand its size. The leaps one would have to make to believe all the superstitions about the ship frustrated Wilbur. He could not imagine why people were so gullible, but then he trafficked in facts as a reporter.

While researching the ship, Wilbur encountered one theory that the ocean itself led to the stranding of ghosts. The paranormal "expert" suggested those dying at sea were unmoored, not unlike some ships. Absent a connection to physical ground, spirits had no path to follow to the afterlife. Wilbur found that angle fascinating but considered such speculation hogwash. Ghosts were not real. He planned to prove as much.

The ship loomed high above him while Wilbur wrestled with his carry-on in the trunk. So vast was the parking lot that it resembled an ocean itself, a sea of pavement. The size of the lot spoke to the popularity of the attraction. Except now the lot was relatively empty. Wilbur freed his carry-on from the trunk.

Hovering above its ocean home, the massive ship was one of beauty and elegance. The structure rose high into the sky until intercepting a cloudless blue sky. The ship possessed a stately grace that evoked simpler times. Nothing from the exterior hinted the ship held dark secrets, never mind a plethora of spectral visitors.

A queue of people climbed the ramp. They wore business suits which stood out in constantly casual California. Wilbur preferred suits himself, but his weight lent itself to Hawaiian shirts and elastic waist pants. The triple-x loud shirt he wore would help disguise him as a tourist for his stay, hiding Wilbur's occupation as an influencer. For added effect, an oversized camera dangled from his neck.

He needed the camera, which he borrowed from their offices, to take the required pictures. There were two things he never confessed to his boss. The first was his recent bout of thumps in his chest, which, if shared, could cause the paper to take him off the food beat. The second was that he still owned a flip phone. His boss was all about the paper's digital future. Wilbur did not wish to out himself as a luddite.

He could make or break restaurants long before the internet was a thing. Now he competed against foodie personalities online. The thought frustrated him, but he tried to calm himself lest a stress-related thump paid a visit.

Not in any shape to climb such a ramp, he was pleased to find elevators at the ready. He entered the nearest, which carried him up to the ship's lobby. The elevator opened to chaos. There were far more people in the lobby than he had initially noticed outside. All wore badges on their hearts and stood assembled in small cliques throughout the elegant space. The limited staff (it was a weekday, after all) fluttered about in a hurry, trying to respond to all the hoopla.

"Are you with the luggage vendor conference?" A woman at the front desk asked.

"Does this count?" Wilbur held up his carry-on.

The woman shook her head with a smile. "Let's get you through then, before we start in on this group."

"Thank you," Wilbur said and handed over his reservation information.

The woman typed on a computer and quickly produced the familiar sleeve holding his room key card. "Gave you a room away from them. Separate deck even. After this group finishes checking in, the world here returns to normal, and we will be available for any of your needs. Restaurants open for dinner later and ghost tours start in two hours."

Wilbur took his key card and a map of the ship, then the woman went about her business. Remembering, he pulled out his phone with the crooked smile man pictures. Too late. Before he could inquire about the internet phenom, the assembled group had crowded the check-in desk.

The outside elevators that delivered him to the lobby level differed from the elevator banks inside the ship. Wilbur crossed the lobby and stepped into one of two elevators available, immediately noticing the mirrored walls that the office intern had mentioned. Never did a ghost appear behind him. The intern also mentioned the woman in the mirror liked to get men in trouble by kissing the necks of their shirts and leaving lipstick prints, when she wasn't busy kissing the mirror itself. No ghosts and no red anywhere. Wilbur vowed to check his collar later, though it would be a scandal to none were he to suffer a lipstick collar. No one would ever notice.

Lipstick was the easiest thing in the world to fake, Wilbur thought. How many tourists kissed the mirror themselves to leave lipstick prints of their own, hoping to freak out other tourists? The thought grossed him out, so he remained in the center of the small space, careful not to touch anything other than the buttons.

With an emphatic ding, the doors opened into his hallway. The hallway extended on both sides further than he could see, giving a sense of how large the ship truly was. Following the flow of nearby room numbers, he eventually discovered his and entered.

The luxurious stateroom was a sight to behold. The well-conditioned but antiquated décor of the room evoked a bygone era. Seaside-facing, it offered a breathtaking view of the ocean through a small port window. It was easy to imagine the ship sailing the seas rather than floating on permanent mooring. The TV was an outlier in the otherwise historical setting. Once upon a time, such accommodations would only have been available to the privileged, but now anyone could book a room. Online no less.

A child's laughter sounded in the hallway, accompanied by running footsteps. The telltale voice of agitated parents never surfaced. Rather than someone scolding the child for acting so rambunctious in public, Wilbur heard nothing more than additional giggling and stomping.

Wilbur opened the door and yelped. The child stood directly in his open doorway as if waiting for him. "Good lord, child. You scared me half to death! Where are your parents?"

The child giggled and skipped away down the long corridor. Her laughter trailed her, yet somehow still rang in Wilbur's ears as if she remained in the doorway. The entire incident unnerved him. Too startled, he observed no details about the child. A mistake, for how could he report the child to staff when there were likely many kids on board?

Grabbing key card and camera, Wilbur entered the ship's corridor in a quest for the girl's parents. Her laughter greeted him as he locked his door. She stood in the distance, taunting him with her giggle. Once his gaze landed on her, she skipped away, so he gave chase while trying to persuade her to stop.

"I don't wish you harm," Wilbur lied, annoyed at the intrusion. He did not wish to hurt her, but he was okay if she took a spill and scraped a knee. A trouble for his troubles. Make her knee hurt as much as his own, which throbbed through the chase. "I simply want to speak to your parents. Can you take me to them?"

Skipping and giggling, she continued leading the chase. Wilbur assumed she would soon scramble into her room to hide from him. If he remained close enough behind, he could catch the room number and knock on the door to confront the parents. But rather than enter a room, (of which there were so many) the child bolted off to one side into an opening midway along the corridor. Wilbur rushed to the spot and found an atrium, which housed ice, soda, and snack machines.

Moving through to the open space, Wilbur came upon a second identical hallway to that of his own, which made sense. When booking, there were options for seaside-facing or landside. There were rooms on either side of the ship. Despite being out of breath, Wilbur snorted through his blocked nose. The size if the ship was much larger than he expected.

Opening his mouth to breathe better, he grunted in frustration. The girl was gone. He felt foolish. The child was on vacation. Did not that earn a little mirth? A little fun? Wilbur shrugged off the disappointment of not finding the parents and decided to tour the ship while he was already out of his room.

The ship was a joy to behold. Every minor detail leaned toward elegance. Even the upper deck stood out as somehow spotless despite the constant tourist foot traffic (one did not need to book a room to explore). Brass fixtures serving mysterious purposes gleamed brightly in the sunlight.

Seabirds circled overhead while avoiding the ship, as if afraid to drop feathers (or other fowl things) onto decks so expertly polished and clean. Wilbur looked out to sea and decided he could get used to such a view. Leaning over the railing caused his camera to bounce against the mahogany rail, so he stood and removed the camera from his neck.

He was about to set it down on the deck when he noticed a small hook jutting off part of the railing near a post. The hooks were placed every few feet along the railing. Hanging the camera on the nearest, he leaned back over the rail and took in the fresh air that only an ocean breeze could provide.

Even when leaving the room to chase the girl, he had the intention of touring the ship after dealing with the girl, so he had grabbed his camera on the way. Initially, he planned to take all the required pictures on his first day on the ship, but the more he explored, the more he decided he would switch to work mode at a later time. For now, he wished only to take in the sights.

Waves lapping gently at the belly of the ship offered a sort of peaceful soundtrack to his exploring. The sea, long the subject of tales of fury and destruction, appeared happy to lift the boat and any (living) spirits within. Wilbur stood mid-deck but noticed something quite odd when he turned to look toward the stern of the ship.

The ship's rear appeared darker than the rest of the deck, as if nestled under the clouds of an oncoming storm. But a quick glance at the sky revealed only sunlight overhead. A quick glance at the front of the ship offered no such optical illusion.

Turning back to the stern side confirmed it appeared unnaturally dark. One did not need to be at sea to recognize a brewing tempest. Storm clouds existed inland as well, and the world at that end of the ship was so grey that Wilbur feared he might need an umbrella. But why was the sky above the ship as blue as the water? It made little sense. Two enormous stacks towered above the ship, but their resultant shadows faced the ship's front, not its back.

Despite the gloom, details of the distant deck remained somewhat visible. Multiple stairwells along the deck culminated with arched metal bars that circled up out of the stairwells and curved until anchoring on the deck. Wilbur made out one such stairwell near the gloomy rear of the ship, from which rose a man, tall and thin. The stranger turned and faced Wilbur. The man wore a crew uniform. Perhaps he was there to investigate the unnatural darkness.

Looking around to ensure he was alone and not play the fool, Wilbur recited a portion of a sad sea shanty he remembered from a college literature course, oh so many years ago. The memory stuck with him because the words haunted him so. The shanty spoke of a crew meeting their fates at sea.

"We'll go down with the ship. We'll go down with pride. For we're sailors of the sea, we'll never hide. But the sea will claim us, in her icy embrace. And we'll be lost forever in this endless place."

The man at the end of the ship nodded. Did he overhear the sorrowful lyrics? Impossible, the man stood too far away. Still, the nod appeared to be aimed at Wilbur. If Wilbur was not mistaken, the stranger had a crooked smile.

Then a blast!

A horn. So loud that it induced a slight thump in Wilbur's chest. Quick pain that vanished once he isolated the source of the horn. It blared from a passing cruise ship leaving from a dock at the far end of the parking lot, ready for takeoff to places unknown.

Then a different thump drew his attention. The wind blew Wilbur's camera about on the rail's hook, causing it to thump rhythmically against the riser securing the railing. He placed the camera back around his neck. By the time Wilbur looked back at the ship's stern, the man was gone, if ever there at all.

As planned, there was no waiting for a seat at the restaurant. The bar was another story. A host greeted Wilbur at the front of the restaurant where stanchions used to create a queue remained opened wide on one side, allowing access for visitors go straight to the bar where a DJ played. So loud were the boisterous conference attendees, packed shoulder to shoulder, that their voices rose above the music. Whether a stipulation of the event or drunken forgetfulness, most still wore their badges.

Wilbur had waited an hour after the kitchen opened to visit. The host showed no signs of a kitchen staff overwhelmed. She earned points for not questioning his solo dining and earned even more points for seating him well away from the loud group while still offering a seat with a view.

Despite the elegance of the ship, the dining area stood out as a hub of luxury. Tables draped with linen tablecloths formed an ocean of white, stretching out as far as the eye could see. Multiple chandeliers lit the wide space, their long chain mounts vanishing somewhere overhead in a ceiling so high it was not out of the realm of possibility that it had a separate zip code from the rest of the ship. Flickering flames of wall-mounted candles lent sparkle to the chandeliers, crystal goblets, and polished silverware.

Wilbur would keep the camera around his neck until the food was served, playing up the tourist angle. Despite not knowing who Wilbur was, the kind waitress remained focused on him, unconcerned with the throngs of drunken people competing for her attention.

Having already had touches of the thump since arriving, he ordered only surf, no turf. Even drenched in butter, seafood was healthier than other options, though more expensive. Wilbur's order was large, as per his usual when working. The waitress lit up when she finished taking his order, her eyes alight with the possibility of a tip as grand as the dining hall.

The meal began with an appetizer of sautéed scallops bedded on a lemongrass and scallion slaw. Cooked to perfection, the scallops melted in his mouth. The slaw only stressed the freshness of the seafood. Next was a velvety soup billed as a noodle-free seafood ramen which tasted of lobster and cognac.

After the stunning soup came steamed dumplings filled with melon and prosciutto rather than the usual chicken or pork. Wilbur questioned why the appetizer came without a dipping sauce until biting into the first. It burst open in his mouth and released a savory liquid. The interior temperature remained cool despite the steam used to cook the dumplings. Stunning. *If this is to be my last meal, I could die a lucky man*, he thought.

While waiting for the main course, Wilbur heard a child giggle. (How was that possible? The crowd was too loud.) Searching, he soon spotted the same child from his doorway. But again, no sign of parents. Wilbur rose from his chair and the child bolted.

Not one to make a scene and run, Wilbur fast walked toward the girl. Wham! A couple collided with him before laughing and stumbling away, unaware they ever struck him. The brief encounter spun Wilbur away from the girl. He looked around and walked forward, only to stop as he moved too close to the music. The bass attacked his chest, bringing on the thump in full force as if a spindly, rough hand had reached inside his torso to give the beating organ a squeeze.

Wilbur froze, trying to work through the pain. Normally stress or food related, the heavy thumping pounded his chest into submission. No longer concerned with the girl, Wilbur fled. The pain only grew and did not stop, so he rushed toward the exit to the restaurant. Moving away from the music provided almost immediate relief. He had learned how to control his blood pressure, breathing deep through a nose that fought to block air (why was he always so stuffed?). He leaned over, hands on his knees for support as he allowed the thump to dissipate into memory.

Lifting his head, he realized he was near the restaurant entrance and could see into the hallway beyond. There in the distance was the girl. The DJ still spun records nearby, and the crowd roared with gales of laughter and inappropriate chatter, but he could still hear the child's laugh.

No, just a memory. Just an old man angered by how the girl caused him to suffer a serious bout of the thump. There was no way her laughter danced around his ears. She did not run, only stood there as if waiting for him to play, to give chase. He would not give the child the satisfaction. Wilbur turned and jumped when he found himself face-to-face with the waitress.

"Sorry. Didn't mean to scare you, but your lobster is getting cold," the waitress said.

The woman wore the look of someone fearing a dine and dash situation. Wilbur put her at ease and let her know he mistook a person at the bar for someone he knew. The relieved waitress walked him back to his seat where his main course waited. The lobster proved spectacular, and he was eager to write up the wonderful experience, but he would wait until after rounding out the menu over the next two nights.

After the meal, his tip (always a write off) delighted the waitress who begged him back every night of his stay. He promised to be there. Then, remembering his phone, Wilbur showed her a photo of the crooked smile man, asking if she knew anything about him. The waitress went rigid, suddenly sad or frightened. Or both. The mere act of sharing the photo changed the night's dynamic.

"I'm sorry, I have to go," she said and rushed away into the kitchen.

Wilbur exited the restaurant, disappointed in himself. He understood how busy the woman was, yet Wilbur attempted to drag her into a conversation about the "haunted" ship. She likely got it all the time and had enough. Like him, she probably knew it was all claptrap.

Wilbur took a deep breath and felt the slight chest tug. Luckily mild. Still, eating so much in one sitting affected him more and more in recent years, but a tinge was less bothersome than a thump. Deciding to walk off the meal before going to bed, Wilbur climbed the nearest stairs to the top deck. Though the view was spectacular, it was the same one from his restaurant seat earlier, so he walked the entire ship's length.

Mostly flat front to back, the ship's middle housed the triple smokestacks, and between those stood a hall that led down to more casual dining options, a museum, gift shop, and the rooms used by the conference attendees. Along the way, there also rose multiple metal bulkheads. The crisp white metal boxes stood waist-high in random spots along the entire deck's length.

Each clean, white metal box was padlocked. They likely contained supplies or served as access points for engine repair. Wilbur had noticed them earlier in the day but paid little mind. It was only at night when he feared possibly walking into one or falling down an unseen open stairwell under the darkness of night that caused him to consider them an issue.

For that reason, he stuck to the railing, following it the whole way. A much safer route, free of obstacles, and the spot on the deck with the best views, anyway. There was minimal lighting topside, likely dim by design to allow passengers to sleep better.

Initially, the night air felt warm and inviting, but inexplicably, the further he walked toward the back of the ship, the colder the night grew. Strange. Looking toward the stern, he noticed an absence of tourists, which fell into his strategy of booking the weeknight. By Friday night, guests would fight for a spot along the rail.

He glanced again toward the back of the ship. Any signs of a storm on that end had vanished, if ever there. But the oncoming temperature decline as he neared the back unnerved him. He felt a strange sense of dread creeping in with every step. Something bothered him about the back of the ship, but there was nothing out of the ordinary as near as he could see.

There was enough light for him to see where the ship's railing curved ahead, rounding the back of the ship. The railing fed into a spot behind one of the white boxes, same as any other. Except this white box was different.

Different how? Wilbur was not even there yet, but the looming white bulkhead caused him growing concern. Every footstep brought with it more uncertainty, more...What? Fear? Preposterous! Wilbur snorted out loud, disappointed in himself for his own odd behavior. He continued following the rail, intending to circle the ship, as many thousands of people had done before, though none likely felt as wobbly in the knees as himself.

As he drew nearer to the mystery spot, he confirmed an open stairwell near the front of the white structure. *Was that where the man from earlier had risen from?* Wilbur continued moving closer, using the railing as a guide while trying to understand the nature of his unease.

He felt similar feelings occasionally in different cities he visited, especially unfamiliar ones when he travelled for restaurant reviews. Those fears were the built-in DNA survival mechanism warning of potential dangers. But his own research confirmed the ship to be relatively crime-free beyond "ghosts."

The only thing that might explain his current irrationality was that he sensed someone hiding behind the last bulkhead on the ship. It could conceal a ne'er-do-well. But who would wait for victims on a section of ship that may not have any foot traffic at such a late hour?

Wilbur finally arrived at the front of the metal box and confirmed it to be no different from any of the others. He was close enough to touch it but refused to, gripping the rail as if his life depended on it. All he had to do was swoop in an arc and spot whatever was between the box and the tail end of the ship's deck. But he could not bring himself to do so.

Though unable to turn and face the dreaded spot, he walked the remaining length of the railing to where it curved behind the box. Once in place, Wilbur leaned on the rail and looked out to sea and ignored the feeling of dread at his back. His camera dragged on his neck and smacked against the rail once again. Fearing he might lose it overboard; Wilbur removed it from around his neck and hung it on the nearest rail hook like he had earlier.

Then he leaned against the rail and took in the sights. The view was stunning and faced further away from the city than the ship's bow, offering a clearer view of the sea. Lights from passing ships, combined with the moon's reflection, danced on the water in a spectacular ballet. For a moment he forgot his brewing fear, but only for a moment.

Foolish. He felt foolish. Knowing there was no such thing as ghosts, how could he feel so frightened over a waist-high metal box? It was time to turn around. Except he could not. Just the thought of looking over his shoulder made him grip the rail tighter. Then it began.

The thump.

A great weight filled his chest. Not a simple thump. This came on quickly and refused to subside. The moment by the DJ had been brutal, threatened to bring him to his knees, but what he felt as he tried to look behind himself felt worse. The more he turned his head toward the gap behind the metal box, the worse his chest felt.

Something told him that if he looked behind that metal box, his life would be over. He could not explain it, but he understood that turning fully around would change his life forever. So, he looked back toward the ocean and followed the rail back to the box's front and the adjacent stairs. He could not understand why the spot terrified him, but he no longer cared. His chest pounded so hard he feared it would burst open from the inside.

Wilbur's fight-or-flight instinct kicked in, and he raced down the stairs, almost falling the entire way. Immediately after reaching the base of the stairs, despite the stumble, he felt immediate relief. The pain in his chest was gone.

Still, his fear kept him moving. Wilbur bolted down the hallway. He was never a runner, even when younger, but the adrenaline gave him momentum. Earlier in the day, fast-walking after the child had taxed him, but now his desire to flee gave him a second wind.

He only stopped when a large group appeared ahead of him, slinking out from one alcove. He likely would have startled them were their backs not turned. They paid him no mind. It was a late-night ghost tour. Wilbur heard portions of the guide's spiel. A man cut in half while playing chicken with a door hatch, another ghost who only appears when someone is about to die. Nonsensical, all of it. Wilbur moved through the crowd and soon found himself back in his room.

Finally, alone and feeling well—good even (maybe he should exercise more)—Wilbur sat on his bed and pondered the events. The cloud of unease he felt topside had vanished. But up on the deck, for the first time in his life, Wilbur felt the smallest tinge of belief in the supernatural.

Earlier, he saw a storm that was not there. Then suffered a massive thump over fear of something unknown to him at the stern of the ship. Except it was not unknown. Wilbur inexplicably feared an innocuous metal box.

As Wilbur pondered the events in their entirety, he broke into a smile. Such an absurd fear gave him his supernatural angle for the paper. There was no need to investigate the crooked smile man or take one of the "haunted" tours. He had his own wacky experience and was done with it. Now he could write about his unease (leaving details about his thump to his doctor, not his boss) and call it a day.

Wilbur had his twofer. The restaurant and the *"Fear of the Rear."* Wilbur laughed at his working title headline. Despite the scare above deck, he felt better than he had in many months. Yes, more exercise was in his future. A brisk run had done wonders. He was relaxed and ready to sleep. A lifelong back sleeper, he lay down as if in a coffin and closed his eyes.

The digital clock read 3:00 AM when he bolted awake with the fear that he forgot to lock his hotel room door. As he considered mere hours before, statistics confirmed the ship's hotel to be safe, but an unlocked door in a public place was still an unlocked door. Before he could rise and find the lights, he heard something.

A giggle.

In the room? The child. Was she there? It sounded too close, but the rooms were relatively small. Perhaps she was in the hall. Then he saw a flash of movement. She was in the room! The moonlight through the window revealed her shadow.

"Hey, you, stop!"

Wilbur was intent on catching her this time. It was overdue. One thing to traipse around the hall and in the restaurant unattended by parents, but to enter his room? Had she stolen anything? The child only giggled and raced into the hallway. Following close on her heels, Wilbur ran after her. He gave chase, unwilling to let her out of his sight.

Not that he needed to. This time she never let off the gas that was her giggle. And she ignored many alcove escape routes along the way, instead leading him straight toward the back of the ship. Until the thump overtook him again, Wilbur planned to keep on the gas himself, chasing her down. He wanted to catch her before she got too far.

"Stop!" Wilbur yelled.

The kid kept running toward the stern of the ship. Why? Had he mentioned the fear in his sleep during a bad dream? He did not remember sleeping, only waking to find her in his room. Before long, they arrived at the same stairs he had escaped down earlier in the evening. She waited until he was close before climbing.

If he refused to climb, he would lose her. But he did not wish to return to the deck. He leaped back in fright when she stuck her head down the stairwell and laughed at him. That boiled his blood. He was going to get her and give her parents a piece of his mind.

He climbed the stairs and arrived on the deck. The giggling had stopped. It took him a moment to adjust to the dark. A rhythmic thump nearby drew his attention. It came from behind the box in that gap that he so feared. He looked off to one side and finally spotted the girl. She appeared less playful and pointed to the area behind the metal box.

"What game are you playing?" Wilbur said, posturing, trying to hide the shakiness in his voice.

He moved toward her, and for the first time, noticed her clothing. What he assumed was a dress proved to be a bathing suit. Wouldn't she be freezing? He leapt toward her, trying to catch her garment, but she shifted away from him while keeping her finger pointed to the same spot on the deck. Before looking to where she pointed, he followed the source of the thump to the stern's railing.

His camera! It hung from the hook he had placed it on earlier and tapped against a post with a rhythmic thump, thump, thump. The child was simply pointing out his forgotten camera! He turned to thank the girl, but she continued pointing toward the spot he had refused to look at earlier.

Wilbur gestured to the camera. She shook her head, confirming that was not why she brought him there. Wilbur followed her finger and gaze to the spot behind the metal bulkhead. His eyes opened wide at the sight.

"No!"

Wilbur's hands shot to his mouth, stifling a scream as he took in the impossible scene. A man lay crumpled on the deck in a twisted lump. His face was blue, eyes wide open, and his hands gripped his chest. The pretzel positioning suggested the man was in full rigor mortis and had been dead for some time. Wilbur stepped back and looked toward the girl, who giggled.

"No. Please, no!" Wilbur yelled as tears filled his eyes.

The man wore Wilbur's face. And his clothes. There was no mistaking who it was on the deck. The girl then pointed to where a man slowly approached, one dressed formally, as if part of the staff. Wilbur felt a rush of relief. He cried out.

"He needs a doctor!" Then Wilbur looked at the fallen body once again. "I need a doctor?"

The man emerged from the shadows. Wilbur recognized the crooked smile. The man from the pictures. And likely the talk of the ghost hunting group earlier. Wilbur remembered the snippet from the hall. "*If you see him, you are the next to die.*" The crowd of ghost hunters had not ignored him. They never saw him.

A woman's scream cut through the night. A couple holding hands noticed the fallen body. The man asked his date to call for help while he checked the body. THE body? Wilbur's body!

"I'm right here. Help me, please. Please do something, sir. I work for a paper. I can mention you, make you famous," Wilbur pleaded to the stranger hovering over the corpse.

The man shook his head and looked at his female companion. The woman was on the phone calling the front desk or an ambulance. Rising, the man took the woman's arm, and they moved away from the scene.

Wilbur was uncertain when the little girl had taken his hand, but she tugged at his arm. He finally noticed her bathing suit was dripping wet. Her eyes were nothing but orbs of white but were still pretty. She led Wilbur away. The man with the crooked smile joined them.

Rather than take the stairs, the pair escorted Wilbur to the elevator. A woman in an antiquated evening dress stood in one corner. Her smeared red lipstick stood out on her otherwise corpse-gray skin. Likely smeared from all the kisses given in the elevator. Red lip imprints lined almost every inch of the mirrored walls.

At some point, they exited the elevator and walked down a hallway. The woman remained behind, inside the elevator, looking sad as it closed. His two companions introduced Wilbur to Half Hatch Harry, a worker halved by a closing door. The man's partial body roamed about, confused as to his whereabouts. There were others who were in better shape than old Harry, and Wilbur understood he had all the time in the world to get to know each one.

They roamed leisurely, traveling every inch of the Queen Mary. There were worse places to be, Wilbur thought. The sea was calm, and the sights were stunning. Wilbur thought he might miss food, but there was one thing he would not miss.

Wilbur was happy to know he would never feel the thump again.

Fynn and the Infersagax vs. the Warmongers

by Richard Squires

I nvading the perfect blue sky, a sooty mass of roiling smoke sailed across and devoured the horizon. Fynn stood on the balcony of his cruise-ship room, ashen fingers clenched on the railing, awestruck by the Caribbean sky on fire. One hundred feet down, below another two levels of room balconies and the ship's hanging lifeboats, the ocean surface bubbled. The cauldron, Fynn could sense, churned under the charred sky with lifeblood.

"Dolphins!" he said to nobody. He'd been hoping to see dolphins and whales ever since Grandpa Sol had presented Fynn and his mother, Sylvia, the gift of a five-day vacation aboard a Future Cruises ship. But these were no dolphins. Within the mud-hued water, over which a netting of white foam heaved and jabbed the ship, creatures glowed. Their shapes varied: winged, sleek, and diamond like manta rays, multi-armed like starfish, eels coiled in infinite spirals, giant butterflies, their wings studded in fiery jewels, patterned veins in ghostly movement, their incandescence pulsing with the water's motion. Every edge was a silty suggestion, sand trailing and dissolving, then reforming, precision balanced against evanescence.

Emerging from the boil, a sea butterfly rose. Its chest glowed from inside; its intricate patterns and spots glimmered. The thing hovered before Fynn, bigger than any man, its wingspan some-thirty feet across. Seawater gushed from its tail, danced off its slowly flapping wings, sprayed and foamed about itself, drenching Fynn's face and t-shirt. He stood there bug-eyed, speechless, gazing upon this gorgeous creature beyond dreams, the ocean water cold on his face. Feverish and shivering, he surveyed the designs adorning it, nature's unparalleled artistry, detailed like a leaf, a spiderweb, a fingerprint.

Do not fear me, it said telepathically, in a voice—rather, an essence—that did not seem unkind. It had the quality of a young man. *Your world is on the brink. Your past wars have been but grains of sand spinning in water that sun rays render invisible and weightless. Civilization after civilization, you have annihilated yourselves from this planet's surface, only to rematerialize equally arrogant and destroy yourselves again. But now your kind wields weapons beyond comprehension. Now my world is on the brink too.*

Understand: we, the Infersagax, came to a cold lifeless rock and set the world in motion. You live because of us. Its mouth did not move as it hovered in the air. *The warmongers across this pearl of a world are fortifying their positions. That is why we have emerged from the recessed cosmopolites below. I speak to you because you are equipped with the sense to hear me. I will guide you through what is coming. We need you, Fynn. Watch for the signs.*

You can call me Moses.

The creature's light faded. By the flash of lightning, Fynn saw the body instantly dry up. Cracks formed across it as on a desert floor. Then the desiccated creature was no more than a damp clump of sand, dropping sloppily to the water, the driest grains riding the wind. But the kernel of light at its center remained hovering, glowing dimly like an ember.

"The signs?" Fynn said.

Don't you smell the smoke? The fires have begun. Look in the distance.

Fynn looked up to see a charcoal-dark cloud filling like a sail, growing and creaking, expanding until it popped. The force hurled debris that propelled him over the balcony.

With a great convulsion, Fynn's sleeping body jarred and dropped from the bed to the floor. Ever since he had changed medications, his dreams had been especially vivid.

"Everything alright in there?" his mother called from the connecting cabin.

It took Fynn a moment to remember where he was: on a cruise in the Atlantic having departed the previous afternoon from Fort Lauderdale and bound first for Ocho Rios, Jamaica—where they had waterfalls!—followed by Cozumel, Mexico. He rubbed his neck where he'd scratched it.

"Yeah, Mom. Fine."

He brushed his teeth in the tiny bathroom, then rummaged in his toiletry kit for his pills, but the bottle wasn't there. Probably in his suitcase. He stepped outside onto his room's balcony and was delighted to see, for his first time, a limitless expanse of ocean, a blue womb cradling the cruise ship, the waves shushing it like a baby. The scene was soft, such a reprieve from thorny life on land these days. The blue horizon split ocean blue and sky blue, and all was quiet. The humidity seemed to suck up sound. Sure, he heard noises, like people mumbling on adjacent balconies, yogurt spoons clinking dishes, a steel drum up on the deck, and the kazoo calls of birds accompanying the ship, probably hunting for French fries. But it was all muffled, no room tone anchoring sound to reality, easy enough to convince yourself you didn't hear a thing. The breeze blowing the curtains was mute.

Fynn sat in the chair, relaxed his eyes, and let his gaze blur into the infinite blue. He had existed for so long without the feeling of serenity, but now that he'd landed on this new antipsychotic, which subdued the voices in his mind, he felt better, more in control than he'd felt in a long time. And he could feel the tropical vacation working on him already, the heat and quiet massaging his pent-up nerves, his strained psyche.

"Yeah," he said to the blue world, "chillin' on a ship in the Caribbean." Today was a full day at sea, a day for boredom, unbothered by any teacher or bully or doctor or soccer coach while taking in the grand vista of boundless sea. A high school junior, Fynn had recently turned seventeen. His English teacher had assigned a short book called *The Stranger*, and even though Fynn was no avid reader, he already knew he was going to enjoy reading about a man who had become disassociated from society and could no longer make sense of the world. Fynn would never let on in class how much he could relate to the protagonist.

He opened the book, but before he could read a word, he looked up to see, maybe three hundred yards away, sea life splashing the water surface and playing. He'd been told he might see dolphins and whales on this trip, that they liked people and often swam beside the ships. But these creatures were too far away to tell what they were.

And then something strange happened: a projectile, dark beige, round like a bowling ball and huge as a car, shot from the water. The ball looked compact and solid, and seemed to be made of sand. Fynn watched it arch away from the ship and begin its descent, but too far away to see where it landed. Two more followed rapid fire.

"What the...? Hey, Mom, did you see..."

He was interrupted by a cacophony of hiccupping static from his mother's new shortwave radio, which could pick up stations all around the world. She'd wanted one forever, so he bought it for her birthday a few weeks earlier. They'd found all sorts of interesting broadcasts: Aboriginal music in northern Australia, African folk music in Zimbabwe, relaxing sitar in India, a slew of cool world music, not to mention all the talk radio in foreign languages. That first night they'd fiddled around with it, they landed on a station that sounded Arabic.

"It's all Greek to me," Fynn said, and they laughed. It became a repeating joke. If they landed on a French station, or a Russian station, or any station that wasn't in English, one of them would say, "I think it's Greek." The joke never got old.

"Think we'll pick anything up at sea?" Sylvia asked when Fynn walked in. She sat at the small desk and stared through thick glasses at the digital numbers on the radio.

And then she landed on something and the static was replaced by talk: "*El diablo, el diablo está en nuestra casa. Ser advertido o estar muerto.*" A Spanish-speaking station. The guy sounded panicked. Something about the devil. And death.

"Sounds like Greek to me," Sylvia said, and burst into laughter. Fynn giggled, but he was bothered by the sight of the projectiles because he was realizing how unbelievable a story they would make if he tried to explain what he'd seen. What if they were—he shuddered to think it—a delusion?

Time to find that medication.

Sylvia dialed through the static soundscape as Fynn searched his suitcase pockets. She found another station. "The devil's voice is working its way into our brains. There is a sickness sweeping through the smoke-stained wind." It was a preacher with a southern twang. His voice was raspy. He sounded fat, breathless, and choking on desperation. "Do you not see the feathered flames fanning up and suffocating the clouds? I can see the smoke with naked eyes. I can hear the demons in the distance coming closer with my naked ears."

Don't listen to him. It won't help.

The meds weren't in the bag. "Mom!" Fynn hollered.

"What's the matter?" she called.

"Change it, will you?"

He lifted his suitcase onto the bed and pulled out his clothing as Sylvia turned the dial and found another station. This one sounded like British news. Fynn hated the news. The smart kids in Mrs. Lutz's Politics & Society class loved it. They gave twenty-minute presentations on the recent hacking of nuclear codes and the increasing popularity of authoritarians and strongmen. Athletes like Fynn, on the other hand, squeaked by on eight-minute talks about bullshit, like a congressman's recent argument that the label "psycho" shouldn't automatically connote such extreme negativity. Psychos weren't all bad people. That was important, especially with psychosis on the rise.

The latest news, according to the shortwave, was almost too dramatic for Fynn to stomach. He scoured his suitcase while hearing about riots in cities on every habitable continent, egomaniacal world leaders who couldn't, or wouldn't, work out diplomatic solutions to global disputes, missing weapons, a sense that the next world war was on the brink—yada yada, what else was new?

But maybe the worst catastrophe of all was happening right there on that cruise ship: it seemed, unbelievably, that Fynn had forgotten to pack his medication.

"Damn it!" Fynn blurted.

Sylvia looked at him through the doorway. "What's going on?" She shut off the radio, hobbled over to him—thanks to a childhood bout of polio, she walked with a limp and wrote like a kindergartner—and took his face in her hands.

"God, Mom," he shouted, and turned away. "I'm not a baby." What was he going to do without his drugs? He couldn't tell her he'd forgotten them. It would just worry her, and he'd still have to go without them.

"What is it, sweetheart?"

He rubbed the scratch on his neck and turned to face her. He controlled his tone, made it kind. "I'm just hungry. Can we go to breakfast, please?"

"This is more like it," Fynn said, cheered by the breakfast buffet extravaganza. At the Belgian waffle station, the cook served up a waffle exactly the size of the round plate, its texture soft and airy with a brittle coating. Luxurious toppings: fresh berries drowning under whipped cream, thick syrup, warm blueberry sauce, and a shake of powdered sugar.

He found a table for two by a large window with a view of the wide sea, and dug in. The first bite sent a tingle of warm pleasure through his body, and he thought of the circuits in his brain, how the senses received signals before the brain registered them, how the whole system was so complicated and fast and, for many people, out of their hands.

Some people's own minds bullied them. The projectiles he'd seen didn't make sense because he knew for sure that the meds were swimming laps in his bloodstream at a healthy clip. This antipsychotic was easily the best fit of any medication he'd tried, and he'd tried a lot. It had started to take effect just as the state soccer championships and final exams had raised Fynn's level of anxiety to a near-alarming pitch. Both he and his mother worried about a potential reprise of the breakdown from a year earlier when he became convinced—*absolutely convinced*—that a clique of his own teammates were conspiring to keep the ball from him. Even during games, they were stealing from him every chance they could. He caught on to their intricate point system, how a steal was worth more during games than practices. It was an obvious conspiracy that Coach Fischer somehow did not see. Which proved he was in on it.

Fynn was so upset that he started to keep the ball from both the opposing team and his own. Coach Fischer benched him, and then word spread throughout school, *everyone* whispering about how Fynn was as big a ball hog as ball hogs get, when truthfully, Fynn prided himself on being a smart passer and playmaker. It was the height of humiliation.

But early this year, the medication kicked in and managed to hush the voices that made so much noise in his head. Fynn had kept his shit together through the end of the semester, thereby helping his mother—who also had a history of psychosis—keep her shit together. His teammates' game fizzled as though it had never existed. Maybe it hadn't; Fynn couldn't be sure.

Grandpa Sol, proud of his daughter and grandson, and perhaps feeling guilty for moving to Palm Springs so far from New Jersey, gave them this cruise as a gift. Fynn had never felt better. So why did he experience a delusion—a flat-out hallucination—like nothing he'd known before?

"I see you've begun," Sylvia said, placing down a large white bowl of yogurt, fancy with granola, orange raisins, fresh berries, and a leafy garnish—mint? In her other hand, a thin flute of champagne. "We're on vacation, aren't we?" she said, sitting. She seemed buzzed already. "Besides, have you ever heard of 'liquid courage'? That's right. I'm planning to make friends on this boat. You are too."

"I am?"

She nodded and drained her champagne, then wiped her mouth. "I'm feeling a positive energy. It's so pretty out here. The air is clean. Your new medication seems to agree with you and mine with me. I'm just so..." She looked like she couldn't believe she was going to say it, "happy."

"Jesus, Mom. Are you speaking Greek?" Fynn said, and they both laughed.

They found two chaises on the pool deck. Still early, the low sun spread over the calm water, painting a stripe like a white road to the end of the cloudless Earth. An easy breeze cut through the humidity but carried on it a faint stink of smoke. Probably a cigar, Fynn figured, although he didn't see anyone smoking. It smelled more like a campfire. "You smell that?"

"Oh, I don't know, Fynny. My sense of smell isn't what it used to be. My sense of sight, on the other hand..."

Fynn looked up to see a family of four strutting across the pool deck, mom and dad with two teenage daughters. The girls' hair, black and silky, shone in the sun. One of them wore a pink bikini, short shorts, and heart-shaped sunglasses. The other wore a blue and red one-piece suit.

"They're twins, my boy. Identical twins."

"Cut it out, Ma. Quit staring."

The mom jingled in clunky gold bracelets, a gold sun hat with a satirically wide brim, and, from this distance, what appeared to be worked-on lips. The dad, in white, fairly short shorts, carried a briefcase with a newspaper tucked under his arm. He seemed strange, like a European diplomat or politician.

"Understand," Fynn said, "home is complicated, vacation is simple. Get sun, read, swim, eat. That's all."

Sylvia cackled, then laboriously got to her feet, and walked down the gangway. Fynn opened his book and looked at page one. He could tell right off that it was an accessible read, but before he finished the first paragraph, he heard a sound, a voice rather, that he recognized from somewhere. *You are equipped to lead us through what is coming. Accept that you hear me. Acknowledge.* He looked around but knew already it hadn't come from anywhere. Now he remembered his crazy dream. Had he heard the voice this morning, as well?

Fynn gritted his teeth and wiped a tear from his eye. A goddamned hallucination, but like nothing he'd ever experienced, because even though voices in his head and delusional thinking had haunted him over the years, his mental disorder had never manifested as true visual or aural hallucinations. The voices weren't sound-voices, they were thoughts. The things that he saw weren't sights, they were ideas misinterpreted through a faulty thinking filter. So what the fuck was happening? Was this the start of an epic psychotic break?

"Shut the fuck up!" Fynn yelled, and then slapped himself across the face.

An elderly couple three chaises down in mega-sunglasses and thick white sunblock stopped their conversation to look at him. They seemed like judgmental people anyway. A waiter walked over and asked if anything was the matter, which made Fynn's face flush hot.

"Sorry," Fynn said.

The waiter said he would return with a glass of water.

Fynn looked for Sylvia. The situation was only getting worse when he saw her down the way trying to make friends with the twins' mother. "Oh, Mom," he whispered. He put his book in front of his face to hide.

After a bit, Sylvia limped back to Fynn. She didn't walk like a well woman.

"How many mimosas have you had?" Fynn asked.

"I should have brought my cane. And do you smell that smoke? I think it's making me woozy."

"Just don't fall," Fynn said. The breeze moved his dark bangs from his face as he returned his eyes to his book, but he couldn't concentrate now.

"Look over there in the pool," Sylvia said. The twins stood in waist-deep water talking to a couple teenage dudes and shooting a basketball at a low poolside hoop. "Their names are Veronica and Dawn. Their mother is Enid. She talks like she's rich." Then she burped.

Irked, Fynn dropped his book on the chair and stood. He needed a distraction, from both his mind and his mom. A year earlier, when Fynn was going through his breakdown, he would have been in no condition to approach a pair of girls. But now, this morning aside, he felt confident. He was in the best shape of his life with all the running Coach Fischer made the team do. Not all that long ago, he'd grown taller than a lot of his peers. He pulled his t-shirt over his head, sauntered to the pool, and stepped off the ledge in time to pull one of the girls' basketball shots out of the air and alley-oop it into the net.

"Two points," he said to the twin in the pink bikini.

She replied, "Goaltending, buddy. Big fat zero points."

One of the boys there in the pool—shaggy blond hair, pimples on chest and shoulders—laughed. "What happened to your fuckin' neck?" he said. "Looks infectious."

Fynn had forgotten he'd scratched it. The blonde dude seemed to be with the girl who'd shot the ball, and another two guys were hanging around too. "You know how the ship has a dance company?" Fynn said. "Well, I hooked up with one of the dancers last night and she gave me a mean hickey. She got her teeth into it."

Everyone seemed confused. The twin with the skimpy bikini top—she had braces too—looked annoyed, while the other one in the one-piece wore a bright smile. She kind of stood apart from the others. "Maybe she was a vampire," she said.

Fynn laughed. "That's what I thought. But then the sun came up."

She smiled again, and Fynn saw she had a patch of thin, dark purple veins crossing her throat. "Well then, I guess you're safe."

"I am safe. By the way, my name's Fynn. What's yours?"

"Fynn?" the bikini twin said. "Sounds kind of fishy. Perfect for an ocean cruise." Her boyfriend laughed at that.

"Don't listen to her," said the other twin. "I like your name. It may be fishy, but it's better than Gil."

Fynn smiled. "And who are you?"

"I'm Dawn."

"But seriously," Dawn's sister, Ronnie, said, "what's that on your neck?"

"Seriously? A martial arts competition last week. Do you know what a spiked ball on a chain is?"

Dawn erupted in laughter, fell back under the water, then emerged with dark hair slicked back and sparkling in the pretty sunlight.

"Oh, I get it," Ronnie said, a crook in her lip. "You're funny."

Dinner in the grand ballroom of king crab legs and skirt steak was delicious. As Fynn and Sylvia dined, Fynn thought fondly about his hours talking with Dawn and shooting baskets in the pool. But then the ship's captain, speaking over the intercom, announced he was sorry to share that fires in Jamaica and vague reports of a political event meant the ship would not be able to dock at Ocho Rios. The plan was to continue on to Mexico, arriving by morning and allowing extra time to enjoy the fine sands of the Cozumel island. For tonight, a reminder about the Elvis impersonator in the theater at nine sharp. "Trust me, ladies. He'll get you all shook up."

And that's when the voice—Moses's voice—returned.

Jamaica isn't happening. Cozumel isn't happening. The cruise isn't happening. I have information for you that you are equipped to receive. Acknowledge.

In a flash of anger, Fynn stamped his fist on his thigh and groaned with enough volume that the couple at the adjacent table whipped around and practically burned him with the devil's stare. It was the same old couple who'd seen him yell to nobody on the deck earlier in the day.

"Fynny," said Sylvia, who'd just begun her second piña colada. "What's the matter? Is there anything funny going on?" She held her palm to her chest. Her eyes were glassy. Fynn could see that panic was in the vicinity.

He thought of his research topic in Politics & Society, today's concept of psychosis and the discrimination against anyone labeled "psycho." According to a few articles, more and more people were hearing voices these days, many of them describing the voices in similar terms. It was almost like a virus going around; catch the virus and welcome a strange inner dialogue spouting conspiracy theories.

"The waterfalls in Jamaica, Mom." That seemed a reasonable explanation for his outburst. "They're all I wanted to see." Now he wanted to see Dawn. A kind light glowed from her. He tossed his napkin to the table and stood.

"Aren't you escorting me to the Elvis show?"

"Elvis is Greek to me, Ma. Why don't you hook up with Enid?" he said and excused himself.

The club was the best place to look. Maybe the twins and their dumb friends would be there. A disco ball strobed lightsabers at the curtained walls and checkered, 1970s-style dance floor. Rainbow lights swirled like oil across the floor, and shadows of dancing feet and legs wig-wagged the twist. The music was loud, but Fynn heard the twins' crew whooping down the hall before he saw them whirl into the club. The guys were laughing loudly like a bunch of drunk jocks. The blonde, whose name was Preston, had his arm around Veronica. He moved kind of roughly, but she liked it, or at least wanted him to like her. Fynn looked at Dawn, who smiled at him and rolled her eyes at them.

"I'm glad you're here," she said. "My sister is such a poseur. It's my mom's fault. She's always treated Ronnie like the older sister and me like the baby."

"But aren't twins born at the same time?"

"Yes, but one comes out first."

"Oh. How much older is she?"

"Thirty-three minutes and thirty-three seconds. If you ask my parents, that's why she got braces before me and has bigger tits than me. They think she's wiser even though I'm in higher classes. They let her in on all the secrets. It makes no sense."

"Hey, I'm reading a good book about a guy having an existential crisis. Nothing makes sense to him, either."

Suddenly a hand holding a silver flask shot between them. "Who wants a nip?" Preston said, laughing. "It's top-shelf vodka." Preston's buddies giggled. "My dad snuck it onto the ship. Isn't that cool? It was the slickest. We emptied big water bottles and filled them with the stuff, then carried them on the outsides of our backpacks. Hidden in plain sight. Boo-yah!"

"Oh my god," Dawn said, a flat-toned deadpan. "But I thought you guys were loaded. Isn't your dad, like, a bigtime lobbyist for the NRA?"

"We've got sick money, it's true," Preston said, "but in my brilliant dad's enlightened words, 'Fuck those bitch-ass losers.' And fuck Jamaica!"

"Gimme that." Dawn took the flask and swigged two healthy gulps from it. She made it look like it tasted good. While tipping her head back, she covered her throat with her hand. She passed the flask to Fynn. He downed a gulp—it tasted like rubbing alcohol, but he quickly felt warm inside. Music dripped from the speakers, seeped into his skin. A smile blossomed on his face. Maybe liquor would help suppress Moses's voice. Then he thought, *Shit, have I really named my imaginary friend?*

Dawn took the flask from Fynn, put it on the nearby table, and pulled him by the hand to the dance floor. It occurred to him that that had not been Dawn's first drink of the night. Her eyes were closed as she grooved to the Bee Gees' "Night Fever." Fynn was not usually comfortable dancing. Most guys were not brave enough to dance at school, and it didn't seem that any of the girls were interested in Fynn. But there was something wild going on, and Dawn was part of it. He moved his shoulders, cycled his bent arms, shook his hips, and twisted his right foot on the toe—disco, baby. Losing his mind or not, he was alive in the middle of nowhere, alive here and now. Feeling silly, he threw his arm diagonally into the air like John Travolta. "Don't do that," Dawn yelled over the music, and they laughed.

The next song was slow. Dawn looked at Fynn expectantly, so Fynn stepped closer and Dawn came into his arms. At school, unimaginable. Yet here, with her, it was natural.

"I didn't expect to meet anyone I actually like on this boat," she said. "These douchbags are so into my sister, it's nauseating. Another day with them and I'd throw myself overboard. You saved the day."

Fynn wasn't sure what to say. He certainly couldn't frighten her with psycho stories. "I'm glad we met, too. It's just me and my mom." Then he added, "And the voice in my head." He regretted saying it when she pretended not to hear.

They danced for another couple songs—while Ronnie and her boyfriends sat around the table watching Fynn and Dawn with dour expressions—and then

Fynn said, "You wanna go look at the stars? The view is going to be out of this world."

Dawn looked at him and nodded. "Let's get outta here."

Ronnie stepped in front of Dawn as they passed the table. "Where're you going? Remember what Dad said: we have to stick together."

Fynn noticed the boys watching, creepily interested.

Dawn patted Ronnie on the shoulder. "Okay, big sister. I'll be just outside those doors right there. In range of your boyfriend's b.o." She pulled Fynn by the hand.

They crossed the pool deck and climbed white metal stairs to a platform that overlooked the pool and surrounded the ship's big white fin. They lay down on side-by-side chaises and gazed up. It was the best view of the night sky he'd ever seen: a band of clustered galaxies wrapping the earthly orb like an epic rainbow, neon in its brilliance. Sparkling pinheads across the rest of the sky punctured the otherwise black dome.

"Weird," Dawn said, "but doesn't it kind of look like it's snowing over there?"

Yes, in the distance, a swarm of white specks weightlessly streamed across the sky. The moonlight twinkled off them as they twirled. They were far away, but they looked like tiny scraps of paper. Or ash, which made sense considering the pervasive smell of smoke that everyone had grown used to by now.

"It's ash," Fynn said. "That smoke smell is stronger now, isn't it?"

Dawn responded but Fynn didn't catch what she said because the voice returned and spoke over her: *It's only getting worse, soldier. The time is approaching. Steel yourself.*

Fynn's face flushed. He jumped to his feet, shook his head out like a dog shaking water from its coat, and walked over to the railing overlooking the ocean.

You think your mind is the problem, but we have real-world problems. The warmongers are gearing up. You can smell the end.

"At least it's pretty," Dawn said, stepping next to Fynn and leaning her shoulder against his.

Fynn flinched. He pressed his thumb and forefinger into the corners of his eyes, then brushed his knuckles across the scratch on his neck.

"Everything alright?"

He turned his face. They were close. "Totally."

"You got some deep thoughts swimming around in there?" Her eyes rose to his forehead.

"I guess."

"That's what I like about you," she said. "And your eyes."

Fynn, praying Moses wouldn't distract him in this moment, said, "I like your smile." Her lips twinkled in the moonlight. He moved closer, and they kissed, and Fynn felt a rolling ball of fire in his chest, an adrenalized edge pulsing above his tailbone, a hot chill rippling from the back of his neck through his fibers into his cheeks, and his eyes filled with tears.

They gazed together at the horizon. The moon hung where a late afternoon sun would and broke into stardust on the evermoving water.

"Holy shit! Do you see that?"

"What?" Dawn replied.

There were creatures in the water, strange and varied shapes that did not resemble ordinary fish. They glowed from their insides. He recognized the butterfly—it was Moses, he realized, again remembering details from the crazy dream where they'd met. Which meant he really was losing his mind—and just when things had become so promising.

"Fuck!" Fynn hollered into the night.

"Fuck is right," Dawn replied, annoyed and pulling away from him. "Ronnie has a boyfriend at school, and he's a fuckin' psycho. I'm not like my sister."

Fynn was looking down at the water, which was bubbling, just as it had in his dream. He knew it wasn't real. It couldn't be. But there it was, Moses the sand-butterfly, starting to emerge and rise, adding white noise to the sound of the ship cutting through the water.

Dawn watched Fynn, then punched him in the arm hard. He looked at her. "Ronnie's boyfriend? I'm sorry to hear that."

She took Fynn's chin in her hand and turned it to her. "I like you, but this game you're playing, whatever this act is, it's really lame. I don't need this shit." She pushed his face away.

Let her go. We're losing time.

Fynn took Dawn's hand. "Hey," he said, trying not to yell over the fuzzy sounds filling his head. "Sounds like your sister's boyfriend is an asshole. You know, there's quite a difference between an asshole and a psycho." As he said it, he couldn't help but smirk.

"Fuck you, fish-boy," she said, and stormed down the platform's metal stairway.

Moses rose to Fynn's height and hovered across from him.

"You're fucking up my vacation," Fynn screamed. "You're not even real." He slapped himself across the face. But the vision of Moses did not disappear. Instead, the vision explained everything.

"I'm feeling charitable. You get one last chance," she said, and then glass shattered. Fynn turned around to see Dawn, her face distinctly pallid against her black hair. At her feet, a smashed bottle of red wine she'd been holding.

Fynn, drenched with the seawater misting from Moses, wiped his face and said, "You don't hate me?"

She pointed. "What the fuck is that?"

He turned to Moses, back to her. "You mean you see him?"

A shriek up above. In V formation, seven missiles carved through the sky on thick tails of fire.

Moses dropped the sand he wore, revealing his naked self, an egg-shaped ember, and darted back into the water. "Oh my God," Dawn cried, her voice tremulous. "What's happening?" She grabbed the railing by the stairs and lowered her head, queasy. On the pool deck below, people spilled out through the club doors, watched the missiles, and groaned with panic.

"They're going towards Cuba," some guy announced.

"Look in the water," someone else yelled, pointing. "I told you I saw monsters!"

Thump! A massive projectile, like a ball the size of a car, launched from the water and clipped the tail of one of the missiles, sending it off course. In the distance, it arced downward, crashed on the ocean, and splintered into a thousand pieces. The cannonball pulverized into a swash of clumpy sand. A second sand cannonball followed rapid fire, clipping another missile and sending it straight down into the water.

"I don't feel so good," Dawn said. "I think I'm losing my mind."

"You're not. And neither am I." They looked at each other. "I understand what's happening," Fynn said. "Moses told me. The war is beginning."

"What war? The one those psycho conspiracists have been talking about?"

"Wait, Moses is talking now. Oh shit!"

Fynn grabbed Dawn by the forearm and pulled her through glass doors into an elevator hallway that connected to the cruise ship's gym. He sat and wrapped his arms and legs around the metal railing lining a gradual ramp. "Quick. Sit next to me and hold on."

Under the water, the missile detonated and its force whacked the bottom of the ship. A radial wave rose, spread in every direction, and rolled across the pool deck. Ocean water smashed through the window into the elevator hall, filled the room, and tried to pry Fynn and Dawn loose from the railing and pull them back out. But they held firm with their legs intertwined. People down on the pool deck cried out and held on. Fynn and Dawn watched as the water carried four of them clear across and over the other side. They were gone.

The water drained out of the elevator hallway. "What the fuck?" Dawn said, pulling kelp from her hair. Far in the distance, the five missiles met their target. Cuba was aflame. Miles away, it looked like a dying candle sending up a strand of smoke. "War against who? The communists?"

"No. Against humanity."

"You mean it's an alien attack?"

"No. The warmongers are attacking."

Exasperated, ten fingers digging in her hair, her eyes popping wide, she cried, "But who are the warmongers?"

"You know, the strongmen." She didn't seem to get it. "Uh...the people who are crazy about warfare. And absolute power. Corrupt leaders and billionaires who have no respect for life beyond themselves. And a few others like them." Fynn shook water from his hair and pulled his wet t-shirt away from his skin. "Am I making sense?"

"You don't mean..." She looked like she was afraid to say something stupid. "...Republicans. Do you?"

"Well, I hadn't thought of it like that. I'm talking about trigger-happy wackos who got their hands on big weapons, and they've been taunting each other about who's got the biggest dick. Your dad, and Preston's dad, they're involved. They knew about it. That's why you're all on this cruise, so you weren't on land when the shit began."

Dawn shook her head. "But that can't be!"

"Moses says I have a mission. He says there's soldiers out there like me who have been recruited to help save the world." Fynn cleared his throat and spat. "I can imagine how that must sound to you."

"Who's Moses?"

Another shriek as a single missile crossed the sky in the other direction, toward Mexico. Fynn and Dawn ran back outside. Two balls of sand catapulted from the water, but they missed the missile.

Below, the Infersagax swirled under the surface in frantic motion. So many egg-sized fireflies. They scattered throughout the water, filling the sea with their light between the ship and horizon. The ones farther away looked like moonlight on water. They manipulated the sand, pulled it around them into the strangest sea creature shapes, and ran their ornate currents through their forms. The ocean looked like an underwater theme park, a glowing city.

A pair of missiles crossed the sky in the distance. "If Mexico is that way," Dawn said. "And Cuba is that way. Then..."

Fynn finished her thought. "Then the U.S. would be that way."

Sand balls shot from the water and missed. And then a wave of sand rose, a glowing wave specked with light, teeming with Infersagax working together to pull sand from the ocean floor, to reach higher than a building.

"You see? They control the sand, as long as it's wet. But they can't do anything on land. They need our help."

The sand swallowed one missile like a beast and took it down to the depths. The other missile continued on into the gulf, toward Texas or maybe Louisiana.

And then the Mexican land, which was closer than Cuba, coughed up a gray and charcoal mushroom cloud.

"I can't believe this is happening," Dawn howled. The flames pulsed in her wide wet eyes.

Down on the pool deck, someone yelled, "Is that a wave?"

Dawn and Fynn turned to see a wall of water rising and coming their way. "Quick, we have to find my mom," Fynn yelled.

They took the stairs by the elevators down a level, then ran through the hallway to Fynn's room. As he pulled the key card from his pocket, the wave reached the ship and tipped it back, pushing Fynn and Dawn up onto the wall, almost horizontal. As it rolled back the other way, Fynn slipped in the key card. The door fell open and they slid along the floor into the room as though on a carpeted slide. It hurt when Fynn hit the corner of the bed base, and again when Dawn crashed against him. People in adjacent rooms were screaming. Somebody in the room directly above fell over the balcony and sailed into the ocean far below.

"Mom," Fynn yelled as the ship rocked back the other way. Dawn scrambled into the space between the bathroom wall and the bedside table, which was fixed to the floor. Fynn looked in his mom's room. She wasn't there, but the shortwave radio was. He grabbed it, joined Dawn, and switched it on. Just static. He turned the dial until he found a voice.

Listen, Moses said. *He speaks for us. His name is Judah, and he is your general.*

From the radio: "When the warmongers are finished destroying everything beautiful on Earth with their weapons of unprecedented magnitude, the pollution will penetrate the depths of the seas. It will flow through the tunnels and recesses that snake about the innards of this great world where we, the Infersagax, have lived for eons maintaining the machinery that spins and warms this planet. The warmonger pollution will likewise spread lightyears to our neighbors and begin the slow process of destroying their worlds, potentially igniting intergalactic discord that the Virgo Supercluster will not soon recover from.

"Less than one percent of humankind is equipped to speak with us. You who can are soldiers, leaders, ambassadors for humankind and all living things, charged with eradicating the warmonger threat. Tonight we head into battle. We are united across a communal frequency of cosmic goodwill to rescue everything that matters..."

The ship suddenly jolted. Unfixed objects toppled to the floor. Everything went dark. The ocean tantrumed outside. "Do you hear that?" Dawn whispered. It sounded like war—guns and exploding bombs. People dying. When the emergency lights blinked on, Fynn realized the ship was no longer swaying.

"I think we're beached."

People ran down the hallway past the room. Some walked in a daze toward the elevators. Fynn and Dawn joined hands and moved down the red blinking hall. There was a feeling between them like a dream, swirling energy pouring from their chests, fusing and connecting them. It was pure, the flavor of a tranquil home.

Fynn stopped and turned to Dawn. "Do you feel that?"

"Yes," she said.

They kissed, their tongues swirling, oblivious to the panicked people crying and running by. Fynn dragged his lips over her salty face, down her chin, and to her throat, where he kissed her patch of veins that he knew she considered her defect, her vulnerability. He loved her. She was perfect as she was.

Seawater trickled down the stairs and leaked from under the elevator doors. The exit light blinked. The ship creaked and shifted. They held each other and remained balanced. "C'mon."

They climbed the stairs. Outside on the deck, they saw that the ship had crashed into Mexican land. They were in a flooded city. The water, or perhaps the sand, had carried the ship far enough inland that the ship's nose was wedged between two tall buildings. The ocean heaved and sent waves rushing up the avenues. Ocean flowed across the deck, and they held fast until it pulled back. They sloshed through water a foot and a half deep. Between the buildings, up close and in the distance, fires danced. Fires waved from windows. Military hurried haphazard from point to point, firing rifles as sand cannonballs launched from the sea into the city. Whatever the sand hit, it destroyed. It smashed craters in the asphalt, chipped chunks of concrete off buildings, flattened men in camouflage. From the ship's vantage point, Fynn and Dawn looked down upon hell.

"Let's go," Fynn said.

Some people were climbing over the side of the ship. Fynn and Dawn splashed over to find an emergency ladder. At the bottom, they waded through water up to their chests, never letting go of each other's hands. They navigated around concrete debris and rebar, avoided live wires and men with guns.

"Where are we going?"

"Moses said this is the way."

"This way?" said a deep, accented voice. "No way, Jose." A man in military garb with a rifle stood before them. He meant to plunder, no question.

Dawn squeezed Fynn's hand even tighter. She held her breath, then looked at him and said, "What now, soldier?"

Fynn winked. And then a mass of sand rose from the water like a cape, curled over the marauder, squeezed him, smothered him, and took him under.

"Thanks, Moses," Fynn said.

They continued inland a block and treaded across a golf course. The terrain was sopping, gloopy with sand, bombs dropping all around and splashing fiercely.

"Dawn! Is that you?" Her father splashed toward them. "Oh thank God. Where have you been?" he said, grabbing her by the arms and shaking her. "How'd you get separated? I told you to stick together." He had a vague accent, as though he'd moved to the U.S. from Germany decades earlier. "We have to go now. A car is waiting for us."

A strange look came over Dawn's face, first of confusion, then a flood of steaming betrayal. "A car? How can that be?" She looked at Fynn.

Behind her dad was the rest of their entourage: Enid, Ronnie, Preston, his parents, and some other boys.

"Fynn!" It was Sylvia at the back of the group. "Oh, darling. Are you okay?" They ran to each other and hugged. Sylvia looked over Fynn's face.

"I'm fine, Mom. Are you hurt? Did you fall?" She was a gaunt woman and Fynn could see her scalp through her thin damp hair. And yet, her face glowed with health. There was a buoyancy to her in all this action that he'd never seen.

"Fynn," she said, and pulled him aside where no one could overhear her. "Listen to me. I know what you've been going through. I understand everything."

"I don't think so, Mom. There's no way you could…"

"You've been speaking with Moses."

Fynn's mouth dropped open. "But how…?"

"Because I'm paired with Esther. They are coordinating with each other. They're looking after us."

"So, that means you're a soldier, too?"

"My mission is to attach to Enid and go with these people. At their hideout, I will kill her husband and communicate the location to Esther."

"But, Mom, I have to go to the capitol and find General Sanchez. He's the one with the launch codes. Moses says I'm going to kill him."

"You've always been strong, Fynn. You've always been a soldier. You can do this, I know it."

"But we have to stay together."

"We will reunite, my love. Esther says I will meet you at the Capitol. Stay safe. And remember: I'm proud of you."

Fynn followed the group at a distance across the golf course to a concrete staircase that spiraled a column up to the highway. Abandoned cars, some flattened under mega-goops of sand, lay strewn about. He watched, hidden in the shadow of the staircase archway, as headlights approached. A large military

Humvee stopped. A mercenary in black stepped out and said, "Mr. Rainer, we're your ride, courtesy of the Sanchez administration." He opened the back door. "All aboard."

Fynn watched as Dawn, her head hunched with sadness, walked around the car to the door on the other side. Fynn's heart sank. He wanted her to stay with him so badly but he knew that was selfish. She would be far safer with her father's people, no matter how evil they were. The whole crowd of them loaded in, and then the Humvee rolled arrogantly away.

Are you ready, Fynn, to do your essential part in saving the world?

Fynn took a deep breath. He tasted smoke on the air. But he also tasted optimism. He'd never before felt that he knew exactly what he was supposed to think or do. But now he felt as he did when he was with Dawn, in alignment with the universe.

"I'm ready," Fynn said, starting to walk. "I just wish I wasn't alone."

I'll be with you.

"I appreciate that, although it isn't exactly what I meant."

"Hey, Fish-boy!" Fynn turned to see Dawn step from behind an upside-down minivan. "Want any help saving the world?"

Euphoria entered his blood and laughter shook his body. Fynn took Dawn's hand. Eastward, daylight was a hazy suggestion. They turned inland, toward darkness, where far-off fires branded the future.

"I hope you're aware that the capitol is like a thousand miles away," Fynn said.

Dawn looked at him and wiped a gob of wet sand from the side of his neck. "Is that all?"

The Deer Serpent

by Genevieve Williams

T he foghorn of the *M/V Kennewick* rang across the water as though in
summoning. Though the crossing from Coupeville to Port Townsend
was not far, from where Matilda and her father stood on the fore passenger
deck there was nothing to be seen but a brief stretch of water vanishing into
thick, gray soup. An *unseasonal* fog, they'd been told, though Matilda was of
the opinion that everything was unseasonal these days.

"Look at that," her father was saying. "Might be anything out there."

Matilda, who had finished out her sophomore year with a major declaration
in marine biology, thought that she had a better idea of what was out there than
he did. But she knew better than to make that argument. Her father had already
expressed his disappointment in her choice, though whether it was because she'd
never make money at it or because she was selling out to, in his words, "obscenely
well-funded" Big Science was not clear.

"Mm-hmm," she said, instead of any of that. "Hey, maybe we'll see some
orcas."

Their actual destination, one of the many salmon runs that fed into the
Salish Sea, ought to be thick with returning salmon. There'd be fishers and

whale-watchers and tourists galore. And people like her dad, for whom the salmon cycle and the beings who fed on it weren't wonder enough.

True to form, he snorted. "Sure," he said, with the kind of condescension that would have offended her even if she was ten years younger. "Maybe we will." He did his little grin, the kind that stirred an uneasy trill deep in her gut, and she looked out at the water and concentrated on calming that trill down. "But look." He got his phone out, one of those ones that was almost big enough to be a tablet. He hated reading glasses and refused to wear them. It was some web-based forum, the kind with lots of emoji and pop-up ads. "There were a bunch of sightings this time last year. They've gotta eat something, why not salmon?"

Why not, indeed, though from the descriptions Matilda was pretty sure what these people had actually seen was a sturgeon. "Sure, Dad," she said. "You've been looking for sea serpents every summer since I was ten without finding them, but this summer'll be different, right?"

"Don't patronize me." Mentioning that she'd been ten had been a mistake. "I don't have to keep paying for that fancy college, you know." As though state university was fancy in any way beyond the price tag. And the money, she knew, was from a 529 anyway. They'd set it up for her, her parents had, back when they still had optimism and her mother hadn't left for another continent. "We're gonna go out there and prove all these stories right and all those scientists you like so much wrong."

She couldn't think of anything to say that wouldn't wind him up further. So she said nothing, even though part of her wanted to.

"I'm going to get some coffee," she said, just to have an excuse to leave. He gave a little smirk in response. She walked away in the direction of the snack bar, trying not to give a shit, snatching the green ballcap he'd given her off her head as she went and wishing she dared chuck it into the garbage can. As it was, she folded it up so no one could see where it said *45TH ANNUAL CRYPTID WATCH AND FISH FRY* on the front.

The snack bar seating area had chairs and tables fastened to the deck. Several of them were occupied by a bunch of people about her own age. She slowed and swerved a little toward them, then turned away from them and the snack bar both and went up the nearest staircase to the upper deck. The noise of the wind and the ferry engines and the occasional foghorn made it impossible to hear anything else, and the deck was all but deserted. She pulled up her hood of her parka and snugged down into it like a turtle. The fog was beginning to lift. Ahead lay an amorphous shadow.

She'd been to the peninsula before, on previous trips with her father. It would be pretty and maybe even fun. At that moment, all she wanted was to get through this trip and back to school.

She stayed up there until the horn sounded again and the announcement came that they were arriving in Port Townsend.

The campground was a nice one outside of town, shaded by Douglas fir and western redcedar, with lower-growing shrubs to make a bit of privacy between the campsites. The campground was full, mostly with RVs and fancy custom-built camper vans. There weren't a lot of converted vans like her father's, which owed much of its existence to salvage yards. Whatever work online he did while driving it around the Pacific Northwest looking for Sasquatch and sea serpents and arboreal kraken and who knew what else didn't pay all that well. She also had her doubts about the kayak riding on top.

"I'm going for firewood," he said, once they'd got the van parked.

Matilda paused in the process of setting up her tent to nod at him. He watched her for a moment, his expression not quite disapproving. The van had two sleeping benches. Technically. It hadn't felt cramped when she was younger, but it did now.

He still wasn't back by the time she had the tent set up, so she went for a wander herself—and was surprised to see the same group from the ferry in one of the larger campsites. They had a whole tent village going, including a few larger pavilions, one of which sheltered a sizable camp kitchen. Glamping at its finest.

She walked on by, thinking about the laptop in her backpack with its incomplete internship application. If she could work on that, she would have something to think about besides the fact that she was here with her father, instead of with a group of friends. But there was no Wi-Fi in the campground, and her father paid for her phone's data plan.

It was getting dark under the trees when she got back to the campsite. Her father had gotten a fire going, and there was another guy sitting there with him. They looked carved from the same mold: middle-aged white guys in beards and flannel, who'd probably turned some heads before life's disappointments, exchanging glory-days stories over beers. She found herself hesitating at the edge of the firelight.

"Matty," her father said. "Come and meet Jim."

Jim raised his beer bottle at her. "Hey, Matty. Nice to meet you."

"Matilda," she corrected him. "Hi."

"Matilda," he repeated, with a glittering look. She knew she was cute, all blond and big-eyed, but this wasn't the way she liked to be reminded of it.

"Jim here's a kindred spirit," her father said, with an expansive gesture that suggested this wasn't his first beer, either. She hadn't been gone *that* long, just a slow circuit around the campground, stopping to read every posted sign she came across and wondering whether it was too early for dinner.

Close enough. She started preparations, mostly as an excuse to stay on the periphery of their conversation, but she couldn't help picking up bits and pieces of it.

"Two summers ago," Jim was saying. "Well, it was only a glimpse, and the pictures I got on my phone are no good." Matilda focused on stir-frying vegetables to keep from saying anything. "Hoping to get some better ones this time."

"Yeah, if we get better pictures—and video—people will have to start paying attention," her father said, as she sliced pre-cooked kielbasa into the frying pan. "Sure, people will say they're fake, but there's ways to prove they aren't. I don't understand why they're so afraid of the truth."

"That's not what they're afraid of," Matilda said, as she held the pan over the fire, stirring the food with a wooden spoon. "They're afraid of what happens when too many people believe lies." Though they were several feet apart with the fire between them, she could *feel* her father tense up at that statement. But he wouldn't say anything too overt, not with his new friend here. She kept stirring and thought about the ocean.

"Then we just have to show them that there's nothing to be afraid of," Jim said, when the silence had gone on almost too long. "Right?"

"Right," her father said, after a pause.

They got through dinner—the stir fry over instant rice, which Jim stayed for—without any more dangerous edges, and Matilda started cleanup for the same reason that she'd started dinner, though it irritated her to do so. Jim and her father had opened two more beers. It was fully dark now, the campsites around them alight with their own campfires, with lanterns and even electric lights lighting up some of them as bright as though they were indoors. If a Sasquatch were lurking in the woods right now, watching them, no one would even notice.

"I'm going to bed," she said. The sooner she slept, the sooner it would be tomorrow, and the sooner it would be one day closer to get this over with. Maybe next school break she'd come out here by herself.

"Brush your teeth," her father said, which was supposed to be a joke, the way he said it...and yet, there was that undertone, the way he often said such things, telling her to do things that she was going to do anyway. Sometimes, when she was younger—not that much younger, the last time had been right before she went away to college—she'd rebelled, refused, wound up confined to her room the whole weekend because she'd been in the act of putting her glass in the dishwasher when he'd told her to do just that, and had shut the dishwasher and put the glass in the sink instead, just because.

So she didn't say anything, but did get the little bag that held her toothbrush and toothpaste, and headed for the bathroom. The big campsite with the tent village was just across the road from it, and when she came out, it was all lit up like a festival. Her and her father's campsite was just up the road.

Matilda walked across the road and right up to the circle of people gathered around a large fire pit. "Hello," she said. "I saw you on the boat. I'm Matilda."

She hadn't thought it was that late, though the homebrewed hard kombucha was stronger than she was used to. She *had* told them that she was camping here with her father; not revealing that seemed like a kid thing to do, even though she didn't really want to. She hadn't said that they'd come to the peninsula looking for sea serpents, though. The group, only some of whom were in college though all of them were college age, were there for the salmon return. Some of them planned to go fishing.

"Thought you were going to bed," he said, behind her, and as she turned everything went slow as though she were in a dream, she stood up and staggered a little, one of her new friends supporting her with a hand on her arm.

"Oh hey, Dad," she said, and her voice sounded like it was underwater.

"Time for bed," he said, as though she were five years younger. Ten. And, over their protests, knowing it would be worse if she didn't, she got up and followed him back to their campsite. Jim was gone.

"Making friends?" her father asked her, making it sound as though it was the worst thing she could possibly do.

"They were nice," she said, and hated herself for sounding weak.

"You've been drinking," he said, as though he hadn't had two beers before she'd left, and probably twice as many again at least while she'd been gone.

She took a deep breath. The air around them seemed to ring.

"Good night," she said, and got into her tent before he could say anything else.

She was not sure how long she had been asleep when she opened her eyes into darkness. She blinked a few times, making out her tent's interior by the dim light that still came from outside. There was a rustling, and then someone shouted, close enough to be in the next campsite, or out on the road. She lay there a long moment more, listening.

Another rustle, longer, and nearer. Matilda sat up, strapping her headlamp over the watch cap she'd worn to bed, and half-climbed, half-flailed out of her tent.

There were fewer fires and most of the lights were out. The beams of flashlights and headlamps swung and stabbed through the dark. She heard the rustling again and turned toward it. Whatever it was sounded huge. Hand trembling, she reached up and pushed the button on her headlamp. Black eyes and a black mask across a pale, furred face stared at her from the bushes. Then the round, furry body turned and ran.

A hand on her shoulder. She jumped.

"A raccoon, Dad," she said. "Just a raccoon."

"Yup." An electric golf cart with a light shining from its roof had stopped on the roadway; the grizzled voice of the camp host issued from somewhere under the bright beam. "Got 'em, around here. Bears, too. Make sure your food and trash are stowed, y'hear?" Without waiting for a reply, he rolled away with a whine of the cart's electric engine.

"Raccoons," her father said, sounding disgusted. His hand was still on her shoulder. She moved away from it and went back to bed, though by the time she fell asleep, the inside of her tent was clear to see, and the birds had started singing.

The kayak was sun-bleached red and felt brittle under her hands. So far, though, it didn't seem to leak. At least they weren't far from land, and there were other boats around.

There had been fog again that morning, and the sky was still cloudy as though it were April or even May instead of July. Unseasonal.

There were a *lot* of boats. Whale watchers, and kayaks like her father's, and small fishing boats and live-aboard sailboats, even some paddleboats circling near a small dock. It had been like this for days, she'd heard when they launched. This was the peak of that year's return, and everyone from people casually seeking to hook a fish or two to boatloads of tourists hoping for killer whales had been crowding the water. One of the pods of the endangered resident killer whales had been spotted in the vicinity; it was hoped that they'd make an appearance. Matilda hoped for that, too. It would make this entire clusterfuck of a trip worthwhile.

Jim was nearby, in a kayak of his own, sporting a pair of binoculars and a camera with the largest telephoto lens Matilda had ever seen. Her own camera was pretty good, and she practiced taking action shots of the seagulls swooping and diving while her father and Jim traded anecdotes: the time her father had seen something walking along a ridgeline in the North Cascades, kind of like a bear in shape but walking upright; the time Jim had been out on a whale-watching boat and seen *something* in the water that wasn't a whale, or a seal, or a fish, or anything else known to live in the sea—Matilda had to bite her tongue at that one. They traded online handles and discovered that they were in some of the same forums and Facebook groups; her father was CryptidKeeper just about everywhere ("Get it?") and Jim was SquatchMan. Matilda took a photo of one of the guys from last night's camp—they'd been friendly to her that morning but more guarded than before, she thought—as he hooked a salmon and brought the fish soaring out of the water as though it were flying. Cries of excitement came from the whale-watching boat and Matilda trained her camera in the direction they were pointing, capturing the moment when half a dozen black dorsal fins emerged from the water all together. She'd read that too many people and boats stressed out the orcas, but just now they seemed to be ignoring everything and everyone except the salmon they chased. One tossed a fish into the air and hurled its body after it, snatching the fish in its jaws and plunging back into the water to exclamations and gasps from the onlookers. Matilda, who'd switched her camera to burst mode, kept her finger on the button through the entire display. She'd seen the killer whales a few times, on class field trips. She never got tired of them.

Jim and her father were watching, too, but didn't train their cameras on anything in the scene. Matilda sighed. Whatever they were here for, she, she decided, was here for this.

Her phone buzzed in the breast pocket of her parka. She started to reach for it; even as she did, a great shock ran through the water, rocking the kayak from side to side almost hard enough to tip it over. The pod of orcas turned as one, taking great leaps over the water as they fled. A few of the smaller boats *had* tipped over, dumping their occupants into the sea, and someone on the whale-watching boat tossed a life preserver over the side to someone who had fallen overboard.

The water sloshed and rolled like it was boiling. Matilda, who somehow still had her camera up, turned it toward the shore, where the trees thrashed as though ripping their roots from the ground to go walking. Dirt and rocks slid from the sheer bluff above the shoreline, throwing up a great cloud of dust.

Something seemed to move within that dust, a formless shadow that rolled with the landslide down into the water, accompanied by the massive groans of stressed architecture that might have issued from some monstrous throat, in rage or in deep despair. The sea boiled as though in answer, and she wondered how deep the water was here—shallow water was dangerous during a tsunami, wasn't it?—and then something burst from the sea right beside their kayak, two somethings, a pair of necks that merged into one like the trunk of a tree, soaring higher and higher until Matilda's head was craned all the way back, her finger flicking the camera's mode over from photo to video.

Even as her camera's autofocus settled into a crisp view, the red circle in the corner of the viewfinder showing that she was recording, she took in the details: the two heads, with angular snouts such as she imagined a dragon's must look, or else a horse's, or possibly a giraffe's—the heads did have horns, short stubby ones she thought at first, only no, they curled back and around like a ram's horns, and the eyes were enormous but she could not discern their shape, and—it was like nothing she'd ever seen, on any field trip, in any aquarium, on any Youtube or Tiktok video, in any of her books.

It went on forever, the boiling sea, the shaking land, trees and houses shaking until they fell over, every boat that could trying to get away. Through it all Matilda gripped her camera with numbed fingers, kept it trained on the beast until, without a hint of a warning, it slid back into the water and was gone.

Everything went still. The water quieted. Clouds of dust caught the wind and drifted over the sea. The sobs and cries of people in pain or shock or sheer relief mingled with those of the gulls wheeling overhead. Matilda lowered her camera. She couldn't help looking at her father, who grinned at her with gleaming eyes.

"*WOOOOOOOOHOOOOOOOO!*" he hollered, his gaze never leaving hers. Then he shook his head, his loose hair wild, grinning like a madman. "Jim!" he exclaimed, to the man in the other boat sitting frozen with an expression of shock on his face. "Jim. That was it. That was *it*!"

On every social media channel it was the same. Youtube, Tiktok, Instagram, Twitter, Facebook, even Mastodon. Tons of pictures, videos, descriptions, people chiming in with their own stories, people who hadn't been there but had felt the quake, or who had seen or even experienced the resulting tsunami. People who *wished* they'd been there. And people who thought the whole thing was bullshit or were just trolling.

And every one of those images or videos, including her own, was out of focus, or jittery and jumpy, or you just couldn't make out details, or something. Though on her own camera, *only* the images of the creature were like that. The shots of the birds, of the killer whales, of the camper hauling a thrashing salmon into the sky—all of those were in perfect focus, just as she'd taken them.

The eyewitness accounts all disagreed with one another, too, even more than eyewitness accounts usually did. The news media mentioned the serpent, but only as a side curiosity. Their main story was the earthquake, which had done considerable damage to Seattle among other areas in the region. A lot of the comments under the videos and photos, or replies to people's stories, insisted that the whole thing was a hoax. She didn't dare look at any of the cryptid forums that her father liked to frequent, but she didn't need to. Her father was right next to her in the Bainbridge Island ferry terminal, his own laptop hooked up to the public Wi-Fi, his face dark as he scanned the forum postings. "Listen to this. *I don't understand how there isn't better video. How do we know this is even real, and not a deepfake?* For fuck's sake."

All around the terminal, similar conversations were taking place: people who'd been there, people who wished they'd been there—why?—people who thought the whole thing was some elaborate ruse or mass hallucination or something. Some of the conversations were getting heated. No one seemed to agree on what had happened. Ferry service had been delayed for hours while the Seattle ferry dock got itself functional again, and Matilda wondered whether it would resume at all, or whether her father would just give up, take the van out of the parking queue, and drive them off to wherever they were going next.

But the boarding announcement came at last, and Matilda and her father went to their van, rolled onboard with the rest of the vehicles, and parked on the port side. Matilda looked past her father, out over the water. Her video was as jumpy and indistinct as all the rest. She'd kept the camera focused and held it as steady as the physical chaos of the moment had allowed, and yet the result looked like one of those movies where they disguised the lack of budget with shaky camera work and jump-cut editing.

The ferry's engines rumbled, and the boat began to pull away from the dock. Matilda's father stared straight ahead, his hands still on the van's steering wheel even though they weren't driving anywhere. Matilda's heart accelerated with the boat's engines. She had to say something. If she didn't say something, he would—

His hands slammed into the steering wheel so hard that she jumped, a split second before the horn sounded. Someone getting out of the car ahead of them turned around to give them a confused look.

"I don't fucking believe it." He sounded so *angry*, as though some injustice had been done. As though something he had laid claim to had been snatched away. He turned to her, and she wanted to flee from the look on his face. No matter how many times she saw it, it raised that flush of alarm all over her. "I hope you're happy."

"About what?" she asked, feeling tired. Just...*tired* of this.

"No matter what we say, no matter what we prove, people will just insist it's bullshit. Even you. You were *there*!"

"I'm not posting that video," she said. Her voice was steady, though it took some effort to keep it so. "I don't know what we saw." She kept feeling like she'd missed something, like the event had some significance that she lacked the context to understand. She kept coming back to a comment that had showed up under several of the posts that she'd looked at, though it didn't seem to have always been by the same person: *It's not FOR you*, the comment said, along with a hashtag using unfamiliar lettering that she couldn't read. "But it wasn't your sea serpent. It was something else."

"You—" He turned away and punched the steering wheel again.

She jumped, and then grabbed her laptop bag where it nestled by her feet, opened the door, and got out. Outside smelled like exhaust and salt and that tarry smell the docks had, even though they were some distance from the terminal now.

"Where do you think you're going!" he shouted. She heard the driver's side door open. She walked up the aisle between the cars as fast as she could until she could cut over to the stairs, then hurried up them to the passenger deck.

He followed, still shouting, and people were staring and she just didn't *care* anymore. People saw stranger and more terrifying things every day and didn't believe them.

When she reached the front of the passenger cabin, where swinging doors led out into the wind, she stopped and turned. Looking up at him. Memorizing every detail: the once-handsome face turned harsh and cragged by disappointment and resentment, eyes full of rage that dared not admit to grief. Her father. No monster, but a being whose frame of reference she would never, in the end, understand, nor allow herself to live in.

"Sure," she said. "Cut off my funding. Stop paying for my phone, if you want. Leave me on the dock in Seattle and let me figure out how to get a bus back to campus." He'd done things like that last before, more than once. She didn't shout, but she didn't keep her voice down, either. A few people had their phones out. She hoped this didn't go viral.

He walked right up to her, got in her space, close enough that she wanted to back away. She didn't. He'd never hit her, give him that. He'd just...always been bigger, always been louder, always worn her down with fear of what *might* happen. Her stomach had twisted into a knot. If she threw up on him, so be it.

And then...he left. Shoved past her, through the swinging door, and outside. She didn't turn to look. She didn't move, or speak, try to accommodate or smooth over or make better. She just let him disappear.

A ferry worker came up to her, all neat in dark pants and a pressed white shirt. "Everything okay, miss?" he asked.

She blinked and looked at him, then nodded.

"Fine," she said, though fine was for later. She went over to one of the bench seats, right by the window where she could look out at the water, and opened her laptop. Her hands were still shaking as she connected to the Wi-Fi and opened the application that she had partially completed. But then she found herself flipping over to her video archive stored on her hard drive and looking at it again. No matter how many times she watched it, the details refused to stay in her mind—and refused to match up with what she had seen that day.

Maybe, in the end, it didn't matter what the being looked like. It was not *for* her, so certain commenters said, this creature that confounded the eye and refused to render in clear image. It hinted at a wider world that would not be bound by her second-year undergraduate explanations, nor yet by her father's conspiracies; but something wilder, stranger, and more true.

Invasive Species

by Karen Menzel (née Bovenmyer)

D own by the well under the linden tree, where wishes were made, I watched my golden pearl sink like the moon into the unfathomed dark. There, on the cool edge of the forest, you boiled up from below, thou green swine, my pearl pinched in your wide, alien mouth.

What was there to do but run from you? Fear pebbling my skin, freezing my blood. To bar the door against the plip, plop, plip, plop of your coming. I should have known there was no stopping this. Freedom never lasts in a story.

Father admitted you because you said you had my promise. You had my pearl. Even as a thick, ugly water-splasher, he let you in. My promise was not the only thing that had been broken.

Father commanded me to share my golden plate with you. That which had always been mine alone. That which had fed and sustained me. And you, pond-squatter, were invited, consulted, honored. A frog commanded more respect than I did, pretty golden bride price that I was. Slime rings rippled from where you dipped your blunt head into my cup.

My tears changed nothing. Once a thing is shared, it cannot be unshared. Documents were signed, land changed hands. No amount of begging could have reversed where the story went next. Father commanded I carry you, fly-gulper, to my bed, my secret seat of dreams, inside my private curtains. I did not bother to mask my disgust as I carried you with just two fingers. You threatened to tell my father if I did not allow you into my inner sanctum.

You pushed against my silk pillows, burrowing wetly, a scream building in my throat. Father was not here, now. Only you and me alone. You did not expect to be thrown, old croaker, with all my might, against the wall. I expected you to land with a wet plop, or perhaps a satisfying crunch of broken bone. I did not expect you to explode into a beautiful prince, as commanding as a mountain, shaking a mane of hair. You leapt across the room, more demanding than ever. How terrible were you, husband, folding me into your arms, pointed elbows still smelling faintly of swamp.

Three things you asked and were given by my father: to eat from my plate, to drink from my cup, to sleep in my bed. The fourth, that I love you and have you as my dearest companion, only I can give. It matters not, paddler-turned-prince, that you shove me into a carriage drawn by eight horses with white ostrich feathers on their heads. I don't care how many servants follow you with dangling bands of iron. I have learned who matters in this kingdom. The princess is at the bottom, like my pearl, like the naked moon, sinking into the well. That lost childlike wish and myself will always and only ever belong to me.

[...] at the end of a stalk

by John Christopher Nelson

W hen the boat became intimate with the time-barnacled rock that was large enough to puncture the vessel's side—but far enough below the surface of the water to remain unseen by the not-fully-trained and mildly inebriated individual piloting the ship—three things happened and one thing didn't.

First, "Space Age Love Song" stopped playing because the iPhone, paired with the Bluetooth speaker assigned its own chair, flew off the side of the boat and into the ocean. The brunch was also worse for the wear, most of it sliding onto the deck, where it was punctuated by shards of broken plates. Memories of partially consumed charcuterie—Iberico ham, Emmental, cornichons, Marcona almonds, olives, Turkish apricots—scraps of morel and chanterelle quiche, mostly finished peach and herb salad, exoskeletons providing evidence of shrimp cocktail, and two neglected deviled eggs for which nobody could accommodate room in already overburdened stomachs.

Kelsey didn't know who Flock of Seagulls were, anyway.

Second, the vessel was now at a twenty-three-degree angle, providing it the illusion of a freeze-framed speedboat.

Third, Kelsey, who had been sitting on the toilet below deck, was jolted forward, smashing her face into the faux-wood paneling that bordered the shower wall. The thing that didn't happen, yet, was the power had not cut out, so Kelsey still had light to ease her return to consciousness.

Oh, and, technically, when listing things that did and did not happen, there's the matter of the other members of the festivities.

Raymond—whose balance was already askew from the six Bloody Marys he'd had—slid along with the boat's new angle and collided with a pitcher of mimosas, impaling his face with varying sizes and shapes of shards of glass. Despite his protestations that mimosas were "just for chicks," he died smelling like them anyway. Though, the pitcher of orange juice and cheap champagne didn't kill him. He lay there, bleeding from his face, slipping in and out of consciousness for some time until the boat upended and he slid under a railing and overboard.

Stephanie had been standing at the railing on the side, when the boat struck the rock. Also victim to the abrupt halt in motion, she toppled over the railing where a spear of wood, that had burst from the boat, post-collision, entered beneath her jaw and exited through her left eye socket. She would remain suspended this way until the boat eventually sank, partially alive until the vessel went under and she drowned, only a quarter conscious for the experience, not even enough to panic when she stopped being able to breathe anything but salt water.

As for Skylar, Kelsey's partner—he hated her calling him that, but boyfriend felt weird because he was a man. They'd fought about it more than once, but that would never matter again. He had a mimosa in hand and was waxing captain behind the ship's wheel—he was the only one qualified enough in seamanship to man the boat rented for Stephanie's birthday—when they struck the rock. It sent him full force against the wheel, breaking his sternum and stopping his heart instantly. He might have survived, but the fracture instantly dislodged a blood clot that had remained hitherto undiscovered and been waiting patiently for a green light. A luckily painless end for him and, impressively enough, he'd slumped over the wheel, never spilling his mimosa.

There's a lot of ways a person can regain consciousness. The way a normal, healthy person wakes up in the morning. Or the way a person who passes out drunk, rather than falling asleep; their morning is that much different. Or when you take the wrong length nap in the afternoon and you do it too long or not long enough and you just can't get back on track for the rest of the evening. Then there's passing out for health reasons, and that cold, thick sweat that layers you, like glaze on a sheet of fresh cookies, when your battery has recharged sufficiently. And then there's a good knockout, which is a strange combination of a few of the aforementioned sensations and more. It's a shame most writers haven't been knocked out and most boxers don't write, because it would be nice to find that perfect overlap to describe that unique sense of seeing stars, as they accurately describe it.

When Kelsey came to, she was still seated on the toilet in the too small bathroom below deck, her head resting against the wall in front of her where it had struck when the boat lurched forward, sending her with it. Before taking her head away from the wall, she blinked, freeing some blood on her face, and assessed the room, everything at an angle.

When she sat up, putting her back once again against the open toilet seat, noting the blood on the wall, she realized that, albeit, less of an angle, the bathroom was still decidedly not level. Also, she must have been out for a minute because the blood from her face had coagulated and pulling it from the wall made the split in the skin on her face start bleeding anew.

There was quite a while spent—one of those fugue states when you're just having a moment, regrouping; could be seconds, hours, minutes, who's to say—while Kelsey just sat on the toilet, letting her head bleed, pants and underwear still around her ankles, staring at the blood on the wood paneled wall that framed the shower in front of her. Luckily, the bleeding mostly stopped, the blood having scabbed up again during her lapse from reality. Any fresh, bright blood was the result of her having torn asunder small fragments of scab when she withdrew her head from the paneling.

She let her face hang in front of her chest for a moment, drawing a breath or two, and finally wiped and stood to pull up her—too fast. Sitting down again, sturdily enough so the toilet issued a complaint. After another few minutes or however long, she stood, slowly, ever so slowly, pulled up her bottoms, flushed the toilet and closed the lid. Then braced herself on the sink. The angle of the bathroom was doing little to help her sense of post-syncope nausea.

Now, carefully, bracing her hands on the countertop, to investigate her wound in the mirror. Not bad, but bad enough to knock her out. She checked her pupils to make sure their size was equal. Well. She had no idea where the boat's first aid kit would be, anyway.

As one does, she absentmindedly pushed against the bathroom door. Nothing. Well. Something. Something was clearly blocking the door. Still weak from passing out and smashing her head, her initial attempts were halfhearted. But after three or four more tries, Kelsey put her full weight against the door, shouldering it with as much force as she could. The gap was enough to maybe slip her fingers through, but nothing else. And this was when she noticed the water on the bedroom floor, water that was making its way into the bathroom. She let up on her weight and the door closed. In this short amount of time, the degree to which the boat had tilted had increased.

Now, the next logical step. "Steph! Sky! Ray!" Kelsey banged on the door, then the wall, then the ceiling, repeating the names of her three friends. Only Ray could hear her, but he was not within his wits enough to respond. Kelsey found herself thinking of that eighties song that she didn't really know, but then she was thinking of other eighties songs she did know that her dad used to play in the car when they ran errands that mom didn't want to join for. He was a big INXS guy and he played a lot of their tapes, but she remembered always loving "Don't Change" the most.

As Kelsey continued yelling, the boat shifted again and the small gap in the door opened. Water pooled into the bathroom. Trying her luck again, she shouldered the door. The gap was now ever so slightly larger. She slipped her fingers through the opening.

For those who have owned a cat, one knows the phantom cat of night. Certainly, they are fast creatures, but not that fast. Yet, somehow when they walk over you, before you can even reach out to pet them, they're gone. This was the fingertip graze. Kelsey felt it and could not pull her fingers back fast enough. Yet, the graze, like a cat's, felt comforting, soft, as though she might get through all of this, after all.

"Hello?" Panic, looking around the bathroom. Looking for what. "Hello? Sky? Steph? Hello?"

A drawer opened in the bedroom. Then closed. Water continued to drift into the bathroom. It was maybe an inch deep now. Kelsey heard the bedroom door open and close. Steps upstairs, then steps overhead. The boat continued to tilt at what could be called an alarming rate.

Kelsey was trying to keep her wits stable and imagine what could possibly be in front of the door.

That fucking bookcase. That goddamned bookcase. Full of the kind of stock books that nobody actually reads, that they fill bookcases in rental properties and boats with. And they never match thematically. Edith Wharton. Tom Clancy. Ayn Rand. Sometimes ironically right alongside Sylvia Plath.

Once at a vacation cabin on Whidbey Island, Kelsey copped *Where the Red Fern Grows* and wrote, in sharpie, "The dogs die" on the cover. She left the book in a Little Free Library. Because, really, who cares? Kids need to learn somehow.

This was all fine and well until the sound of crustacean on acrylic from underneath the bathtub, a steady scrape of multiple limbs. This was getting to be time to leave. The skittering around the bottom of the tub sounded of acrylic nails against an empty gallon of milk. Somewhere water attempted to start. From the sound, of its own accord, it was as though the water in the boat was attempting to avoid drowning itself. But being something without a soul, the boat was too stupid to know it was making matters worse.

How could Kelsey not glance toward the tub? Who wouldn't? And as she did, two long crab legs reached up and over the edge, accompanied by bubbling over water from the drain. In simultaneity, water started to overflow from both the sink and the toilet, and the water intruding the bathroom from under the door was also entering with more urgent rapidity.

There's that thing that happens. We have all done it, at least those of us whose lives haven't been especially privileged, when we are desperate for something to work and nobody else is around to be ashamed of that desperation, and we keep repeating a word or phrase over and over, without taking a breath between, sometimes with increased rapidity, like, "Open, open, open, open," and we may lose count of how many times we say, "Open."

Then, maybe after a pause, to catch a breath, to fill the lungs again with the air that fuels desperation like a hot air balloon, "There has to be a way, there has to be a way," but your lungs lose their power each time you exert your strength against the door. Eventually, it becomes the refrain of defeat, the ever slowing, "Why, why," longer pauses between, "Why." When "Why" becomes a statement, not a question. You don't get to ask anymore. Why tells you.

But one eventually accepts, as one often has to, is forced to, a realization that all who have identified their circumstances as dire and insurmountable, that there is not a why, that life is naturalistic. It is not malicious, but it also does not care. There is not a why. The bookcase is simply blocking the door in front of the bathroom where water continues to rise, where the angle continues to steepen, because it is. Things just are. That is simply what happens. It does not mean a thing. It is not a vendetta. Not like the intentions of other living things on the boat.

The problem with being alone is never having a true guarantee of being alone. Is it not the worst fear of many to be in a well-lit home, at night, and to look out a window, into the dark, a position whence anyone could see you clear as day. It is terrifying, however, to imagine, seeing there, somebody watching you. Being alone is one thing. People are not always afraid of being alone. That can be comfortable. Nice, even. What people are afraid of, that they sometimes cannot articulate, is thinking they're alone but, in reality, having an unknown companion.

For the time being, there were, at the very least, a crab or crabs, somehow, under the tub. And someone on the upper deck that had been in the bedroom.

The water was now overflowing from the tub, the sink, and the toilet. The clawing sounds from under the tub continued and, in one spot, Kelsey heard a crack in the acrylic.

And then, subtle as that exact moment when the sun crests the hills and the morning coffee you're enjoying on the porch is ruined by your being blinded, the boat pitched sharply, sending Kelsey slamming against the door, which splintered somewhat, pushing further open than she'd been able to manage thus far. The knob on the door broke a rib or two and one of the shards of wood punctured the opposite side of her abdomen. All of the water that had been pooling up dumped onto Kelsey, temporarily suffocating her.

It would appear the boat was pointing upright, like when shit went haywire in *Titanic*. Even through her pain, she could feel the boat sinking. Faster now than before.

Stephanie, half conscious and half blind, finally started drowning as she submerged with the boat's wound. Skylar tipped over at the wheel and finally dropped his mimosa. Raymond had been doing a pathetic job of crawling along the deck—making it only a foot and a half—looking like bad modern art, and when the boat pitched totally upright, he dropped against a wall that broke his right hip and drove the glass further into his face. He vomited and the spew went into the cuts and his eyes, but it was soon washed out when he rolled overboard like the wet towels of a person he was.

Kelsey was dealing with another moment of regaining her bearings. On one hand, a doorknob had injured her and a shard of wood had penetrated her. There was also the matter of the water that had dumped on her from above and the water rapidly rising around her from behind the door. The boat was clearly sinking. It wasn't just the rising water. Kelsey could feel the downward motion. And in fact, she was right. Just fifteen feet and two walls away from her, Stephanie was being torn in half as the downward motion of the boat pulled her impaled body alongside the rock that had initially maimed the boat. Oh well. More for the fish to eat.

Could Kelsey see her way through this? Logic. Reason. Step by step. First there was the shattered piece of wood from her landing on the door that had fortunately not penetrated her side any worse than cutting oneself while juli-enning a carrot. She bit down hard on her right knuckle and rolled to her side, allowing the wood to slide out of her like it had never been there. Just a large splinter. She did feel the blood immediately start to drip like a leaking faucet and worked at tearing a piece of her shirt off. She had no tape or anything similar to use but bit her thumb again and stuffed the fabric in the puncture. Now, the doorknob.

The two ribs it found its home between were both certainly broken, luckily without any compromise to the flesh covering them. But what could be done about that now? Fuck all. Kelsey waited, cowardly, ashamed of her cowardice, to try to roll off the knob, afraid of the newly refreshed pain with which the effort would congratulate her.

And there was the touch again.

The spider man.

Gentle as a compassionate lover, the kind who insists you're pleasured before they are. That light graze of a fingertip, through the shattered wood of the bathroom door against which her body was resting. A fingertip gentle as gauze, as the wish one makes on a dandelion, as a sprinkler rainbow. She knew, without knowing who he was, what he wanted. It was the spider man, caressing her earlobe through the door, through the wound in the wood. And she immediately rolled away from the touch, even though something felt comforting about it.

She was being reassured, even if against her knowledge or want of reassurance.

The pain was excruciating. The doorknob had sort of found its way between the two ribs it broke, so the abrupt movement away renewed the pain of that injury. But even through and past that, Kelsey's first thought was to turn behind her toward the gap in the door, terrified of her certainty of seeing a reaching hand. But there was none.

All of this. This had fucked her mind. She was imagining things.

Then that sound of a car accident. Neither metal, nor plastic, nor anything manmade. The sound of chaos and discomfort, of disrepair and entropy. And with that sound, the lights went out. The bathroom was as black as it could manage, save those few motes of light that are reflections of atoms bouncing off one another in even the darkest of spaces. Never fully black. Never even allowed that peace. True blackness never has the privilege to exist.

Who, Kelsey wondered, struggling to push herself up from the door, from the rising water, had ever seen full black. Nobody, maybe. God?

The water was almost covering her entirely now as she lay against the door. Solution.

Not the help she was looking for, but more scraping from the tub above. The sound of small bits of plastic breaking off and landing here, there. Wherever. It didn't matter.

The bathroom had no window, so the door was the only way out. So, think Delany. No, no. Kelsey. Her thoughts were shutting out like when a television set starts to turn off at random interims. She had a head injury. She was in the dark, in the cold water. She was Delany.

No. Debra. Who? Kelsey. Kelton?

A large crack above. A chef's knife size piece of plastic landing on Kelsey's back. And then a more alarming sound as she resisted the urge to succumb to the fear of putting her hand through the hole in the door and feeling a hand touching her hand in return, embracing it, caressing it, holding it like you would walking your date onto the dance floor at prom. *What am I even looking for?* she wondered, hearing the crabs in the tub above, knowing that however absurd it was that they'd made their way not only under but through the tub, the important part was getting out of the sinking bathroom before she was sharing the rising water with several or one or three or whatever number of crabs.

Thinking of The Cure, "that the spider man is having me for dinner tonight."

Recurring dreams are common enough for most. We all have these scenarios, and a psychoanalyst would tell you that they mean something. Psychoanalysts will insist, to the point of annoyance, that all details in all dreams are important, that they are reflections of the specifically curtailed conscious lens through which we are forced to experience our particular iteration of reality. This may be true. Also mayn't.

More interesting than dreams that return unwelcome and on habit are recurring settings in dreams. Dream maps. Kelsey had often thought about trying to draw hers out. There were five or six places she always returned to. The scenario of the dreams may have been different, but the setting was always familiar. Her psychoanalyst told her drawing out maps of them could be overwhelming but writing out descriptions not as much.

One of them is a locker room or a bathroom, something like that. It's labyrinthine. Dimly lit. Everything wet, filthy. Nobody else ever present. But, an energy, nonetheless. A feeling. Something not right, something after her, but she never sees it, never hears it. It's just a sinister force that intends both to remain hidden and to harm her.

Oh.

Oh.

The most important part of the plan that the desperation in her mind had just birthed was a tool. She doubted her hands would be strong enough, but she could try. It would be a start. She pulled herself up against the wall, feeling the contrast in temperature of the warm blood from her wound against the saltwater still rising around her legs, above her knees now. She felt a caress on her bare foot somewhere along the door but ignored it. Again, it was somehow, inexplicably, a comfort.

More important things now. Her wedges were long gone and any initial fear of stepping on this or that or the dirty water had also escaped her.

As the intensity of a situation grasped higher like the hands of demons in a Doré painting, it's important to keep one's wits about them. To focus on what matters, which is survival in the moment. Some infection in Kelsey's feet could be dealt with later. Hell. She was bleeding out of her torso, had at least two broken ribs, and who knew what had happened to her head. And now there were bathtub crabs and some weird door hand that she just kept telling herself, "You've been through a lot and had a head injury on top of drinking earlier. You're hallucinating. Focus," as she started grabbing onto the sink and dragging herself through excruciating pain. "Your goal is to get the fuck out of this bathroom, Kendra." Fuck. No. Kelsey.

Suddenly she threw up in her mouth, but swallowed it, not wanting it in the water below her that she would have to be in once again, soon enough. The bathroom sink was sturdy enough to balance herself on and have easy access to the toilet. She removed the two plastic caps from the base of the toilet that kept restrooms looking classy by hiding the fact that screws are used for keeping things in place. Now, the hard part.

Presumably no tools in this rental boat bathroom, but definitely washcloths. And with a strong enough grip. Maybe. Kelsey played softball in high school. She could do this.

The nuts came off easy enough, but Kelsey took for granted the toilet was caulked to the floor and was also sitting on a wax ring. It took some negotiating the counter, but Kelsey picked standing in the sink and pulling the toilet from there. With her wounds, this was asking a lot, but desperation is an amazing experience that way.

You know, the stories of the kidnapped children who are held captive in unthinkable circumstances for years in a basement, and somehow, one day, make their way to what must be blinding daylight. The animal desire to live is one of the most impressive things nature has to offer. We take for granted that we are still animals. We have our sentience and technology and influencers, whatever. But we are still animals. An animal trapped will chew off its paw to escape because, sans paw, life will be decidedly more difficult, but, nonetheless, livable, and, better than being dead. Most people don't realize the amount of pain the human body can endure, but in a survival situation, it's quite a lot.

Kelsey was not weak by any means but also didn't have an abundance of weight to toss around. She wedged her feet into the sink and pulled the plunger so she wouldn't cut her feet on the trap. She reached over, cringing against the pain on both sides of her torso, and pulled hard on the toilet. The tank lid fell off first and smashed against the door below. Kelsey wondered where the residual light was coming from but realized a seashell shaped night-light had been plugged into the sink near where she'd planted her feet. It made no sense that, given the power on the boat had cut out, this silly nightlight was still on, but she was grateful for the scant illumination it was allowing her in her attempt to survive. One, two, like you mean it Kelsey. The toilet came loose but landed against the side of the bathroom counter. Kelsey shifted her position and weight again to push the toilet past the sink so it would hit the bathroom door and maybe do something about making an actual exit.

But, best laid plans, or however they say. With the disproportion of her balance, Kelsey went down with the toilet. The intent of her mission was half a success. The toilet shattered against the door and opened the gap in the wood fully—although this allowed the water to rise in the bathroom all the faster. The opening in the door was now more than large enough to squeeze through, past the part blocked by the bookcase. However, Kelsey had landed atop the shattered toilet and incurred an additional injury where a shard of porcelain cut her forearm.

It's funny how some wounds don't seem as personal as others. Like, a cut from a broad piece of porcelain certainly does more damage, but it feels un-intentional, like it isn't personal. It's just incidental. Large shards of porcelain just do that. They can't help it. But when you slice your hand on the edge of the lid of a SpaghettiOs can, say, it feels personal. That lid meant to do that. Or anyone who has ever grated some of their knuckle into the cheese knows that the cheese-grater had it out for them.

But here was no time to think about any of this. There was only time to swim and hope to find a place with air that wasn't further than the length she could hold her breath.

Drawing in a gasp deep enough that felt as though it would last her to where the stairs out of the room were—opposite her and not fully submerged—she heard an eggbeater constructed from bone scramble on plastic above her, and looked up in time to see six black beads, like marbles—emotionless, empty eyes, not reflecting empathy, reflecting only the nightlight from the seashell that their mirror quality allowed. The several sets of limbs were all wrapped over the side of the tub, eager. It was now or never. The sound of the crabs falling into the water just a finger's reach behind her was the last thing she heard before her deep inhale of air and diving under.

There was somehow enough light from the seashell above the sink to make out some things. She watched her blood in the water behind her, closer to the light, swirling in slow motion, and it reminded her of adding dye to vinegared water for Easter Eggs. There was something truly gorgeous about the crabs swimming toward her, through her blood and the seashell light. She thought it would be nice to have a painting of, one day, if she lived.

But before she could dwell on it any longer, a crab arm slipped into the wound in her ribs and another in her arm, mounting her. She started thrashing, darkening the water with more blood. That dark, arterial blood, like melted fudge.

Then someone pulled the crab out of her and took her by the forearm, pulling her to the stairs.

He was not a man. He was, well, what, she didn't know. He was a man and not a man. He was not frightening or sinister, despite being clearly dead and not, well, presentable for public. He was not intending harm. His touch, his grip on her wrist was as gentle as his earlier surreptitious caresses. He led her up the sideways stairs with all the care of a nurse walking a patient down a hospital hallway.

He turned as they topped the stairs, the water still rising behind them, the boat still sinking. She hadn't seen his face before this. No nose, or eyes, no ears or lips, hardly any teeth, most of the flesh gone from his cheeks. His remaining gray hair obscured most of the remnants of his face. He was, on paper, terrifying, and yet, even with his hand still wrapped around her wrist, bones exposed in his forearm and fingers, she felt no fear, for there was a warmth in him. She felt, even, him pitying her. She could tell he felt fear for her and wished he could do more for her.

"I'm sorry it's the way it has to be. You see. Sometimes, they mix it all up and there are mistakes made." He ran an index finger, the tip all exposed bone, along the wound on her arm, and somehow it didn't hurt. "I have to stay for my mistakes to try to correct them. Or, well. I will never correct them. Wait them out. I sinned more than most, long before anyone in your bloodline was likely alive. This is now what I do until I'm completely dissolved by the saltwater." He looked up toward the deck, the two stairs further above them, and somehow there was a longing in his empty eye sockets. He was seeing more with his empty sockets than Kelsey ever would with her intact eyes.

He turned, with his collapsed cheeks, exposing the few remaining teeth, most of the remaining, unstolen gold. "Soon enough. But then, I suppose it will be some new punishment. And. I'll have it coming. We all do. Well. Here, come." They took the two last steps up and Kelsey was taken by the image of standing on a sideways deck, watching the boat rapidly sink. She initially felt panic, but given a rotting escort, she assumed she would somehow be safe, whatever that meant, in these circumstances.

"You got lost somehow. Misplaced. There's mistakes. No system is perfect. Ask any seaman. And where you're headed isn't pleasant, but know one thing: life guarantees for everything, from minnows to a sperm whale, that it's never without pain. None of us escape uncut. And," fingering an empty eye socket, "You can take it from me. There are fates worse than you can imagine. Be well." He put two of his rotten fingers to her lips and suddenly she felt a calm she'd never known. Her eyes closed. She felt him catch her form as she collapsed.

When she came to, she was underwater again, but this time in a tank. There were two others like her, but they didn't communicate with one another. Nothing beyond glaring with those marble black eyes and grappling with their mouths like chipmunks without nuts or hands with which to hold them. Before long, she was retrieved from the water, and held by her limbs. She wondered where and how she'd learned as much as she had about being human. Had she been a crab all along? Or was she meant to be a crab and the mistake was caught too late? Being held for a brief moment over the boiling water, she could feel warming her stomach, and she wondered if this was the dream. She thought she'd been told once that crustaceans did not sense heat the same as humans. Perhaps, even now, she'd been rescued from the shipwreck, injured, delirious, and was asleep in a hospital bed.

Then, excruciating pain of boiling water removed life and sentience from her shelled cage of consciousness, and, in those tenuous seconds, she thought: was it better to have been a crab dreaming of being a woman or a woman who died as a crab in her dream? Perhaps, in a moment, she would wake.

But perhaps it wouldn't matter.

The Keepers of Deerback Isle

by Joseph Carro

FROM A 1789 US BOOK OF COMMON PRAYER

PRAYER TO BE USED AT SEA

T HOU, O Lord, who stillest the raging of the sea, hear; hear us, and save us, that we perish not.

O blessed Saviour, who didst save thy disciples ready to perish in a storm, hear us, and save us, we beseech thee.

Lord, have mercy upon us.

Christ, have mercy upon us.

Lord, have mercy upon us.

O Lord, hear us.

O Christ, hear us.

God the Father, God the Son, God the Holy Ghost, have mercy upon us, save us now and evermore. Amen.

Our Father, who art in heaven, Hallowed be thy name. Thy kingdom come. Thy will be done on Earth, As it is in heaven. Give us this day our daily bread. And forgive us our trespasses, as we forgive those who trespass against us. And lead us not into temptation; But deliver us from evil.

Amen.

FROM THE MANUAL "INSTRUCTIONS TO LIGHTKEEPERS, JULY, 1881."

Treasury Department,

Document No. 158

Light-House Board.

GENERAL INSTRUCTIONS TO ALL LIGHT-KEEPERS

The keeper is responsible for the care and management of the light, and for the station in general. He must enforce a careful attention to duty on the part of his assistants; and the assistants are strictly enjoined to render prompt obedience to his lawful orders.

In the absence of the keeper, his duties will devolve upon the assistant present who is next in rank. No keeper shall leave his station without informing the assistant present who is next in rank of his intention, and of the probable length of his absence; and no assistant shall leave without the previous knowledge and consent of the keeper; but this regulation will not justify the keeper in denying an assistant any proper leave of absence.

An accurate report of absences, with the reasons therefor, must be forwarded monthly to the Inspector by the keeper.

Watches must be kept at all stations where there is an assistant. The keeper on watch must remain in the watchroom and give continuous attention to the light while he is on duty. When there is no assistant, the keeper must visit the light at least twice during the night between 8pm and sunrise; and on stormy nights the light must be constantly looked after.

No keeper can excuse an assistant from his regular share of duty, except on account of disability. When such disability continues, immediate report thereof must be made to the Inspector.

Light-Keepers may leave their stations to attend divine worship on Sundays, to procure needful supplies, and on important public occasions. As no specific rules can be established limiting the times and durations of absences, keepers will be held to strict account for any abuse of privileges.

In case of sickness, keepers must provide sufficient attendants for the lights; but when a keeper is, or is likely to become, incapable of duty, the Inspector must be informed at once of the need for assistance.

A LETTER FROM JOSEPH CAMDEN TO HIS SON JACK
October 11, 1900

My wonderful boy,

Today I am sending you this birthday letter. Mr. Harlan is to be delivering it to the post when he reaches shore in Portland. I wish you very many happy returns of the day. It would have been better to all be together. Lord knows your mother frets about it, but it can't be helped this time. We shall all meet again soon, and I will give you enough treats to, I hope, make up for it. I have also sent you a picture book, from your Daddy and your Mummy both, about a Wizard in a land called Oz. And I have also sent you a toy whale that I carved from wood here at the lighthouse. I painted it, and she should float. Tell Mummy to bring you to the old fort where Longfellow used to walk as a boy just your age. Set the whale in the water there, where it's calmer.

Be a good boy for your Mummy, and I will soon be on leave for shore to return for a fortnight as always. Mr. Harlan will have his turn first as Mr. Hadleigh just returned from London.

Goodbye for Now,

Your Loving Daddy

A LETTER FROM LAURA CAMDEN TO HER HUSBAND JOSEPH
October 14, 1900

My Dearest Joseph,

I've received your letter in the post, and I do always appreciate your letters when you're gone. I miss you, and you'd likely think I was a fool or a liar if I told you how much I think of you. I'm only twenty-odd miles away, and yet it may as well be twenty thousand. Jack has been over the moon about your whale, it makes me laugh. He bothered me to bring him to Longfellow's walk near the old fort on the East End, and you are right. The whale floats, but we almost lost it to the tide. I had to fetch it as it was pulled out to sea, wetting my skirts, but we did not lose it. Hurrah! Thank you also for the book of poetry you sent to me in the post. I hope to read it together with you when you return home. Yeats has a very particular style that I enjoy. I agree with what you said about the one poem, I believe it was entitled "The Sorrow of Love". It's very good. Although it did make me sad to think of you all alone, looking at "a climbing moon upon an empty sky." We have candles in the window for you, and Jack helps me tend to them with great enthusiasm. He never lets them burn out and always fetches me.

This week, I'll have you know, I am embroidering one of your handkerchiefs and if given time, I shall embroider them all with your initials before you return to us. I wish you were here right now. I have so many things I want to say to you, none of which I want to say here. Take care of yourself, please, until you come back. I know how hard they work you, and the skies have been stormy lately.

Forever Yours,

Laura

TELEGRAM FROM CAPTAIN KEENE OF THE PHAETHON
OCTOBER 26, 1900

Camden and Oscar Hadleigh, are nowhere to be found on the island or in the Lighthouse. Upon our arrival today, the island was empty, and we were not greeted. We fired flares and when no response came in any form, I sent three of my men to shore, whereupon they went up to the Lighthouse, but they found no keepers there. They reported strange things from the inside quarters, and outside the quarters were dead gulls and other birds so much so that it was described by the men as being impossible to step around their carcasses. The clocks had stopped, which indicates that whatever transpired was more than a week past. Other curiosities included a circular pattern drawn with coal throughout the crew q uarters, and a locked door with hatchet marks and a broken hatchet nearby. The locked door belonged to a closet storeroom, and no one was inside when my men opened it. I have left Bentley, Harlan, and Middleton on the island to keep the Lighthouse working until you can make other arrangements and to clean up the bird carcasses. I will not return to port until I hear from you. I will remain at the telegraph office tonight until it closes, if you would please wire me.

Captain Keene, PHAETHON

LETTER FROM ERNEST HARLAN, ASSISTANT LIGHTKEEPER, OCTOBER 28, 1900

Sir,

It is with deep sadness and regret that I must inform you of some sad affair that has taken place here during the past fortnight on Deerback Island. The two lightkeepers, Mr. Camden and Mr. Hadleigh, have vanished.

As you already know, we landed on the 26th for relief. That day, as on other days before, we came to anchorage under Deerback, and not seeing the Lighthouse flag waving, we thought at first they did not see us arrive. The Phaethon's horn was sounded several times, but we only received silence in reply even after the firing of flares. Finally, Captain Keene deemed it prudent to lower a boat and land three men: myself, Mr. Middleton, and Mr. Bentley. Mr. Bentley was left in the boat until our return from reconnaissance on the Deerback Lighthouse. Mr. Middleton and I came to the entrance of the gate and found it closed, and we were met with an unholy stench as we found hundreds of dead gulls piled up around the lighthouse. We made our way to the kitchen through the entrance door and found it closed as well, but when we entered, we noticed the storeroom door just inside was marked by huge gashes made by a nearby hatchet. Mr. Middleton remarked at the fireplace while I opened the storeroom that the fire had not been lit for several days. The storeroom had been strangely locked from the outside but was empty when I opened it with a key. We then entered the rooms in succession and found each bed empty and left just as they would have been in the early mornings. What concerned me, sir, were strange and disconcerting circular patterns scribbled on the walls with coal, of which there were several expired nubs strewn throughout the quarters. The patterns covered most of the walls and even some of the glass windows. Coal powder prints of bare feet were tracked throughout the bottom most floor of the station. I am enclosing some quick sketches of the coal markings done by Mr. Middleton in case they prove of value.

We did not take the time to search further, as the hatchet and the coal marks indicated something sinister had to have occurred. We darted out and made for the landing. When we reached there, I informed Mr. Bentley that the place was deserted, and Mr. Middleton and I recounted what we had seen. We walked back to the Lighthouse accompanied by Mr. Bentley this time, so as to make sure the island was indeed empty and to verify what we had seen. Unfortunately, our first impression was only too true. Mr. Bentley and I proceeded up the stairs to the lightroom, where everything was in proper order. The lamp was cleaned, the fountain was full, and the blinds on the windows were all intact. We left and proceeded to rejoin Mr. Middleton downstairs and made our way back to the landing, and then rowed back to The Phaethon. On arrival, Captain Keene ordered us once again to the island where we were to do duty until timely aid should arrive. We went ashore and proceeded up to the lightroom and lit the light that night at the proper time, and every night since. The following day, each of us took turns traversing the island from end to end but still nothing has been found. The ropes and supplies are all in their proper places and untouched.

Now, to be sure, there seems to be nothing aside from the hatchet and its gashes in the storeroom door that would indicate the poor men may have met violence somehow, but the dead birds are very concerning, and we have yet to find the logbook, which will perhaps give us more context. We do know that Mr. Camden has his seaboots on and oilskins, but we know that Mr. Hadleigh has left his wearing coat behind him, which shows, as far as I know, that he went out in shirt sleeves. He never used any other coat on previous occasions, only the one I am referring to.

Mr E. Harlan,
Assistant Lightkeeper,
Deerback Island Lighthouse
October 28, 1900

EXCERPT FROM PORTLAND DAILY PRESS, DATED OCTOBER 31, 1900

MYSTERY IN THE ATLANTIC

—

LIGHTHOUSE KEEPERS MISSING

—

MAINE LIGHTHOUSE MYSTERY WORRIES FAMILIES. The United States Lighthouse Board has received a telegram stating that Deerback Island Lighthouse's two principal keepers, Joseph Camden and Oscar Hadleigh, have gone missing on Deerback Island, which is about twenty-three miles southeast of Portland. Typically, the lightkeepers are relieved every fortnight. There are three lightkeepers attached to the station, two of whom are always present and attending to the light. These remain in the lighthouse five weeks at a stretch, with each receiving a fortnight leave on shore. The Phaethon left its port in Kittery, Maine on October 25 to make the ordinary relief at the station, taking with them the keeper who was to relieve one of the others. On arrival it was discovered that the two keepers had vanished from the island. Searching for over an hour, there was no sign of any life. A horn was blown, and flares were shot into the sky, but there was no response. The captain landed a boat full of men to go to the station, but they found no keepers there. What they did find were hundreds of dead birds piled around the lighthouse and curious dark circle markings drawn with what appears to have been coal from the fireplace around the insides of the walls, and finally a broken hatchet next to a locked closet, the door of which had for some reason been repeatedly struck by the blade of the tool. The blade was reportedly broken. There were also stopped clocks which indicated the men had been gone at least a week. No one truly knows what happened to these unfortunate fellows, but there are many theories including that they may have been swept away by a freak storm, or perhaps had gotten into some sort of row or had even simply gone mad. Joseph Camden, principal keeper, is married and has one child. Oscar Hadleigh is unmarried, and both Oscar and Joseph are native to Portland. Deerback Island is uninhabited. It is locally known as Deerback and covers an area of about two miles by two near a precipitous area of sea known for its high number of shipwrecks. Deerback Island rises to a height of 200 feet above the sea level, with vertical rocky cliffs on all sides. There is only one landing spot on the entire island at the time of this article. Aside from some interior damage, Deerback Lighthouse seems to have been left in complete working order with no damage to the light itself or to any of its structure. Just four years ago, a charter ship was running along the coast in the same vicinity and was lost with all hands in a freak storm and of course fourteen years ago was the unfortunate wreck of the Annie C. Maguire relatively nearby at Portland Head Light. Inquiry at the offices of the United States Lighthouse Board elicited that the Phaethon reached Deerback Island on Friday, October 26, 1900, and that the observations of the officials on the scene of the disappearances came to no firm conclusions as to what fates might have befallen the men. The families have been notified, and as the mystery spreads so too does the hope that the men are to be found safe.

EXCERPTS FROM DEERBACK ISLAND LIGHTHOUSE KEEPER LOGS WRITTEN BY JOSEPH CAMDEN

October 11, 1900: Breezy all day. Winds coming from South West, water choppy during first part of twenty-four hours. Sent out the mail today with Harlan to Portland. He will return after his fortnight leave along with needed supplies. General duties today. Hadleigh will take the cover off of all the oil cases. Second part of 24 hours, wind lessened and sea smoothed.

October 12, 1900: Light wind from North East and sunny most of the twenty-four hours, though in last part of twenty-four hours a strong gale and heavy rain kicked up from North West. Some of the glass panes in the kitchen were knocked out and shattered. General duties for the day. I organized the stock room to make way for new supplies when Mr. Harlan returns.

October 13, 1900: First part of twenty-four hours, the sea was very rough. Lots of rain and wind pulling in from North East. Hadleigh and I stayed inside due to rough conditions, but we repaired a burned-out lamp pipe. Second part of 24 hours, light East to North East wind and small showers.

October 14, 1900: Light variable winds and some showers first part of twenty-four hours, but then switched over to very fair weather. Sea became very smooth. I went fishing, Hadleigh fitted panes of glass the storm knocked out in the kitchens. General duties otherwise.

October 15, 1900: Sea quite smooth today in first part of twenty-four hours, with some variable winds again. Fishing boat, the Claire Holmes, passed through to Portland at around 9am. Hadleigh went fishing. I cleaned out an old store closet off the kitchen. General duties otherwise, but the lock on store closet is old—needs to be repaired and cleaned.

October 16, 1900: Light East wind these past twenty-four hours dry and cool until latter half when sea turned rough. Rough winds, too, from North East but the new glass held up. Hadleigh said he heard wailing and shouting but I did not, though he seemed quite perturbed by it and was distracted in his duties. The sky was a shade of color I've not seen in my years, but perhaps there was a fire on the mainland which by its lights echoed into the sky. Sent Hadleigh to sleep to rest his nerves. General duties, as far as could be accomplished.

October 17, 1900: The first part of twenty-four hours, I didn't mark weather as I was distracted. Woke to hundreds of gulls on the grounds and Hadleigh wailing. A man's body was washed ashore, most likely from a wreck, overnight, which Hadleigh discovered among the rocks. The gulls seemed agitated and stirred themselves into a frenzy when Hadleigh and I picked up the body and brought it inside. They began bashing themselves into the lighthouse and falling dead within minutes. Very odd and did not help Hadleigh's constitution. We exchanged words, but I wrapped the body in linen sheets and placed it in the storage closet I'd just cleaned out, out of Hadleigh's sight. No general duties but kept the light. Placed the new lock on the closet door, to assuage Hadleigh's superstitions.

October 18, 1900: Massive storm. Woke to banging and shouting, which was Hadleigh taking a hatchet to the closet. Luckily the hatchet blade broke, for I think he was about to come for me with it when I shouted at him and we exchanged words. I subdued Hadleigh, as he had covered the interior in "charcoal sigils and circles of protection." This is what Hadleigh called them, and he said the body was a demon sent by an Aleister Crowley. I tried to talk to Hadleigh and talk sense into him, but I kept him tied to a chair as he would not stop ranting and raving. More birds today, too. Will send word with the next fishing vessel or charter boat we see about what has transpired, but so far the sea still rages.

October 19, 1900: Hadleigh missing, will go out to search for him. Slept terribly due to Hadleigh's constant wailing, and I had a nightmare the young man we found was hovering over me in my sleep. I could not look into his eyes.

Poor Hadleigh, his stories and ranting are getting to me. Will report back when I find him.

—THERE ARE NO FURTHER ENTRIES FROM JOSEPH CAMDEN—

TELEGRAM FROM CAPTAIN OF THE PHAETHON SENT ON OCTOBER 29, 1900

Very concerning news from Deerback Island about the disappearances of Joseph Camden and Oscar Hadleigh. The lighthouse keeper's log was found among the dead birds by the men, and within the log contains new information that was previously unknown. Mr. Hadleigh seems to have become violent and unhinged, according to Mr. Camden, and there was a report of a body washing ashore, possibly from a shipwreck. We will look in the area to see if we can find a vessel that may have crashed during the recent storms. Will report back if we find anything new, and the men will conduct a more thorough search of the house with the new information that has been brought to light by Mr. Camden's log.

Captain Keene, PHAETHON

LEAFLET FROM CIPHER MANUSCRIPTS, FOLIO 4—A RITUAL DESCRIPTION PERFORMED BY THE HERMETIC ORDER OF THE GOLDEN DAWN (THE ORDER)
FOUND LOOSE IN HIS JOURNAL AND WATERMARKED 1809
(Translated Inside Margins Using Key and Cipher by Oscar Hadleigh)

Nought = Nought

I am in Darkness.

My robe is black, I carry a sword of judgement

My banner = twilight

I am fortitude

I sit on a throne of the Rising Sun
I rule & Govern the Hall & members
Of All grades
My robe is red, I hold Scepter & all banners
I expound mysteries
I am Power, Light, Mercy, & Wisdom
Purify with Fire
Consecrate with Water
Let all Circumambulate in Light
It is accomplished, let us adore
Holy art thou Lord of the Universe whom
Nature has not formed, the vast & the
Mighty one lord of Light & Darkness
Proclaim the Temple Open
Proclaim the Sun has Arrived
Close

EXCERPTS FROM PERSONAL JOURNAL OF OSCAR HADLEIGH

Thursday, Oct 11/1900: Well, Ernest Harlan left today for Portland. I can't wait until my next leave already; this lighthouse has become stifling in its lofty perch out in the sea even after my extended leave and my trip to London near two months ago. Today I polished the glass on the lights, and I took the cover off all the oil cases for Joseph. I didn't know that the man was a fan of poetry, which came up in casual conversation. He's from Portland, so of course he's a Longfellow man as all Portlanders must be proud of their poet, but he also surprised me in that he reads Yeats and so he has heard of him. Yeats is an Irish nationalist, and of course I met him in London when I decided to leave the Order on my last trip home, though Joseph can't know of my dealings with them, the Order. Neither can Ernest, or especially the Light House Board.

Crowley is filled with a darkness I've not seen the likes of in all my days, and the way Crowley treats the Order – the way he wants the Order to become, I could be no more a part of it. I saw Yeats kick Crowley down the stairs as the two of them cast spells and curses at one another, and ever since...I know Crowley has wanted revenge on the Order for laughing at him. It sits uneasily in my stomach, and I see him in my dreams. It's funny that I cannot escape Yeats, Crowley, or The Order even here in Maine where I came to be away from everything. Anyway, Joseph seems a good man and he has told me so much about his home life that at times when speaking with him, it makes me wish I had taken up with someone and gotten married. Alas, it wasn't meant to be. "A pity beyond all telling is hid in the art of love."

Friday, Oct 12/1900: Today started out rather nice, I will say. However, toward evening the weather soured a bit and a raging storm took its frustrations out on our poor kitchen windows. Some of the glass panes broke. Luckily, we keep a few down in our storage area. I suppose Joseph will have me take a look at them when the weather lets up. I didn't see him most of the day as he was organizing the storage closet while I tended to polishing the light and I did notice one of the lamp pipes needs to be fixed but we'll keep an eye on it for the time being. The storm raged something fierce and, at the time of writing this journal entry, it's now 11pm and the sea has not stopped its outrage at our little lighthouse standing as a testament to the hubris of civilization against nature. Since I didn't see Joseph most of the day, I couldn't help but practice the Order rites just as a way to say goodbye. I didn't see him until dinner, over which we ate fish and talked some more about poetry. This time it was less about Longfellow or Yeats, and we both connected over Byron. Joseph does have some surprises left in him, to be sure.

Saturday, Oct 13/1900: What a dismal day today has been, but I suppose a nice change of pace. The weather was bad all day, and so Joseph and I had to keep busy inside the Lighthouse. I showed Joseph the broken lamp pipe and he helped me to fix it while the rains beat against the windows and sea spray crashed against our little Lighthouse trying to knock it into the sea. We were both chilled to the bone, even with our fire, and to pass the time after dinner

I showed Joseph a few of the card tricks I'd learned. These tricks seem to have impressed him, of which I'm glad, because I could see the two of us becoming friends. He's very open and genuine, and he also gives respect where it is due which is rare in society and must be coveted.

Sunday, Oct 14/1900: Today, the day began with some frothing waters and remnants of the storm, but then by around noon had given way to fair weather. Joseph informed me he was going to go fishing to try and catch us dinner, as our stores would be low until Ernest gets back, and while he did that, I set about replacing the panes of glass that were broken during the storm. There weren't too many, and the sunlight shining down on my work made it more enjoyable. Joseph was away quite a while. I can tell he wants to return home to his wife. I don't blame him, as each day on this rock feels like a fortnight all on its own.

Monday, Oct 15/1900: I did a terrible thing. I woke up in a cold sweat, and I could feel a dark presence over me, and I couldn't move a limb. I opened my eyes and I saw that I was looking directly into Crowley's dark, imperious eyes. I stifled a scream. Joseph began work on the closet sometime after breakfast, of which I could eat none, and all I could think to do was to take a piece of charcoal from the fireplace and draw protective Wards under my bunk. I know seeing Crowley was more than just a dream. Crowley is crafty, and experiments with dark magic. He's careless and perhaps he's out to get me for laughing at him. I certainly wouldn't put it past him. If so, he will likely come for me again in my sleep. The Wards should help, I hope. I heard word just last month that Yeats himself was attacked in his sleep, but rumors fly faster and farther than the albatross and so it's hard to know for sure. Still, better safe than to be sorry. I told Joseph I was going fishing and instead of fish, I stood just out of sight and made a small cut on my hand and cast protective spells over our island, putting my blood on various rocks. I saw a fishing boat go by and my heart flew, my mind thinking it was already time for Joseph's leave so that mine could be next. I didn't see Joseph much during the day, by design, and kept busy with my work. I hope I'm able to get some sleep.

Tuesday, Oct 16/1900: Crowley's war on my psyche has begun in earnest. All through the night I was tormented by Crowley's voice in my thoughts. He told me that I was going to burn, that I was going to rot in the ground for laughing at him and that the Order would be destroyed. I woke with dark circles under my eyes, and my nose ran red with my own blood from the strength of Crowley's mental assault. The protective wards under my bed were perhaps too weak against a man like Crowley. I need to make bigger ones. I went about my duties as best I could, but soon I began to hear a snickering in my ears as I polished the light. It persisted, and then when I shouted at it to stop—either Crowley or whatever entity he'd summoned against me with his black magic began to wail and shout and carry on, at first frightening me but then angering me at Crowley's audacity. My blood wards on the rocks surrounding the island held true, however, at least tonight and I know this because the sky turned blood red. Joseph at last noticed my behavior was off, and I cursed myself for being so obvious. I explained to him that I thought I heard wailing and shouting, and I think he could see how tired I appeared, for he told me that I should get rest and he'd finish with the light. I obliged, if only to get back to my wards and their protection. Thus far, Joseph doesn't seem to be affected.

Wednesday, Oct 17/1900: I woke again to Crowley's attempts to invade my psyche—THE RAT! I heard a great commotion outside, more laughter and mockery—indistinct words but a feeling of intention and tone in them. I raged out at the early morning sky as the winds kicked up. I hoped to cast another protective ward, as the sea had washed away most of my blood, but as I set about cutting my own hand with a hatchet—I was set upon by a swarm of sea birds. I flailed about as they flew into my face and body, scratching at me with their beaks in the hundreds. I ran back to the Lighthouse, screaming, and that's when I saw the body on the rocks. It was bloated, and waterlogged, and naked, and a shade of light blue tinged the skin. It was a man, and his body was scratched and beaten most likely by the rocks. Soon, Joseph found me and helped me bring the man inside before I could properly begin to wonder what the man was doing there. As we did, gulls began careening into the Lighthouse walls and I could see the confusion and incomprehension in Joseph's eyes as I told him what had happened. I also swear when Joseph was wrapping the body in a linen sheet, that it smiled at me—a grin covered with bloody teeth, and that same imperious stare of Crowley's. I wanted to destroy the body, right then and there with the hatchet but Joseph said he'd lock the body away out of sight and did just that as I tried to calm down. I explained to him what I thought I'd just seen the body do, and he told me I needed sleep and he placed my hatchet on a stack of crates near the closet. It was hard to sleep, for the gulls smashed over and over again into the Lighthouse, and I slept very little, if at all. Not sure if I did fall asleep as everything is blending together. I hope I no longer dream of Crowley; I can't take any more.

Thursday, Oct 18/1900: It's happened. My wrists hurt from being bound all day, but for posterity's sake and for the sake of the questions others no doubt will ask once this is all over, I must write what may be my final entry. I don't blame Joseph for subduing me and binding me to the chair, for he couldn't possibly know what I'd seen. The smiling, bloated corpse had somehow escaped the closet as I lay in bed and scratched at me, drinking of my blood with greedy, gulping, slurping noises, flicking a forked tongue along its lips and making a mess of my bed sheets. It taunted me and told me that it was coming for Joseph next. I managed to loose one of my wrists from its grasp and throttled the creature, who crawled on all fours across the floor of the kitchen and apparated back through the closet door. I took the opportunity to draw on the experience I had with sigils from being in the Order and I used large pieces of charcoal to scribble them all along the inside of the kitchen. From the inside of the locked closet, the creature cackled and told me that my mother was burning in the fires of hell and the fat was sizzling off her body and into the hungry mouths of lesser demons. This filled me with a deep rage, and I tried my hardest to hack down the door, so that I might do the same to the bloated, cackling corpse inside. However, Joseph had woken at the sounds of my hatchet striking the wood and emerged looking extremely haggard. There were two puncture wounds at his neck, and I knew immediately it was the demon that had done it. I tried to warn him, and tried to tell him about the corpse, but the monster had ceased making noise and so I appeared to him to be insane. I struck the door a final time, breaking the blade on the hatchet and rendering it useless, whereupon Joseph subdued me and bound me to a chair. I managed to loosen one of the ropes during the night, after Joseph fell asleep, and untied myself. Joseph, if you're reading this, just know that I have begun to think of you as a friend. I hope that you go on to live a full and happy life with Laura and your boy, Jack. Anyone else who may read this, just know that occultism is real, magicks are real, and Aleister Crowley is the antithesis to healing and love. Wish me luck, and may God

—THE JOURNAL ENTRY STOPS HERE ABRUPTLY—

You Always Have a Choice

by Elizabeth Beechwood

I didn't understand what was happening to me at first. First, my brilliantly emerald scales turned to the pale grey of decomposing flesh, then the luxurious veil of my tail shredded and tattered like the flag of the losing army. I wasn't in pain—I'd never felt pain. I wasn't afraid—nothing could hurt me.

My sisters didn't know what was happening to me, either.

"I'll Google your symptoms," Sister Two said, retrieving her latest cell phone from behind a clump of ferns.

Sister One rolled her eyes. "You had better not be contagious. Who knows what the humans are carrying these days."

We'd had a hard time when humans first became hooked on electronics. Those who hiked to our pond didn't see us and were only interested in taking selfies by our waterfall. Or they were trapped in their own soundtracks with earbuds feeding them music, podcasts, and audiobooks. The siren song of social media was far more potent than ours.

But we were survivors. We learned to stay relevant in the world beyond our Mirror Pond. We took to dating apps and social media to make connections, singing our siren song over 5G. We expanded our reach to encompass the world and kept a tally of how far away a human traveled to find us. Sister Two was in the lead with a bloke who came all the way from Sydney, Australia.

"I'm not contagious," I told my sisters. As my tail rotted away, the outline of legs took shape beneath the disintegrating muscle. As the tail withered, my hips loosened.

"Maybe you're Ariel from the Little Mermaid movie. Did you fall in love with a prince? Did you trade your voice for legs?" Sister One taunted.

Sister Two chimed in. "Maybe you have ichthyophonus hoferi. No, wait, that's a fungus for saltwater fish, so it can't be that."

"But she has *legs* under there. Sounds like a sea hag spell to me. What was the price of those legs, Sister?"

They were cruel and angry beings, my sisters. But, to my shock, I realized I no longer felt that way. When had that happened? Maybe the regaining of my legs was taking away my rage. Or maybe it was the other way around.

"I did not make a deal with a sea hag. I don't know what's happening to me."

We had legs, long ago. The three of us, dancing in the moonlight, naked, the water swirling around our ankles. We brought the winter floods that fertilized the fields. We were revered. We did as we pleased and served no human, took lovers as we saw fit—and they were honored at being chosen. But then fear took hold of the humans, fear of our power, fear of our sexuality. They encased our legs in a single tail and we were left with our newly formed rage. A rage that carried us through all the centuries. Instead of bringing fertility, we brought death. Instead of lovers, we took victims.

I hauled myself onto my favorite rock. The rough texture bit into the raw new flesh that was replacing my protective scales. I stretched my lower half out in front of me, and the last of my tail fell away into the water.

My sisters swam closer, and, for the first time, I felt fear.

"Oh, *gross*," Sister One said as she reached out to touch my new legs. "What's wrong with them?"

I pulled my new legs away from her.

"Ew! You have old lady legs. Look at those veins! Good luck luring humans to you now. You're so screwed!"

They screeched and laughed and held hands as they swam in a circle chanting, "Old lady legs! Old lady legs!"

I tried to stand but the rock was too rough, too round, my legs and balance too new. I fell into the underworld of bones and stolen treasures. I thrashed and kicked, got my legs under me, and propelled myself to the surface. I climbed out onto the mossy bank and looked back at the pond that had been my home. My body shook from cold—I'd never felt cold before.

The leaves of the lindens above our pond carried a new song, deep and sonorous and salt-encrusted. It was the call of some sort of siren. It caught up with my heartbeat and vibrated along my new old lady legs, urging me west.

I fumbled through the clothes that had piled up along the boulders. I pulled on some jeans and a brightly striped sweater.

"What are you going to do now?" Sister Two asked. "Where are you going?"

"I don't know," I said. But I did know. Wherever the siren song led me.

"Well, don't think that you're taking any of our stuff with you when you walk away," Sister One sniffed. "This is our stuff, and you don't deserve any of it anyway. You haven't lured a single human to their death in a long time. Don't think we haven't noticed. We've been doing all the work and sharing with you out of sisterly kindness."

"At least give me enough money to get started," I said.

"No one uses *cash* anymore." Sister One rolled her eyes but tossed me the Gucci purse the victim from last week had been clutching when my sisters dragged her to the cluttered bottom of Mirror Pond.

I fumbled through the bag and took some cash that at least this one human did still use, but I left the credit cards. We'd never gotten caught using them before because who would find us here? But now I would be traveling through the land of humans. "Give me some jewels to pawn. Nothing big or traceable."

Another huff and a few bits of gems thrown at me, and I zipped them into the pocket of a red rain jacket I pulled on over the sweater.

"That's all you're getting from us, *Ariel*."

I looked over the peaceful surface of Mirror Pond, the dark water reflecting the trees above, their golden leaves floating on the surface like bits of gold.

Higher up, the leaves of the birch trees moved gently in the breeze, carrying the siren song that was vibrating through my legs, urging me to walk on.

"Too good for us now that you have legs? Do you think you're human? Because you're not. Can you still sing?"

The last question caught in my chest. Had I lost my siren voice? My ability to draw victims to me? To get money and all the wonderful things in the human world?

I was too cowardly to try to sing, though. If I didn't have it, I would be leaving with nothing but what was on my back, what I could carry, what I'd been given. Could I make it? Could I do it? If I did have my siren song, did I still want to use it?

My new old lady legs shook. Fear—this new emotion that both held me in place as well as pushed me to run away—was everywhere.

But I had legs.

And I was a survivor.

I straightened my back, squared my newly released hips, and stepped into the unknown.

I pushed the skiff out into the water as the tide ebbed. The old oars were heavy and rough in my hands. A plastic kayak would have been easier, but I liked the hollow thumping of the waves on the wooden bow. I braced my feet against the floor of the skiff and leveraged my weight backward, rowing with long strokes. The siren call vibrated through the air and my body, urging me forward. I rowed out of the bay under the full moon, taking advantage of the outgoing current. The pleasant scent of decaying vegetation filled my nose as I rowed past the tall marsh grass growing out of the now-flooded mud flats. I moved on, past the sandy dunes with more grasses and past the sandy beaches on either side of the inlet. It was a clear June night, and all was quiet. Only the slap of my oars on the water echoed across the calm water. Above me, the stars shared the sky with the moon.

It was going to be hard as hell to row back, a voice in the back of my mind said. I pushed it away—the siren called, and I had no choice but to follow.

You always have a choice, the voice said.

Again, I pushed it back into the dark and kept rowing.

It took me years to get to this place, so many years of traveling toward the siren call, working at jobs to make more money to move ahead, to buy my cottage just above the mudflats, to live simply and to be happy. I even made some friends in town. I joked with myself that I was well on my way to becoming a swamp witch, a thought that I loved.

When I was too tired to row any further, I pulled the oars in. The siren call continued—I just needed to rest for a few minutes. I stared out across the dark surface of the ocean as I rested my tired shoulders, guessing what the shifts in water's surface could mean. Two currents colliding. A school of herring passing by. The undercurrent wake of an orca. There was a lot going on below the surface.

A vision of my sisters surfaced in my mind.

The wind shifted.

The siren call was no longer in front of me, calling me forward. It came from above. Below. All around. I was surrounded.

A slow beating thumped against the hull of the skiff, vibrating the craft and my body. My own heart picked up the rhythm. Ripples moved out across the water's surface with each beat. I reached out to touch them...

A dome of water lifted and rolled back as the creature surfaced slowly. Its smooth skin was dark and mottled, although it had a silver sheen in the moonlight. As it rose up above my skiff, one eye leveled with my head—a large eye with a long horizontal pupil. I was certain another eye was on the other side of its head, and the creature was too large to look at me with both eyes when it was so close. Its siphon was just below the surface, circulating salt water.

The creature regarded me silently with its one giant eye that held an intelligence I hadn't expected.

I wondered if there was a sharp beak on its underside, ready to snap me into pieces.

I stared back into that one eye and refused to scream at it to get it over with already, to drown me, to eat me, or leave my body to sink, then bloat. Whatever it intended to do to me, I just wanted it done. But my voice was stuck in my throat, and, in that moment, I wondered if this was what Ariel had felt.

But I hadn't bargained my voice away to a sea hag. I was just terrified.

I cleared my throat and croaked, "What do you want?"

A single tentacle, at least a foot in diameter, its underside lined with suckers, slipped up from beneath the skiff and delicately wrapped itself around the bow, pulling it down with its weight. I grabbed the sides of the skiff to balance myself, fear swamping me.

"Are you the siren?" I managed to squeak. Its eye moved, the pupil looking down. I looked into the water but saw nothing beyond the dark.

"Is the siren down there?"

A second tentacle rose up, grasping a white plastic jug. It placed the jug in my skiff. Another tentacle deposited a large swath of netting into the skiff. And then an old bike tire. A shoe. A plastic water bottle. A flat soccer ball. Over and over, the creature added more trash until the weight nearly sunk my skiff.

Then it stopped and stared at me with one eye.

Its siphon hesitated the pulsing movement. Then the rhythm started again, the same rhythm of the creature's heartbeat and of my own. The creature sunk down into the ocean, disappearing into the depths as silently as it had appeared.

"Wait! What do you want? Why did you call me all this way? To pile trash into my skiff?"

My sisters and I had wanted the jewels, the cell phones, the fear and lives of the people we'd called to us. This creature didn't want any of those things from me. Instead, it gave me trash.

I sighed and took the up oars again.

The lights of town were far off in the distance.

"It's going to take me forever to row back with all this trash weighing me down," I called out over the water. "I'm an old woman, you know."

Something solid bumped into the bottom of the skiff, nearly throwing me overboard.

A wave rose beneath me, lifted the skiff, and delivered me and the trash to the shore.

While I pulled the skiff further up the beach where it would be safe until morning when I could get help, I thought about the path my life had taken. Of how I had regained my legs, lost nearly everything I had, and made it all the way to this spot at this moment. But why?

"Why?" I yelled out across the ocean's surface.

A single tentacle waved in the moonlight as if to salute me.

Then it disappeared.

Everything was silent except the lapping of the ocean on the beach.

The siren song was gone.

I felt naked without the constant vibration of the siren song. It felt like a best friend had suddenly left, or died, and I'd never hear their voice again. At first, I streamed music or a noisy TV show to keep me constant company. But, slowly, over the months, I started to enjoy and appreciate the silence. It was never completely quiet, there was always the scurrying of a mouse, the scratching of the fledgling owls under the eaves, or the slow unfurling sound of the philodendrons that draped from bookshelf to bookshelf in my home.

Now that my journey was over, I didn't know what to do with myself. What had the creature meant for me to do with the trash? That morning, with my skiff filled, I'd been lucky enough to run into my friends, Trish and Steve, at their coffee shop, and they'd helped me bag up the trash and take it to the landfill. They asked me why I'd gone out at night to collect trash when it was so dangerous, and I had no real answer for them. They were friends, but they certainly wouldn't believe me!

"We should get a group going on MeetUp to collect trash every week," I suggested. "We can put up a flyer in the coffee shop."

"That's a good idea. But it's not enough to pick up the trash," Trish said. "We need to educate people to not create more."

"Did you know there's an island of trash twice the size of Texas in the ocean, caught up in this current vortex, just swirling around?" Steve added.

Excitement caught hold of us—the excitement that we could actually do something about the problem. We could educate people, collaborate with other organizations, host a beach clean-up day, and build an interpretive center. It wouldn't solve the problem, but it would be something! As we ran through all the things we could do, I saw the creature's great eye looking at me, its tentacle saluting.

"But that would take a lot of money," Trish said with a sigh. "Where would we get that kind of money? Do they even give out grants to start an interpretive center? It's just such a huge problem."

This time, I saw something else in the back of my mind. Jewels dotting the bottom of Mirror Pond. Piles of cell phones that could be wiped clean and resold. Cash that could buy supplies. Purses that could be sold online, no questions asked.

I pushed those thoughts away. I wasn't like that anymore. I was good and kind and wanted to live a quiet life.

That night, I dreamt of my sisters. They had been in the back of my mind all day, but I'd kept ignoring them. When I fell asleep, my subconscious dropped its filter and let the memories come crashing in of when our rage and desire for more and more had hooked us. In my dream, I sang my siren song and lured humans to our pond in the mountains, and they happily waded into the dark water to me. And I laughed, as I'd always laughed, as they handed over their money and I led them down deeper, deeper, until they ran out of breath and Mirror Pond filled their lungs.

Life settled into a new quiet cadence. I walked along the rocky shore looking for any odd movement along the ocean's surface that suggested the creature was nearby.

I was walking along the rocky tidepools one morning, talking to the hermit crabs, when a woman dressed in expensive outdoor gear came clambering along. She stomped on the vulnerable barnacles with her well-treaded boots while taking pictures with her latest-model phone. Something in my gut shifted, and the little voice in my head told me to look at the size of that diamond ring flashing on her finger. We could pawn it.

"Go away," I whispered to the voice. "I'm not like that anymore."

Then the woman pulled a protein bar out of her pocket. She ripped open the wrapper, removed the bar, and threw the wrapper into the wind. It flipped and dove like a bird on the current until it settled in a tide pool filled with green anemones.

Rage rose up in me, a rage I'd thought I'd banished. But, no, it had been slyly hiding away, waiting for just the right moment to emerge.

I opened my mouth to yell, to tell her to get down there and pick up her trash, but instead of those words, the rage came out as my beautiful song. My siren song, so long silenced.

I led the woman around the rocky shore to a secluded cove and brought her to a cliff by the water's edge.

Another song joined in with mine – the song of the creature. It lifted from the water, and I saw its powerful beak open and close, beckoning to be fed. All I had to do was to take all the woman had and then send her to the bottom of the ocean with the creature. No one would ever know.

The creature's tentacle moved to grab the woman.

I had no choice—it was the only way to get the money for the interpretive center.

You always have a choice, the voice said.

You always have a choice.

I grabbed the woman's arm and hauled her back.

"I can't," I told the creature. "I won't do that anymore. Not for the interpretive center, not for Nature, not for you. I'm not like that anymore. I won't let rage rule my life."

Its siphon opened and shut, faster now and with more force. It surfaced higher, its beak snapping out its displeasure at being denied.

Another tentacle struck out of the water, snapped around my middle, pushing the breath from my lungs.

So this is how it ends, I thought dispassionately.

I looked back at the woman and used the last of what breath I had to sing a song of safety up among the trees and grass and road where she could find her way back to her car. I sang her away from me, away from death.

I looked the creature in the eye. "At least I know what's real in the world," I said. "At least I'm not shocked by the truth like all my victims had been."

The creature hesitated. It took hold of me and held me aloft for one quiet moment. It felt like time stopped. Then the creature put me gently back on the shore and sunk down into its dark abyss, taking my rage with it.

Westward Wind

by Shane R. Collins

B y now, they were all dead. When it first started, a doctor on television explained that it was a virus, a type that no one had ever seen before. The church said it was the End of Days—that the Lord was judging us for our sins. The tabloids claimed it was a plague started by alien invaders. I suppose any of them could have been right.

I looked out over the bow of the sailboat. Natalie lay on a towel baking in the sun. It was a warm and clear July day with a steady breeze coming from the east over the wide blue Atlantic. I sipped the margarita and wished for the thousandth time we still had some ice. The mix was syrupy sweet and had warmed in the sun, but the tequila was top shelf. I looked at the bottle and wondered at the Spanish words. I shrugged and took another sip as Natalie stood and stepped down to the bridge. She shuffled through papers, loudly moving around our baggage, searching for something. I pretended not to hear and returned my attention to the salty air and the sound of our boat cruising through the water.

"Have you seen that Grisham novel?" she asked.

"I thought it was by the coffee pot."

"It's not."

"Well what about those two Stephen King books?"

"I've read those two already."

I shook my head dubiously. "There's a manual on knot tying under the captain's chair."

Natalie gave me a look that meant she was unimpressed. "Jesus, Tom, are you drinking?"

"Sure."

"It's eleven in the morning."

"I'm on vacation," I said. "I can have a noon cocktail."

When it happened, no one knew what to do. No one was prepared. There were only a few isolated cases at first. It spread from infected avian population through mosquito bites. That was before they realized it had gotten into the water supply. And it was contagious as hell. The hospitals were flooded with the Infected. I saw it on the news, the night before the cable went out. The dead and dying lying on stretchers. The virus attacked the victim's circulatory system they said, turning fatal after about a week of agonizing pain. It began on the East Coast, but reports of outbreaks came in from Los Angeles and Seattle as well. Just before broadcasting stopped, there were cases in Madrid and Hong Kong.

I couldn't believe how quickly everything fell apart. After a week and a half, infrastructure became a thing of nostalgia. No one wanted to go to work. Television stopped. The radio followed along with cell phones, telephones, newspapers, and of course the power. If it didn't run on batteries, it became a paper weight. The only news was from neighbors and people passing through. Natalie and I stayed at her father's house, Doctor Travis Brohman.

The first incident happened two weeks after the initial outbreak, from what I could gather anyway. A mob at a closed grocery store turned violent. A woman was trampled to death after the door was smashed in. No, but three people were shot to death, one an old woman. It wasn't three people; it was a dozen and the whole store was burned down in the riot. One man said the National Guard was deploying. Everyone's story was different. It was frightening, but we felt removed from it in a way. We were safe in Doctor Brohman's house. No one was sick in our neighborhood, and the riot at the grocery store, if it even happened, was far away from us.

One morning at the Doctor's house, someone knocked. It was the middle-aged father that lived next door. "Mrs. McCarthy at the end of the street is sick," he said. The man awkwardly stood there for a few moments. He shook his head and returned to his own house. He did not come by again.

At dinner that night, the three of us ate by candlelight. We had canned beans and purified water. We ate in silence until Doctor Brohman looked up from his bowl. Natalie's father was intimidatingly tall. He had brown hair and a reddish beard that had streaks of gray. He always shirked typical Radiologist attire in favor cargo shorts and flip flops. Even now, at the end of the world, his flip flop smacked happily across the hallway's wood floors every time the Doctor went to the kitchen for a cup of tea.

Doctor Brohman dabbed the corners of his mouth with a napkin and said very solemnly, "We ought to board up the house." The next morning we did.

As I held a two by four in place, hammer in hand, I squinted through the window. Thick, black smoke was rising from somewhere down the street. Natalie's father saw it as well and grimaced. "Come on," he said. "There's some more wood in the attic."

We took stock of our food and water. Before the utilities had stopped, Doctor Brohman had filled his bathtub with water. "Twenty minutes of boiling and any water can be safe to drink," he assured us. His pantry was filled with canned food, enough for three months. None of us talked about what we would do after that.

One night, after Natalie had fallen asleep, the Doctor took me to his study. Bookshelves lined the walls with a lone cherry wood desk in the center. He opened a drawer in the desk. There was a revolver there wrapped in cloth and a box of cartridges beside it.

"What's this for?" I asked.

"Just in case you need it," he said. "Do you know how to use it?"

I shook my head and he showed me how to load it. He gave it to me to hold and taught me how to aim. I was surprised by how heavy it was.

"It's a .357 Smith and Wesson," he said.

I looked at its oiled gunmetal body with awe and reverence.

"If someone tries to break in here, I don't care what they say; you don't do any of that fancy bullshit you see on TV."

My skin shivered as I looked at him, unable to look away. I had never heard her father curse before.

"You level this at them and give them two in the chest," he said in a flat voice. "I've a rifle in my bedroom as well."

I nodded. Doctor Brohman wrapped the weapon back up and closed the drawer. We did not speak of it again.

By late afternoon the sky began to turn gray. We dropped the anchor and fastened a tarp on the bow to collect rainwater. It didn't taste good, but it was safe to drink. I looked over the starboard side. The shore was never very far away; we always kept it in sight while cruising because neither of us knew much about nautical navigation. A chart was laid out on the table on the deck. I stood over it and tried to decide where we were. Maryland? Maybe we were in Virginia already; the wind had been very good for the last week or so. I looked through the binoculars. There were rustic cottages spread over a green hillside with white sand beaches in front of them. I saw a large water tower in the distance and the hints of high-rises half obscured by clouds. The only motion at all was from a pair of smoke plumes. When the rain began, we went inside.

Natalie turned on an electric lantern and read through a tired magazine. I looked out the porthole for a time, watching the rain and listening to the monotonous patter it made against the fiberglass hull. Eventually I went to the sailboat's oversized kitchen and opened a cabinet. It contained a proud and boisterous collection of wine and spirits. "I think I'd like something tropical,"

I said and picked a white Caribbean rum. I broke the seal and smelled it before pouring a few fingers. "Would you like any?"

Natalie looked up. "No, you usually drink enough for the both of us, dear."

I took a good swallow and sighed. Perfection.

She did not stay up long. It was best to use natural lighting; batteries were a luxury and we tried not to overuse them. So many things we had to live without, but I think music was the hardest. We could, of course, turn on the generator and power the boat, but only for a short time. Tonight I thought about it, just for a little while, just to listen to music for a few minutes, but in the end, it would have been too wasteful. Natalie closed the door to the main bedroom, which she had taken for herself when we first boarded the boat.

I poured myself another good one and rolled out my sleeping bag on the small couch. Things with Natalie had begun to fall apart, even before all of this happened. Now we barely spoke to one another, usually only a few words each day. I finished the drink and fell asleep to the rocking tide.

The next day was overcast but dry. Natalie made coffee while I siphoned the pooled water from the tarp. I hoisted up the main anchor and readied the sailboat to leave when she called my name.

"Look, over there!"

I looked to where she was pointing.

"Someone's coming."

I saw a small rubber boat with someone inside paddling it closer. The person waved to us and cried, "Help!" It was a woman. Dark red spots where blood was pooling beneath the skin covered her. The worst of them were scabbed over, scaly, and weeping blood. "I saw you yesterday," she cried.

"Don't come any closer," I called to her. "Natalie, raise the sail."

"Please," the woman said, and I saw that she was not alone. A young girl was sitting beside her. She had blond hair and wore a pink dress. She looked scared. "Please, take my daughter with you. She's not sick!" When the rubber boat was nearly beside us, the woman picked up the girl and held her out to us. The girl in the pink dress began to cry.

I couldn't tell if she was sick too. "I'm sorry lady, but we can't help you. Natalie, raise the goddam sail!"

Natalie stood rigid and gray as a statue. She stared at the Infected woman and was consumed with inaction. "Tom," she whimpered. She began to move toward the little girl on shaking, unsteady legs.

I hastily climbed around the side of the sailboat to the mast and raised the main sail, angled it so it filled with air, then hurried back to the wheel to direct the rudder. Natalie was on her knees, dangerously close to the woman in the raft, and I feared she would reach out to the little girl. The boat pulled away from her, and I heard the woman cry out after us. When the rubber boat was far enough away that I could no longer see the woman's arms flailing in distress, I inhaled and tried to recall how long I had been holding my breath. Natalie was sitting now, leaning against the side rail and shaking.

I walked downstairs into the cabin and found a cup. I filled it half full with a fifteen year old single malt scotch. It was one of my favorites. I finished it in one sip and thought for a moment before pouring a second.

Natalie was still sitting when I came back up. She looked at me with red, accusing eyes. "We should have taken the little girl."

"She was sick."

"She didn't have any marks."

"Her mother was infected," I said. "She was too. I couldn't save her. They were dead already, no matter what I did. All I can do is protect the two of us." I remembered an alleyway between two redbrick buildings and hoped that I had concealed the guilt from my voice.

"You're a coward."

"It's kind of you to say so," I said.

"You're a coward," she repeated with more conviction.

"Go to hell."

"How old do you think that little girl in the boat was? Three? Maybe four?"

"Shut up."

"And how about that woman in the alley?"

"Shut up, Natalie."

"Do you think about her, Tom?" she asked. She began walking toward me, her voice growing louder. "I hope you do, Tom. I hope you dream about her every night for the rest of your life! You're the most selfish man I've ever met. You don't care about anyone except yourself!"

"Natalie, shut your fucking mouth!"

She slapped me hard across the face. Natalie shook her head. "How do you do it? How can you just stand and watch people die and do nothing?"

I did not move but stood, rubbing my face and tending the wheel, looking out over the southern horizon.

After a long silence I said, "We'll need to stop soon, tomorrow probably. We're running low on food."

Natalie nodded. It had been two weeks since we had stepped on solid ground and restocked the pantry.

I will never forget the day Natalie's father died. I was still in bed, dreaming of a cheeseburger, draft beer, and running water when she woke me. "What is it?"

"My father," she said. "He's sick."

Doctor Brohman had locked himself in his bedroom. We stood outside his door, listening to him vomit noisily. Natalie knocked on the door. "Dad, let us in so we can take care of you."

"Dear, there's nothing you can do for me."

"Don't say that. You might not have the virus."

"I do," the Doctor said. "You've been a wonderful daughter."

Natalie began to sob.

"There is something you can do for me."

"What Dad? Anything you want."

"You and Tom, take all the food you can carry and head down to the harbor."

"No, Daddy."

"Take everything. You get to the harbor and take the sailboat and you go south," he said. "Wait out the virus, find an island somewhere, but you leave."

"No," she cried. "I can't."

"Do it for your mother and me. I want to know that you're safe."

"I love you, Dad."

"I love you too, Natalie," he said. "Tom, do you remember what I told you in the study?"

"Yes."

"You keep my daughter safe."

Natalie banged on the wooden door. "We won't leave you, Dad. Come with us."

"Goodbye, Dear."

Natalie screamed for her father, trying to turn the locked doorknob and hitting the door. Suddenly there was an explosive sound from the locked room, like a car backfiring, and a moment later the sound of a sandbag hitting the ground. Then nothing. Natalie stopped knocking and stood silent. Neither of us breathed. I tried to think of something to say, anything at all, but they did not make words for such things.

At last, I turned to Natalie and all I could say was: "I don't know how to sail."

We filled two duffel bags with all the canned food, clothes, and batteries we could fit and threw them in her father's black sedan. I took the revolver and cartridges from the cherry oak desk, and we left. As the automatic garage door opened, I realized I could not remember how long it had been since I had been outside. Natalie cried in the seat beside me as I started the engine.

Abandoned cars filled the road. We had to weave between them slowly and, at some places, had to drive on lawns to get around. And the dead. There were bodies in a couple of the cars, some lying on lawns or in rocking chairs on porches. Trash was everywhere. Windows were broken, and some houses were burnt down entirely. It looked more like a bombed-out war zone than a quaint New England suburb.

When we got to the commercial district near the harbor, we saw the living, and they were more frightening than the dead. Fires burned everywhere. People looted anything they could from shops. They threw rocks, shattering large store windows. Two men were in the middle of the street fighting over a television. I wondered if they knew the power was out. We sped around them as they began throwing rocks at us. One cracked the passenger side window, and Natalie shrieked. One of the men chased us but soon lost interest. A mile further, a school bus lay on its side and blocked the rest of the way. The harbor was just around it.

"We have to go," I said. "Can you walk?"

Natalie nodded. We stopped and grabbed the duffel bags from the trunk. I brushed my hand against my pocket and felt the revolver.

"Come on," I said. We walked around the bus and down the small street, diligently looking over our shoulders. Up ahead I saw the marina where the Doctor's sailboat was kept. Before it, on the left, was a pair of red brick buildings with a narrow alley between them.

I heard voices coming from there. I held up my hand, and Natalie stopped. I peered into the alley. There were three men and one woman. The men had her surrounded, were shoving her, laughing, and taunting her. She slapped one, and he hit her. Another grabbed at her blouse, and I heard it rip. She screamed. One of them grabbed at her and forced a kiss on her. She shoved him back, flailing her arms at the men like a wild animal.

"Tom," Natalie pleaded quietly beside me. "Do something."

I watched in horror as they pushed the woman to the ground. One of the men was infected, the others I couldn't be sure. They tore her skirt, the soiled fabric ripping away from her body. Natalie turned away, unable to watch.

One of the men kicked at her on the ground while another climbed on top of her. The third turned around and saw me. He did not appear to be infected. He looked at me and I back at him, and I shivered. He was not alarmed. The man did not look threatening but rather curious at our being there and made no motion to alarm the others or threaten us.

I felt the weight of the revolver. It was too heavy. "We have to go," I said.

"No," Natalie whimpered, but I pulled her arm and she followed me. We half-ran down to the marina. It was a mess. One of the docks had collapsed and only a few wooden planks remained. Many of the slips were empty, and most of the boats left were broken into. Natalie led the way down one of the wooden docks where we were relieved to find a large sailboat tied up and untouched. It was at least forty feet long with a light blue hull. We carried the bags on and untied the boat. The name on the back of the ship was stylized in curvy gold letters: *Westward Wind.*

The skies were still overcast and there was a cool breeze. I lowered the sail as Natalie started the underpowered inboard motor and eased us into an empty slip. I grabbed the empty duffle bags, headed up the stairs to the deck, and thought I ought to bring the revolver.

We tied up her father's boat and walked along the dock. It was a small island – only a few miles wide – but had several houses on it. I decided it must have a grocery store on it. Less than a mile down the road, we saw a small country store. One of the windows was smashed, but it looked otherwise intact. There was no one in sight. A bell jingled as we opened the door, and I winced. It was very dark inside and, once the bell stopped, was eerily quiet. A tower of sunglasses was knocked over, glasses spilled everywhere. We each took a shopping cart and went separate ways. I filled the cart with cans of baked beans, soup, canned vegetables, tuna, boxes of pasta, and bags of potato chips. All of the produce was rotten, and hordes of flies infested that side of the store. I took some soda and spent a few minutes browsing the liquor aisle. The aisles were stocked for the most part, and I wondered where everyone on the island was. Maybe they were just vacation homes.

I took handfuls of batteries and piled some magazines on top. There was a swivel rack near the cash register filled with maps, brochures for camp sites, and information on attractions in South Carolina. I filled up the empty spaces in my cart with candy bars and packs of gum. As I sorted through them, I heard a jingle.

"Can I help you find something?" The man had a thick southern accent and a shaved head. He wore gray pants and a dark shirt with the sleeves torn off. One eye was black while cuts and bruises covered the rest of his body. He held a baseball bat.

"I was just getting some food," I said. "I'm running low."

The man with the bat stepped forward and two more men came in behind him. None of them seemed to be infected. I wondered how they had survived so long. "That's our food you's taking."

"I'll give you something for it."

"What would you have that I'd want?"

"What's going on?" Natalie was startled to see the three men.

One of them gave a slow whistle. "Pretty lady. She with you?"

"Yes."

"Tell you what," the man with the shaved head said, taking a step forward, "you keep the food, and we'll keep the girl."

"You're not taking her," I said.

"I wasn't asking." He took another step toward Natalie, and I put up a hand to stop him. He cracked his bat across my head. I reeled forward and collapsed onto the linoleum floor. My vision narrowed, and I struggled to stay conscious. Natalie lunged to help me, and they grabbed her. She screamed, but just as I was beginning to come to, something hard hit me in the back and then the stomach. I gasped for air.

"We're gonna have fun with her."

As I lay struggling to recover on the ground, I remembered the revolver. Amid the flurry of my beating, I pulled it from my pants pocket and remembered nothing except how to pull the hammer back and four words; *two in the chest*. It only took one. I pulled the trigger at the man with the bat as he stood over me, poised to swing again. It sounded like a cannon. The bullet caught him just below his sternum and he lurched backward, skidding across the floor. His two friends watched his shirt soak [1] with blood as a single wisp of smoke rose from his chest and vanished. They stood and looked in awe, unable to move.

"Let her go," I said.

The one who held Natalie released her, and she ran back to my side whimpering. The two men looked at me with fear. I pointed the revolver at the nearest one. "Go," was all I could say. They sprinted out of the store and down the street.

Natalie put her arms around me and cried. I had not held her in a long time. "Come on," I said. "We've got to go."

We ran down the road back to the dock with the shopping carts bumping in front of us. I looked back, but no one was following us. We loaded the boat with all of our loot and left. The afternoon skies began to clear up and some blue showed through the clouds as we untied and set sail.

"It's the end of the world," Natalie whispered.

"We're still here."

"It's not enough," she said. "What if we're it, Tom? What if we're the only two?"

"The men at the grocery store weren't infected. There must be others like us."

Natalie had a far away look. "What are we going to do, Tom? Where are we going to go?"

I shook my head. I tried to think of something reassuring to say, but I could not get the image of the man I killed out of my mind. I thought of the shirt and the way the blood slowly soaked it, the thin wisp of smoke rising from the wound and how it evaporated in an instant, the sound he made as he exhaled for the last time, his body going slack and the silence that followed. I did not feel anger or concern or guilt. I did not feel anything except my bruised ribs and my split lip and throbbing head. At last, I looked back at Natalie and said, "We'll keep going south, like your father wanted."

She nodded and smiled. The look she gave me was no longer accusing. She went downstairs and brought back a small first aid kit. Natalie carefully rubbed some ointment over the gash in my forehead after wiping away the dried blood.

"Are you alright?" I asked, looking at the bruises on her arm where one of the men had held her. She nodded.

I stood at the wheel, making small adjustments in our course from time to time. Natalie looked out over the side of the boat toward land. "Why do you think we haven't gotten sick when everyone else has?" she asked.

We hadn't caught the virus. We had been careful. We were lucky. I realized that none of these seemed right. Perhaps we were immune, but in the end, it always returned to the same question: why us?

"I don't know," I said.

"It doesn't seem fair," she said. "That everyone else dies and that we should live on."

I nodded.

That night I did not sleep on the couch. Natalie asked if I would sleep in her bed. It was good to lie on a mattress under blankets and out of the sleeping bag, to sleep beside her again and to wake in the night and hear her breathing, to feel her beside me, to be wanted and needed and—for the first time in a long time—not hated, and to not feel alone. Sleeping beside her, it did not feel as though we were the only two normal people alive, and it did not matter if we were. She kissed me goodnight and we forgot.

The next morning, Natalie was sick. I heard her vomit in the bedroom while I was making coffee. I ran. I tried to open the door, but she had locked it. "Let me in."

"I can't, Tom. I'm sick."

"Open the door, Natalie," I said and violently rattled the door handle. I heard her throw up again. "Let me in and I'll take care of you."

"I'm sick, you can't take care of me."

"Goddamit, Natalie!"

"Take the food and the gun and the rubber boat. You can find another sailboat and keep going. You have to leave me though, Tom. Someone has to make it. Someone has to live."

"Unlock the door or I'm going to break off the fucking lock." I waited, but she did not unlock it. I heard something that might have been a groan and returned to the kitchen. I took a fire extinguisher from under one of the cabinets, held it above the door handle, and smashed the handle off in one downward motion. Natalie cried out, and I walked in.

She looked like hell. Her skin was covered with perspiration, her eyes were watery, and she was very weak.

I walked to her and said, "Come and lie down."

"Don't touch me," she cried, but she was too weak to resist. I helped her into the bed and under the covers. I grabbed the waste basket as she began to dry heave. I touched her forehead.

"You have a fever," I said. I got a ginger ale from the kitchen.

She sipped at it, but it was difficult for her to keep any down.

"How did this happen?"

Natalie shook her head.

"Maybe it's just a stomach bug," I said.

"I'm sick," she said. "Like the others."

Natalie stayed in bed all day. She dazed in and out of consciousness, and I held her hand.

It's not fair. How could she die now, after all that we had survived? I had thought we were immune, but no one is immune. No one's ever immune. It was never fair. She could not die, not now. Don't leave me, God don't let her leave me. I could not go on without her—the last man alive. Oh God, don't let her leave me. Who was Adam without Eve? Please, God let her live. And the worst, I know, is that no one will be there to hold my hand at my end.

I laid my head down on her chest and cried, feeling reassured by her persistently beating heart.

"I'm sorry," she said.

It startled me. "You didn't do anything wrong."

"I shouldn't have said those things, darling."

I stayed with her all that day, sitting beside her, checking her fever. By that night it had not gone down. I fell asleep in the chair with my head down on the bed. I had trouble sleeping, waking up from awful dreams but always relieved to wake up and hear her breath.

I woke up the next morning when Natalie touched my head. "What is it, Natalie? What's wrong?"

She smiled at me. "I think my fever is gone." I touched her forehead and it felt normal. "I feel better. Maybe it really was just a stomach bug."

I sighed and hugged her. "I thought you were going to leave me." I could feel that she was weak. But she was alive.

"I haven't gone anywhere, darling."

I climbed up to the deck. It was the first time I had gone outside since she became sick. I pulled up the anchor and raised the sail. We were going south again. A pair of seagulls flew over us and landed on a large buoy up ahead. The sun felt good on my skin. Perhaps it was the end of the world, but I did not believe it. It could not be the end of the world on this day with a strong wind blowing west, the sun bright and the skies blue with the smell of salt, and Natalie in the cabin heating up a bowl of soup. I wondered where we would go now and if it even mattered. We had followed the eastern coast, but maybe we could venture away from land into the Caribbean. I smelled the air, smiling, and guided the ship around the buoy with the seagulls. It was a fine day.

The Beast

by Rebecca McKenna

F airies don't belong on the water. That's what my mother told me. Water is for sprites. Water is for naiads. Water is for mermaids. Water is for the bold, the fearless. Water is for those lucky enough to be born with gills.

I didn't want to be on the water. But there I was. On a ship. On my way across the water because of an obligation.

When we started out, the motion of the waves made my eyes hurt. The smell of the seaweed turned my stomach. The salt dried out my nose. The cold made my fingers ache. And, all of that aside, I was afraid of the water. When we had been out there for a few weeks, my discomfort had gone away, and I felt at home on the ship. Except for my fear. There was no shark, no kraken, no giant crustacean that was as fearful as the water that they all breathed.

There is a myth that says that if you catch a fairy, it will grant you three wishes. The myth also says that the fairy has to give you those wishes, even if you don't make them all at once. That a fairy who owes you a wish is in your debt until it is paid.

I didn't owe anyone wishes. And the whole wish thing is just a myth anyway. But it is true that, like all creatures, we sometimes are in debt to others, and those debts cannot be ignored.

A little over three hundred years ago, Max saved me from a gambling debt. I didn't want him to do it; I had the awful feeling that owing him would be worse than owing anyone else. But he wouldn't take no for an answer. He paid up for me before I realized what was going on.

And then six weeks ago, he had come to find me. Himself. Max hadn't sent a go-between, just showed up at The Angry Snail, sliding in beside me at my usual corner at the bar. Really, it was my own fault for being so predictable; I'm sure he'd had no trouble finding me.

"Aster," he said, signaling for a drink as he eased his long body onto the stool. "How are you feeling, my friend?"

I should have told him I was failing. That I'd been ill for months, years. That I could barely hold my head up. But Max would have known those were lies. Why would I be at The Snail if I were sick? So instead, I turned my brightest smile on him and pushed my empty glass in his direction. "Dry," I told him. "Very dry."

Two glasses of red beer frothed on the bar in front of us. Max picked his up and raised it in my direction. "You won't be for long," he said, and my heart fell into my stomach. He drank deeply and, without looking at me, asked, "How do you feel about going to America?"

The Stone of Elfame is as big a myth as the idea that fairies grant wishes. No one had ever seen it. Elves, fairies, and even goblins had hunted it for time immemorial without any luck. But myths must have been coming to life because I was on that ship granting a wish: Max's wish for me to go and fetch the Stone home for him.

"It is said to be guarded by the souls of a thousand dead fairies," he'd said to me in the bar.

I only blinked at him. Fairies do not fear the dead.

"It is said to be guarded by the fiercest of mermaids," he'd said to me.

I blinked again. Fairies do not fear mermaids.

"It is said to be housed in the depths of a cave and in the firmament of the sky," he'd said.

I stared at him. How did he expect me to get to the sky?

We were sailing south and had been doing so for a month since we left New York. Shortly after we had set sail, I had been regularly feeding sacrifices to the open waves, dropping pieces of flesh overboard whenever I felt that the waves were rising, that the winds were blowing harder, or that we were being followed by a curse. And out there, those things seemed to happen all the time.

Herkel was the first to offer himself up, so to speak. I was looking for a sacrifice that would cause the least impact. He was the laziest. Really, it was his fault. I caught him skipping out on his watch our second day, already making extra work for others and jeopardizing everyone's safety. I lured him to my room with a promise of brandy, but when we got there, I tied him in a chair and gagged him. Then I took him apart, piece by piece, and fed him to the ocean. While he lasted, the weather had been good, the winds had been fair, and we were not followed by anyone or anything. Herkel proved himself to be helpful after all.

But humans are weak, and their bodies only last for so long once they begin to be parsed up into useful pieces. Herkel was only good for five days. Then Schmidt. He lasted six. Then Curran, who stuck around for eight days. Mercer, Walling, and Geno all did their part for six days, too. But then we were seven hands down, still a few weeks out from where I hoped to find the Stone, and the remaining crew were getting frantic about the missing sailors.

I had meant to stop feeding the ocean. After Herkel, I did not make any offering for two days, despite my growing uneasiness. Dark shadows appeared under the water, following along beside the ship. The waves grew larger, almost imperceptibly, but I felt the increase in the swells. My fear gripped me by the throat, and I did what I had to in order to keep the ocean happy, to keep the water at bay.

While I was not a sailor, I found that it was easy to be accommodating to the others. The *Marie Celeste* was a fine ship. Her rigging responded to the lightest of touches, her keel was straight and strong, and she was incredibly solid. As everyone was expected to, I did my duty on the deck with the crew. Indeed, once Mercer was sacrificed, I was the only one who was willing to go up into the crow's nest at night. Because they were men and I am a fairy, they didn't understand that, while I was stronger, faster, and nimbler than any of them, I was seasick for the first few days. I kept this information to myself, both about my sickness and about my being a fairy. They hailed me as a great helpmeet and trusted me, until more and more men disappeared.

While I was not made for the sea, I did love the height of the mast and the freshness of the air. I also liked being on top of the mast because it put me that much further away from the dreaded water. My eyesight is keen, and I was often able to see whales, sirens, sea scorpions, and other citizens of the deep while they were out playing on the surface.

One day, McAllister caught sight of a water horse off the port side. He wailed and screamed to the captain, to anyone who would listen, imploring that the beast be harpooned. Fortunately, no one else was close by, and I decided that McAllister would make a good sacrifice. Instead of parceling him out in pieces, though, I just threw him overboard. The sharks took care of him.

The difficulty in a task such as finding the Stone was not the journey itself. Fairies can, of course, travel in so many different ways. But the issue with using ley lines or fairy rings, or even corpse roads, is that you need to know where you are going. In the case of the Stone, I was following a feeling, although I did not know where it led. The crew had been told that we were sailing to the West Indies to pick up cargo. The captain knew that I had a separate plan. He was paid handsomely to follow my lead. I pretended to give him coordinates from a private map, although I really just directed him based on where I felt the pull.

It had been three weeks since McAllister, and only the captain and the first mate were left. They eyed me with distrust, although they were unwilling to ask questions about the missing crew. At first, there had been lots of questions. Then there was only fear. If more crew members were left, I imagine that the captain would have tried to turn around. At that point, though, his only hope was to forge on ahead, and so we did.

The Stone of Elfhame only calls to certain beings. I live in the fairy world and often venture into the human world. A family secret is that my maternal great-grandmother was an elf. The Stone called to the elven part of me, but the sensitive fairy part of me picked up on the call so much faster and easier than any full-blooded elf would have. Hell, some elves would never have heard the call at all, never have felt the pull. Somewhere along the line, Max found out about my little impurity, and he used it to his fullest advantage. And there I was, less than two days away from the Stone. The need for it was tremendous, and it urged me onward. I was nervous, though, about the weather, about a presence which I could not name. I went in search of the captain to give him new directions. After that, I went in search of the first mate to make the necessary sacrifice. I couldn't let the waves begin to rise again.

It had just passed the darkest moments of the night when the jolt came. I felt it in my blood, although there was no ripple on the water, no shift in the wind. We were there. To the north, there was a small cluster of islands. To the southeast, a large landmass loomed on the horizon, although I could not tell from there if it was an island or a mainland. What I did know was that a force was below us, and that force was tied to the Stone.

There was a screeching of something dragging across the hull and a shuddering as the *Marie Celeste* came to a halt. The captain, who had come up from his berth about an hour before, stumbled backward and fell onto a pile of folded sails. I had been swinging on a rope, high up near the top of the mast, on the lookout for something, anything which might indicate the presence of the Stone. The rope swung wildly, and I was thrust out over the waves.

Fairies do not scare easily, but as I have said, I was afraid of the water. As I swung out over the never-ending black waves, I lost my breath. In the water was something else that scared me even more.

I did not fully understand what it was. It was water, and it was darkness, and it was cold, and it was energy. And all of those things had bound together the detritus of the ocean into the thing that was now rising above the surface.

It had broken through a valley between two wave crests, and I could see it because of its darkness against the black waves and sky. A void. The beast was long tendrils of seaweed: kelp and sargasso wound together into thick, impenetrable cords. Jagged chunks of coral stuck out here and there between strands of seaweed. A megalodon's mouth gaped open, row upon row of teeth sinking into a hole of swirling black water. It looked at me with the unnerving, mirrored and irregular eyes of a squid, huge and unblinking.

I do not believe the captain could see the beast from where he lay, but he must have suddenly become aware of the smell, because he leaned over and retched up whatever remained of his dinner. Even to me, the stench was dizzying. It was as if the rot of a thousand years of fish and seaweed had been encapsulated in one sulfurous bubble which had burst when the creature opened its mouth. Putrid, stagnant water just beyond the rows of teeth held the smell, fermented it, offered up its suffocating shroud.

My fear was thrilling, the pull of the Stone intoxicating. I knew then that the Stone did not lie on one of those remote islands, as I had thought, but rather within this beast. The creature must have been its protector and keeper for eons. No wonder the Stone had been lost to time.

Humans have a quaint story of a man who is swallowed by a great fish after he is thrown into the ocean. The man's shipmates sacrifice him when their strange god brings up a storm because he is unhappy.

This ancient beast brought its own storm. Winds screamed and whistled. A maelstrom began around us, the beast at the still center of the raging swirl of water. The *Marie Celeste* threatened to tip over. It was apparent that a final sacrifice was needed.

As my rope swung back over the deck, I slid down and grasped the captain by his collar. He was too cowed to resist, and I almost hated to give such a meek offering to this tremendous spirit. Still, the captain would not be the only item on offer.

Again, the ship pitched and we were thrust out over the water, hanging on to the rope. I'm not sure if it was the creature or the wind that screamed. Perhaps it was both. Perhaps it was a cosmic warning.

The infinite mouth was now the only path ahead. I opened my fingers and released the captain into it. There was a sliver of peace, of stillness, of acceptance, and then I opened my other hand and dropped from the rope, following the captain into eternity.

I fell fast. Within moments I had passed the captain in his descent. I fell past the undead bodies of sailors who had been descending for fifty years, a hundred years, two hundred years. A fairy who had been plunging down for six thousand years was left behind me in an instant.

While fairies do not feel time in the same way as humans, I had no way of describing the duration of my descent. It was boundless, even by fairy standards. My being was wrenched apart, my consciousness parsed out in much the same manner as I had offered up the piecemeal sacrifices of the sailors. But the pieces of me were minuscule. Somewhere along the way, my fear was separated out, encapsulated in its own sphere. I let it go, dismissing it from the mucosa which was now me. I travelled on and on, through the proverbial belly of this beast, which was water and fear and time. I was drawn ever faster toward the Stone.

Whether the Stone was at the center of the beast, or at the bottom, I cannot say, and I don't believe it matters. But finally, there it was, and I was beside it. I was still not in the physical shape I was used to, but I was whole, except for my cast-off fear.

The myths about the Stone of Elfhame are as myriad as stars. They had seemed so unreal, so ridiculous, that I had not really believed them. What appeal is there to a stone which gives eternal life if you are already immortal? Why should you want endless power if you don't even use all that you were born with? If even half of the stories of the Stone were true, it seemed to me that finding the Stone, guarding the Stone, and wielding the Stone were all much more effort than it was worth. I had never, in all my endless years, been so wrong.

For weeks, my thoughts had focused on the plan to get the Stone, to get home, to give it to Max, and to never be in debt to anyone again. Now, that was all insignificant.

I was in the belly of the beast, and I was the beast. My energy and consciousness swirled and mixed with the water, the seaweed, the sinews that held time and power in this dark form. I felt myself expand. I moved throughout the tendrils and the spaces between them. I inhabited the falling bodies of men and fairies who were trapped here. I surrounded the Stone, encasing it in a shell at the core of my being. I was the beast. I was me. I was the Stone. I was the universe.

I awoke lying on the deck of the *Marie Celeste*. The sun beat down upon the ship, which was adrift on calm seas.

I knew, instinctively, that it was the morning after the maelstrom. That I had been asleep for a few hours, and that barely any time had passed in this world while I had been on my journey to the Stone.

Standing and stretching, I faced northeast toward home. I could be there in the blink of an eye. I didn't need the ship anymore.

There was no Stone to give to Max. The Stone was within me. Either I would find a different way to repay his debt, or I would leave it unpaid. Obligations be damned. I owed nothing. Not to anyone, to myself, or to the universe. I was the Stone Bearer. I was burdened, and I was free. I harbored the souls of a thousand dead fairies; I had become the fiercest of mermaids; I contained the depths of every cave and the firmament of the sky. I was the Beast.

Disappearance of the Dawn Bringer

by Devin J. Gaither

The APV submersible series was engineered by OceaniX, a division of Edom Technology Corporation, in late 2022 in response to the success of commercialized space travel. The tragic accident of her maiden voyage with paying passengers has many asking how we could safely send average folks into space but couldn't manage to safely take them to the bottom of the ocean—

Cary opened her car door and the radio jockey's voice cut off mid-thought. She was tired of all the depressing news stories, but if she didn't listen to them, then how would she take an active part in conversations at parties or online? Having a social life really was emotionally exhausting.

She pulled her shoulder bag from the passenger seat across the center console and juggled it and her Cricut-emblazoned coffee canteen as she got out of the car. She knew it was probably rude to take the spot on the street right in front of the clinic where she worked, but the patients probably didn't know it was her car.

As Cary pushed the car door closed with her hip, her phone vibrated in her back pocket. She sat the reusable coffee mug on the roof of her car, blue sparkling decal facing her. It read "Boss babe? More like Beach Babe." It was tacky and she loved it.

"Good morning, Sunshine," she said.

Her friend, Denise, groaned in response. "Feeling that good, huh? I shouldn't have had that last Tequila Sunrise," she groaned. "Who even ordered those anyways?"

"Apparently you, at 1 am on a Tuesday." Cary pinched the phone between her ear and shoulder, grabbed her coffee, and walked up the concrete steps leading up the front lawn of the clinic.

"Is Doctor Dreamboat at the office yet?" Denise asked.

"Oh my god, shut up. I should have never told you," Cary said. She cringed at the memory of drunkenly confessing to having a crush on one of the therapists that rented office space in the clinic. "He's not a doctor, he's just a therapist, and, no, I like to get in early on Wednesdays so that I can leave by three-thirty."

"How very responsible of you," Denise said.

"Yeah well—" Cary stopped. As reached the top of the front stairs to the clinic door, she noticed the welcome mat was wet, sopped through with dirty, foul-smelling water. "Oh for Christ's sake," Cary said. "It didn't rain last night, did it?"

"I don't think so, but everything past a certain point is just an abyssal void so, who knows," Denise said.

"Ugh, gross. I think a pipe burst or something. I should go," Cary said.

"Bummer. Call me when you get off," Denise said.

Cary pulled her keys from the front pocket of her shoulder bag and unlocked the door, careful to stand as far to the side of the disgusting puddle of stagnant water so that she didn't get it on her shoes. She pushed the door open gingerly, expecting to see the hardwood floor of the ground level flooded, but...it was not. The stinking water was relegated to the exterior of the front door. It was as if someone had stood at the front door for a long time, dripping onto the stoop and welcome mat, but didn't come inside.

Cary took a small leap over the mat and into the entryway of the clinic. She checked her feet, careful not to track any of the stinking water onto the hardwood floor, and as she pushed the door shut behind her, she saw a wet pile of mail sitting on the floor, pushed against the wall from when she opened the door.

That's weird, Cary thought to herself. *I gathered up the mail when it came yesterday...someone must have stuck this through the slot in the door after we closed.* She quickly gathered up the soggy pile of mail to take it to her desk. Hopefully it wasn't anything too important—she'd have to try to catch the postal carrier today and figure out what in the world happened. She needed this job, and the last thing she wanted to deal with was taking the heat for someone else's carelessness.

She let her shoulder bag drop onto the floor by her desk, sat her coffee and phone next to her computer, and began sorting through the pile of papers. Most of them were bound together in a stiff folio, wrapped with leather cord. They looked like personal papers, and there didn't seem to any sort of address or identifying writing on the outside of the folio. It was probably notes from another doctor, or maybe something a patient dropped off? She couldn't tell.

She then saw that a smaller, tri-folded pamphlet lay on her desk. Was it meant to be part of the folio papers, or was this a separate piece of mail that had just gotten stuck to the back of the soggy mess? Certainly the latter—this was a brochure for a cruise line—and it was addressed, as it happened, to Doctor Dreamboat.

The front of the brochure was emblazoned with the words "Tasteful Indulgence aboard the Minos," followed by a beautiful sunset photograph of a luxury liner on a tranquil sea. At the bottom of the image was a section that looked like a two-dollar lottery ticket from the gas station. It said, "Scratch the Squares to Reveal Your Prize!"

Cary plucked her keys off the desk and used her Class of 2013 keychain to scratch at the silvery gray masking. Little icons of squids, octopuses, boats, and submarines appeared from beneath and, to her surprise, three smiling devil icons, all in a row. She had won a free ticket; or rather, she supposed, Doctor Dreamboat had won a free ticket. He didn't have to know that, though. If she presented it as a gift (his birthday was coming up), maybe he'd ask her to come along. Or at least take her out for dinner to show his appreciation. In any case, what could it hurt?

Supplemental Document #787384

Case #1976399200: Investigation into the Death of Edom Technologies Investigative Analyst John Meade

Document Type: Audio Transcript

The following is a written copy of Recorded Session AISHD-6539, interview of Bradford [last name redacted] by Edom Technologies Investigative Analyst [name has been redacted]

Begin Recording

Analyst [name redacted] : "Do you mind if I record this interview?"

Bradford [name redacted] : "Seeing as you've already hit the record, I guess it's fine."

Analyst [name redacted] : "Excellent. I'm here today to ask you about your patient, John Meade."

Bradford [name redacted] : "Well, this will be quick, then. I can't talk about my patients. Especially not with their employers."

Analyst [name redacted] : "Unfortunately, in this instance, I think you can. Mr. Meade was killed in an accident on his latest assignment."

There is a long exhale, followed by the sound of an office chair squeaking and settling.

Bradford [name redacted] : "I'm sorry. I need a glass of water. Would you like one?"

Analyst [name redacted] : "Oh, yes, please."

Sounds of movement. The shuffling of paper cups, dispensing of liquid from a water cooler.

Analyst [name redacted] : "Thank you."

Sounds of gulping, then the sound of a presumably empty paper cup being sat on a desk surface.

Braford [name redacted] : "If you were that thirsty, you should have said something."

Silence.

Braford [name redacted] : "What happened to John? And why are you interested in speaking to me about it?"

Analyst [name redacted] : "We have reason to believe that John suffered a mental health episode while on the job. As I'm sure you're aware, the nature of John's work was...is...delicate. Edom Technologies is worth a lot of money, Mr. [name redacted]. It's practically a household name."

Braford [name redacted] : "And I guess you're worried about a lawsuit."

Silence.

Bradford [name redacted] : "I'm guessing you want me to say that John was stable and mentally well when last I saw him?"

Analyst [name redacted] : "Tell me a little bit about your relationship with John. Why did he start seeing you? What was bothering him?"

Bradford [name redacted] : "John has been one of my patients for approximately four months. He first came to me as a referral from a friend and colleague that was retiring to Florida. I didn't know much about him when he first walked into my office. I try not to read too much about my clients before meeting them, I don't like to make subconscious assumptions about them, and, if I'm being honest, I'm not sure I could help it if I knew much more than their name."

Analyst [name redacted] : "What did you talk about during that first session?"

Bradford [name redacted] : "During our first session together? That session isn't much more than an intake, so we don't get into much detail on things. I learned that John spent some time in the Navy and then the DoD, before taking up work at a big-name theme park working as an investigative analyst for ride-related accidents. After a few years of that, he started contracting as an investigator for high profile accidents at a very private, but very profitable contracting company. I guess now I know which one."

Analyst [name redacted] : "And what else did he tell you about his line of work?"

Bradford [name redacted] : "That it was a macabre business, which perhaps accounted for John's generally somber attitude most of the time. After a few sessions together, it became clear that John was here because he was required, or rather, *strongly encouraged*, to attend regular therapy sessions due to his frequent exposure to upsetting and graphic accidents. I was also aware, as it was passed along by his previous practitioner, that John had been involved in a drunk driving incident ten years ago, so I suspect that also was a contributing factor in his choice to seek therapy."

Analyst [name redacted] : "To your knowledge, did John have a drinking problem? Either before he was under your care or presently?"

Bradford [name redacted] : "I don't think so. I think it was a dumb accident. Maybe he had too much to drink after a particularly hard day at work, or maybe he just went out to a bar, acted like an idiot, and accidentally killed someone. It happens."

Analyst [name redacted] : "What makes you so confident his drinking wasn't a way of drowning away his work stresses."

Bradford [name redacted] : "Generally speaking, he seemed disaffected by his work. Not in a concerning, sociopathic way, but more in the way that a stoic father is unbothered by accidentally running over a possum nest with the lawn mower. John had issues with desensitization and compartmentalization, but he wasn't mentally unwell."

Silence.

End of Recording.

Bradford sat stiff in his chair. When the man had reached forward to turn off the recording app on his phone, Brad wanted to scramble back, away from his outstretched arm. Something about him filled Brad with revulsion and he wanted to put as much space between as he could as quickly as possible.

"Is there anything else I can help you with?" Brad asked. Please, please let him say no.

The stranger slid the phone into his pocket and pulled a pristine handkerchief from somewhere in its depths. Brad noticed the moisture pooling on the man's forehead, in the crevices beside his nose, and along the cavity of his dimpled chin. Drops slid down the sides of his face and neck. *He must have some sort of condition,*Brad thought. *No one sweats that much, even in September.*

The stranger dragged the kerchief across his forehead and the cloth came away gray and streaked with what Brad imagined must be dead skin and dirt. Brad swore he could smell a brackish, fishy odor in the air. Was that even possible? For someone to sweat so copiously that you could smell the salt from their skin?

"Did you see John after his time on the Herosphoros?" the man asked. He slid the soiled handkerchief into his pocket, and as he turned his head back up to look at Brad, a smile split his face. His teeth were gray and discolored and...it seemed as though his spittle was thin and gray too, pushing its way between his grotesque teeth.

"Yes, I saw him once after that," John said. He felt his bottom clench in his chair. He could feel the threat underneath the question, the threat in that hellacious smile.

"And what did he say about his time onboard the Herosphoros?"

Brad fought to keep himself from glancing at his bottom desk drawer, fought to keep himself from stealing a glance to make sure that the folio of wrinkled, handwritten pages were still there. The stranger must know; he must know they were there in the office somewhere. Or if he didn't know, he suspected.

"Nothing, really," Brad said. "Just that he enjoyed getting to travel for work."

The stranger inhaled sharply, a wet and sudden sound, before letting out a gurgle of laughter. John wasn't so sure what was funny.

"Excellent," the man said, standing up. He reached forward and grabbed Brad's paper cup of water, from which he'd previously taken a single, solitary sip, and downed it in three gulps. The stranger took both cups and, strangely, stuck them both in one of his jacket pockets. From another, he pulled a business card and deposited it on Brad's desk.

"I may be in touch," he said, making deliberate eye contact. Brad felt his already frozen stomach drop into his groin.

"Well, if I don't get back to you right away, just leave a message. I'm going on vacation in a few weeks."

"Oh? Anywhere good?" the stranger asked.

"Just a cruise. Gift from a friend."

"That's a very generous friend," the stranger said. He smiled once more, and Brad could have sworn that the man's teeth were longer than those of the average person. "Enjoy yourself." The stranger turned and swiftly walked out of the room.

Brad released the breath he had been choking on for the last several minutes. He waited until he heard Cary say "have a nice day" and then front door close before opening the bottom desk drawer. The folio of papers were still there. Brad bent over his computer, opened one of the folders on his desktop, and scanned the files for Meade_Session_3_Audio.mp3. He double clicked the file and hit play.

"Well, how was the Pacific," he heard himself ask John as he walked into the office. John didn't answer, he simply shuffled into the leather chair across from the desk and awkwardly shrugged off his coat. Brad pictured John at that moment, looking up at him expectedly as he rounded the desk.

"Sorry, what was that?" John's voice said.

"Your trip—you were heading out to the Pacific last time I saw you."

"Right," he said and left it at that.

"You seem distracted today, John. What's on your mind," Brad's voice asked.

"Nothing, I'm just preoccupied," John said.

"Forgive me if I'm wrong, but it generally seems like the point of therapy, for most people, is to empty their brain of those preoccupations and examine them a little bit."

"Right. Well," he said. *"I'm really only here because the company..."*

"...strongly encourages it." Brad said. *"So why don't you tell me about the job you did, John. What happened?"*

"Well, that's the thing. I'm not really sure what happened. And that's what I can't stop thinking about. Like a thorn in my damn paw, or a splinter in my sinuses."

"Let's start from when you arrived at the site. You said it was an oil rig? Like in the ocean?"

"Yeah, like in the ocean."

Brad stopped the playback of the recording, grabbed the folio from the open desk drawer, and walked to the open door to his office. "Cary," Brad called down the stairwell. "You got a few minutes? I need you to make some copies for me!"

Supplemental Document #787397

Case #1976399200 - Investigation into the Death of Edom Technologies Investigative Analyst John Meade

Document Type: Firsthand Account (from the notes of John Meade)

*The following is an excerpt from the notes of John Meade, taken from the private practice of Bradford [name redacted]. These documents were recovered from a privately rented office in the [name Redacted] Clinic for Mental Wellness in [Town Name Redacted], Maryland in the course of the investigation into Bradford [name redacted]'s disappearance (**Case #1976399202**)*

Transcription of Document Contents:

July 8, 2026

I have never kept much of a record of my work, save a simple logbook of basic details for my own record keeping (and that is more out of habit than anything). In this instance, however, I feel moved to provide more details and context concerning what I have experienced, to give it a skeleton, a scaffold on which to stand - then perhaps I can figure out what really happened aboard the Herosphoros.

What follows is a combination of memories and suppositions based on research, interviews, and first-hand experience.

I didn't know much about oil rigs and drills when I got the email about an upcoming position on an investigative committee tasked with looking into events that transpired on the Herosphoros. I know the guys who work on board are sometimes called roughnecks—I heard that in a movie once—but I know that they probably don't look like Ben Affleck, and Liv Tyler definitely isn't hiding under anyone's bunk comforter.

I first received word that I would be investigating a mass disappearance on an oil drilling rig on a Tuesday morning, and by Tuesday afternoon I had completed my preliminary research such that I felt like I knew enough to sit in on a Wednesday briefing without sounding like a dumbass. The briefing was short.

"The Herosphoros was built as part of an initiative to expand the life of oil fields until 2050," he said. "It's estimated that the Herosphoros could net a revenue of over 6 billion dollars over ten years of operation. It was outfitted with a highly advanced security system and rescue boats capable of accommodating 25 workers in case of an accident. The platform features a helipad big enough to land 2 helicopters capable of carrying 23 workers in case of a weather event or other emergency. Generally, occupants of an oceanic drilling rig spend 2-3 weeks aboard, 2-3 weeks on shore. When on the rig, it's 12 hours on, 12 hours off. Video calls are limited to living quarters, for safety. I recalled a job I worked several years ago where a young woman stepped right off the edge of the Grand Canyon trying to take a selfie and understood the reasoning—damn cell phones."

I was shown some grainy, jumbled footage of video communications that came in from the Herosphoros early the night before communications from the rig went silent. Most of the footage and recording were unintelligible, minus approximately thirty seconds of clarity, where one crew member can be heard asking "Is that a light? What the fuck is that?" before beginning to scream.

When I asked what it was the man was screaming (the recording was cutting in and out, it was difficult to hear), I was told that the crewman was screaming the name of his wife.

It should be noted that the crewman in question was a widower, actively under investigation for the death of his late wife.

Just before the recording cut out for the final time, it sounded as though another crew member (or potentially it was the same one—it's impossible to tell) could be heard yelling "Oh god, its teeth" or perhaps "Oh god, you see?" I'm not sure which, and this was the extent of my knowledge upon boarding the Herosphoros.

I arrived by helicopter in the mid-afternoon and was greeted by a Navy officer. "This way," the officer yelled as he crossed the helipad in long, confident strides. I don't often get to travel by helicopter these days, but I flew on my fair share when I was in the Navy. I had forgotten how loud the damn things are.

The contract officer opened a door into a glass-walled galley-type office. As he shut the door behind him, the sound of the helicopter became muted, as though it had been trapped in a jar, the lid screwed shut.

I immediately flipped through the possible scenarios.

"Based on what I've heard so far," I said, referencing my own notes, "I'm going to be looking into two major scenarios. Scenario one, the crew was abducted by a terrorist organization. Scenario two, the crew was swept overboard during a rogue weather event." I proceeded to walk through both possible scenarios with the officer managing the investigation.

Scenario number one: the Herosphoros had begun drilling nine months earlier. Much of the technology aboard the drill was new and she almost immediately drilled too quickly at too far a depth. The consequences of this were that a large fissure, the largest man made one in known history, cracked its way across the Pacific Plate. While there was initially substantial spillover from the oil reserves being targeted by the Herosphoros, much to Edom Technologies energy division's surprise, the oil quickly dissipated into the surrounding ocean beds and left behind a deep and empty fissure. While the ongoing oil spill concerns were alleviated, several environmentalist groups (who were already up in arms about the oil rig) became rabid with fervent protest. It could be possible that one of these environmentalist groups had crossed the line into terrorist cell territory and had somehow kidnapped the crew to prove a point.

"Unlikely" the officer told me. "I follow your reasoning, but we've already looked into that group and there's just no way they have the capital to get out this far into the open ocean, nevermind kidnap or kill nearly a hundred men. What about scenario number two?"

Scenario number two: the Herosphoros had been hit by a rogue storm or wave, sweeping the entire crew overboard without, somehow, damaging the larger structure.

"Seems more likely than scenario one," he said once I had finished my explanation. "Doppler didn't show any weather events, but a rogue wave makes as much sense as anything. But what in the Sam Hill were they all doing out on the deck at the same time, especially that time of night?"

"Hell if I know," I told him. By this point, the sun had started to set. "Why don't you give me the tour and then show me where I can set up shop for the night," I asked. The officer led me out of the glass-walled terrarium of a room into a dimly lit stairwell.

The living area of the rig spanned four floors and included pantries, gymnasiums, and a small first-aid room with medical personnel and emergency evacuation equipment. The room I was to stay in was on the first deck of living spaces. It did not escape me that the room had recently been cleared of belongings from its previous occupant. The bunk had not been remade. There was still a rumpled towel tossed over a wooden chair in the corner. I took the towel and threw it on the floor, sat myself up at the small wooden desk, and started transposing my notes from the afternoon.

Rogue Waves travel at 12.1 meters per second. The largest in recorded history was in November 2020 and measured 58 meters high. The North Pacific has the highest percentage of rogue waves compared to the other oceans of Earth. It wasn't impossible that one had come just a little further south than usual. Who knows, perhaps the change in the Pacific floor was somehow to blame for causing a rogue wave. I'd planned to research as much when I got back to land with a better internet connection.

I glanced at my watch and saw that it was nearing 2:45am. It wasn't unusual for me to work into the night when I was on location for an investigation. I could feel my legs cramping up and decided I would walk out onto the deck and at least try to get an idea for what the crew could have been seeing or thinking in the hour leading up to the incident.

I slipped on my trench coat, descended the stairs, and walked out onto the deck. The air was chill, and the wind was stronger than I expected. The deck was well lit enough to safely traverse, but beyond the white tubular railing, a black velvet abyss yawned forth into nothingness. I estimated I could see maybe 40 feet beyond the railing before the glow of the deck lights was swallowed by the endless dark of the open ocean.

I tried to imagine what it would be like, standing on the deck of the Herosphoros, staring out at the nothingness, only to see a hundred-and fifty-foot-tall wall of water racing towards you at the final moment. There wouldn't be time to react. It would all be over before you could even take a deep breath.

My mind went back to something the officer had said. What in the hell was everyone doing out on deck? If the wave hadn't been strong enough to damage the structure of the Herosphoros, then how was the ENTIRE crew lost? At three in the morning, shouldn't at least half of them be sleeping? It was an impressive feat of engineering for a rig to survive a rogue wave of that size, even one as state of the art as the Herosphoros. For that, at least, the Edom Technology Corporation could be proud.

It's at that moment that I began to hear it. An awful caterwauling coming from beyond the railing. I raced forward, expecting to find that someone had gone overboard, but as my eyes scanned the perimeter of water visible from the deck, I saw no one; but still I heard it. An all-encompassing shrieking, like tires on asphalt; or was it screaming? Perhaps both? I reached up to cover my damn ears with my hands because it was so loud that I thought my eyes might burst, but even that didn't help. It was almost like it was coming from inside my head.

That was when I saw it.

Just where the light from the deck began to fade, I saw something crawl from the depths onto the surface of the water, almost as though crawling from an open grave. It hefted itself onto the surface of the waves. Yes, the surface, rolling gently with the rising and lowering of the wave pattern. It was on all fours, limbs sticking out at odd angles, almost like a spider missing limbs.

It began to crawl.

It floated on the top of the water like a cranefly on a puddle, and as it got closer, I could see that it was a woman. Or something like a woman. Her hair hung down in her face, but not enough to block the terrible visage completely from view. Her soggy, bloated skin was gray and, as she reached the bottom of the ladder that led from the water up to the deck, she paused on all fours and looked up. Looked at me.

Her bottom teeth were so long that they nearly reached her nostrils as her mouth snapped open and closed. I made eye contact with the thing, and it stopped, mouth snapping open and closed in a regular rhythm.

"What in the hell are you doing?" I heard the lead investigative officer yell from behind me. Reflexively I turned back to him and said, "There's...there's something in the..." As my face turned back, I saw the thing, the drowned woman thing, crawling—no, SCRAMBLING—up the ladder at an alarming speed, its mouth snapping and grinning.

I heard myself scream and felt the force of it burn my throat as I threw myself back from the railing. I hit the deck hard and began scrambling backwards on all fours, but before I got very far the officer grabbed me and hauled me. I fought him, trying to tell him, "No, no you don't understand! It's in the water. There's something in the water!" But before I could warn him, before I could get it all out, he hit me square in the throat and knocked me out.

By the time I woke up with a massive headache, it was dawn, and we were meant to be boarding the helicopter back to the island where we would catch our respective flights home. In the end, everyone blamed my episode on lack of sleep and stressful working conditions.

Now that I'm sitting in a well-lit airport terminal, I find myself questioning if I truly saw anything, or if perhaps this job is finally catching up to me. I haven't craved a drink in nearly ten years, but right now, with the airplane bar only thirty feet away, I feel that urge. One, I think, will be okay.

It's not as if I'm flying the damn plane.

Something has come back with me.

It started the first night back from my most recent contract in the Pacific. I had come home, eager to be finished with the never-ending series of journeys required to get me home. From the Herosphoros to the nearest island base, the island to a larger island, upon which I boarded a plane (with enough gin in my system to sleep most of the flight), upon which I then landed in a city, caught a layover to another city (where I replaced the gin with red wine), and then traveled in an Uber for 90 minutes, finally arriving back at my condo.

I deposited my bags, threw my coat over one of the barstools, and immediately made for the single bath on the main floor. I turned on the shower, eager to scrub away the grime of my trip, sober myself for the first time since I stopped drinking a decade ago, and try to ground myself back into the real world. While the water heated, creating wisps of steam, I turned the sink on full blast and grabbed my toothbrush from its cup on the counter.

Once I finished, I shed my clothing, throwing it into an unceremonious heap behind me, catching a glimpse of myself in the mirror. Not just myself. There was someone in the shower. I did not scream. I was not fast enough to scream. I whipped around to face the glass doors, and...there was nothing. I gulped in a chest full of air, a startled and belated strangled sound choking from my throat. I was exhausted, I thought to myself. I needed sleep. I needed to shower and sleep.

I stepped into the hot shower, defiantly fighting the flight response rising in my body at the feeling of stepping back into a tight, enclosed space. The water pooled down my face, aggressively invading my nostrils and ears as I tipped my head up. As it moved over me, so too did the thoughts I had been keeping at bay, which came issuing forth like a wall of water through an opening flood door. Rogue waves. Siren songs. Abyssal ghosts. What has the Herosphoros awakened in the deep? What door have we unknowingly, in our hubris, knocked on? What, to our great horror, has answered?

As I opened my eyes to search for the shampoo, I felt like I was floating in a sea of warm condensation. The steam hung so heavy in the air that it was like fog on a lake, so thick that I couldn't properly see the far side of the room. If I didn't know where I was, it could conceivably stretch on for miles. Just like the darkness of the world beyond the rails of the Herosphoros.

And then, suddenly, an invasive thought: "What if I see something crawling through the steam, crawling toward me from the dark hallway."

I turned the water off without shampooing my hair or so much as grabbing the bottle of soap. I toweled off, found some fresh clothes, and laid down in an exhausted heap on the living room couch. The room was dimly lit by the light of a development-installed streetlamp bleeding in through the sheer curtains. The early, yellow glow gave everything a dark, sickly sheen, as though...underwater. I laid staring around the open room—around the cluttered living room, the kitchen, the dining room.

I felt the weight of exhaustion settling into my bones as they, in turn, settled into the worn springs of the ancient couch. As my body settled, my eyes roved, adjusting, picking up on details in the dark, something under the dining room table began to take shape. There was something...crouched under the dining room table, contorted around the legs of the chairs, resting its upper extremities on the seat of a chair, and it was staring at me. Grinning. With those teeth.

My heart leapt into my throat, and I choked on the breath I was taking in. I blinked a few times, rapidly, trying to will myself to move, and by the time my brain and body had caught up to themselves...it was just...gone. Its afterimage burned into my brain. I tried to retain the details of it so that I would not forget them. I could not forget them; I must remember them because it was THERE. I lay perfectly still, etching its gray, decaying skin, its too-wide grin, its stringy, matted wet hair to my memory...I drifted off on the tides of sleep. "Surely" I thought to myself, "surely it is my eyes adjusting to the light. Surely it is the exhaustion of the trip. Surely I have scared myself senseless and I just need to sleep."

Sometime in the night, I awoke suddenly, startled that I had even managed to doze off. I opened my eyes and let my gaze travel across the room as it adjusted, and, I swear to you, there it was again. This time it was in the kitchen, peering up over the edge of the counter, just the upper half of its horrifying face. Its eyes were dead and malevolent and slowly began to crinkle up at the edges as it, presumably, smiled. I lay frozen, unable to move. Sure that if I moved even slightly, it would leap over the cabinets and race toward me on those horrible, twisted limbs.

The thing sunk, hidden now, behind the kitchen cabinets. I did not sleep again after that, remaining certain that if I moved, it would dart from behind the cabinets and drag me into its maw of teeth.

It has been a few days since then, and while I've convinced myself that it was a series of hallucinations brought on by exhaustion and drink, I can feel that my body is dehydrated. I feel my lips cracking, my skin flaking, but I can't bring myself to so much as fill a glass with water, lest something in that shallow glass, that telescope reflection, see me. Be seen by me.

I say I've convinced myself that all I've seen was a hallucination...but would I be writing all of this down if that was truly the case?

What if, for a moment, we imagine that the fiery pits in Dante's Inferno are the same as that molten core at the heart of our Earth. Is this why mankind has always seemed so sick? So dark in its heart? Has this darkness been seeping into the waters of our earth for thousands of years, slowly infecting us—infecting our very bodies, which are, in themselves, primarily composed of water?

Herosphoros. The Dawn Bringer. And that it was. As best as I can tell, the fissure of the Pacific Plate created by the oil drill opened something far worse than an oil-filled trench. Whether this fissure already existed and was too small to measure with our current technology or was somehow hidden by some sort of...malevolent energies...I cannot say. But I fear that it is open now.

Supplemental Document #78731

Case #1976399200 - Investigation into the Death of Edom Technologies Investigative Analyst John Meade

Document Type: Personal Notes from the Desk of Bradford [name redacted]

The following is a transcript of handwritten notes found with the papers of John Meade recovered from the office of Bradford [name redacted] in the course

*of the investigation into the disappearance of Bradford [name redacted] (**Case #1976399202**)*

I lied to the investigator from Edom Technologies.

Besides telling me that he had been losing sleep after his time on the Herosphoros, he also told me about the job he would be taking on next. Now that I've seen the news coverage and spoken with whoever it was that came to speak with me from Edom, I feel it necessary to record all I can remember from our conversation that day.

Somehow the audio files of my sessions with John have been corrupted and I can't help but feel paranoid that my computer was somehow hacked and the files compromised. Edom Technologies Corp is one of the biggest companies in the world, and I suspect if anyone could do it, they could.

The APV3 Submersible (full name being Abyssal Plane Voyager Commercial Submersible #003) was the third of its kind and met with its tragic fate on its maiden voyage six weeks after the disappearance of the crew of the Herosphoros. In the press, the accident was compared to that of the challenger shuttle explosion, which, in my opinion, was completely tasteless.

At the time of whatever happened down there, the APV3 had an operational crew of twelve and a passenger roster of six. Passengers paid upwards of six million dollars for a spot on the maiden voyage. The APV series was created not many years after it became clear that ultra-rich adrenaline junkies would rather spend millions on experiences usually reserved for the mega-accomplished than humanitarian efforts, it didn't take long before someone found a way to commercialize deep sea expeditions.

According to notes from his previous provider and based on what I could obtain from public enlistment records in online databases, John Meade had spent some time on a nuclear-powered submarine during his time in the Navy, and, by his own account, was unsurprised when he found himself pulled into a conference room for a briefing of the accident. He had heard a few of the basics on cable news already (the news broke early and has been featured prominently in headlines ever since, especially after the loss of the rescue vessel), and he had been uneasily waiting for the call.

"It was only a few hundred miles from the Herosphoros, you know. When whatever happened on that submersible happened," he had said.

Looking back, I can't be sure if he already knew, already suspected, that the two tragic occurrences were related and was trying to gently feel out how I would react if he said something to that effect. I could have chosen to crack a joke in the moment, but something told me not to do so. Humor can, occasionally, come across as dismissive, and this was not a moment to dismiss, but one in which to learn.

"Do you think there could be any connection between the two?" I'd asked. "In your expert opinion?"

"That's the million-dollar question, I guess," John said.

Supplemental Document #787389

Case #1976399200 - Investigation into the Death of Edom Technologies Investigative Analyst John Meade

Document Type: Personal Notes from the Desk of John Meade

*The following is a transcript of handwritten notes found with the papers of John Meade recovered from the office of Bradford [name redacted] in the course of the investigation into the disappearance of Bradford [name redacted] (**Case #1976399202**)*

Transcript of Document Contents:

It has been three weeks since my time onboard the Herosphoros. I have managed to hide my paranoia enough that I am still employed and have been put onto a new contract which will take me back to the Pacific.

The first thing I noticed in the press images of the APV3 was that it was clearly not built by the U.S. Military. It was sleek and made every attempt to be aesthetically pleasing.

The APV series had been constructed specifically for high-paying stakeholders looking for a once in a lifetime opportunity and was, therefore, outfitted with an interior built for comfort and that looked good in promotional footage and selfies.

We will be descending in the APV-Support Unit, which was built to assist in repairs, taking external footage of the APV-3, and, in emergency circumstances, rescue efforts. The APV-Support Unit utilizes the latest in private sector diving technology to connect to the APV3 using a specialized designed pressure-equalizing bridge, allowing cramped but reliable and safe access between the two vehicles. Seeing as the APV has been completely depressurized, flooded, and it presumably covered in the gory remains of the crew, we will not be utilizing that function.

From the exterior, the APV3 looks to be about the size of a double wind trailer. On the inside, however, it felt roomier and more modern than I expected. Small cots were tucked away, almost all of which were neatly made, save one with the blankets thrown aside and trailing onto the floor.

Three engineers from the parent company responsible for the design and construction of the APV series will be descending with me, as well as two crewmen with experience piloting this specific type of submersible.

I cannot believe that my presence on this submersible is a coincidence. I believe that I am being placed there as a convenient means of removal. Upon my return from the Herosphoros, my colleagues noticed my mental decline. The dehydration, the smells from lack of showering, the increasingly strong smell of booze on my person.

I haven't dared utter a word of my paranoia aloud to anyone. I keep telling myself that it is a delusion. But at night, as I lay and try to sleep, I see it—whatever it is—inching toward me. Sometimes crawling, sometimes just standing and staring. It seems so real.

And what is inarguable are the puddles of water I find each morning. Under the dining room table. In the kitchen. In the corner of my bedroom.

I can only hope that it cannot follow me back to the depths of the Pacific Plate. I can only hope that, now that it has escaped the doorways through which it came, it does not want to go back.

Supplemental Document #787393

Case #1976399200 - Investigation into the Death of Edom Technologies Investigative Analyst John Meade

Document Type: Audio Video Transcript

The following is a written copy of on-board security footage recording AISD-7855, recorded upon the APV-Support Submersible.

Recording begins ten minutes after the APV-Support vehicle reaches its lowest intended depth.

[Recording start]

Support Crew 1: "There had to have been some kind of mechanical failure, then. Right?"

Support Crew 2: "I mean you don't just decide to try and walk out of a sub that's so far down. You'll be flattened instantaneously."

Support Crew 3: "You don't, idiot. You pretty much explode."

Investigative Analyst John Meade: "Or you get spaghettified."

Support Crew 3: "Say what now, John?"

Investigative Analyst John Meade: "Have you ever heard of the Byford diving bell accident?"

Support Crew 2: "Oh, dude, yeah. That was gnarly! I saw a video online about that."

Support Crew 1: "Yeah, well, not everything you see on the internet is true."

Investigative Analyst John Meade: "The Byford Dolphin accident happened in the North Sea in the early 80s. The diving bell of the drill suffered explosive decompression and three of the crew died from the blood boiling in their veins.

The fourth guy was pretty much spaghettified. The pressure caused his body to be sucked out of a sixteen-inch crescent-shaped hole."

Pilot 1: "Jesus Christ! Could we not talk about this until we're back topside."

Support Crew 3: "And what the fuck caused that?"

Investigative Analyst John Meade: "Human error and lack of safety valves. The families made out with a hearty chunk of change after years of litigation."

Silence.

Pilot 2: "There she is."

Silence. In the video, the support crew and Mr. Meade can be seen leaving their seats and moving to the starboard side of the support submersible. It can be assumed they are making visual confirmation and observations of the wrecked APV3.

Video signal begins to cut out intermittently before blacking out completely. Audio remains.

Investigative Analyst John Meade: "Oh gods, it's out there. It's down here with us."

Pilot 2: "Well, yeah, that's the point. We came down to find her."

Investigative Analyst John Meade: "No, no! It's here. It's crawling toward us. Don't you see it?"

Support Crew 1: "Holy shit! What the fuck is that?"

Garbled dialogue.

Support Crew 2: "Is that a person?"

Support Crew 3: "It can't be. Look at the teeth. Holy shit! Is it an angler fish?"

Pilot 1: "Absolutely not. We're going back up."

Garbled dialogue. Audio cuts in and out. Silence.

Support Crew 1: "I thought we were going up. Why are we moving sideways?"

Pilot 1: "The risk mitigation system won't let me ascend—I'm trying to get it to reset, but until then we're going away from whatever the fuck that was."

Pilot 2: "[name redacted], are you seeing what I'm seeing ahead?"

Support Crew 2: "Dear God."

Support Crew 1: "It looks like a doorway. It looks like...it looks like fire."

Support Crew 3: "How can this be?"

Silence.

Several voices quietly praying and sobbing.

Investigative Analyst John Meade: "Abandon all hope, ye who enter here."

Silence. Signal to APV-Support Submersible lost. This is the end of the last known contact with the APV-Support vehicle. Contrary to reports given by major media networks, it was never recovered, but the HPV-3 was.

At this time, Edom is allowing this particular piece of misinformation to spread in order to provide a narrative for what happened to the APV series.

—the APV-Support Submersible sent to locate the HPV-3 Commercial Sub has been found. Early reports suggest that one crew member, an investigative analyst known to have issues with alcohol addiction, may be responsible for either an accidental or intentional depressurization of the cabin. At this time, Edom Technologies has no plans to send another submersible down to the locate the HPV-3. All passengers and crew aboard both vessels have been declared dead. The APV Commercial Division has been shut down indefinitely—

Cary turned the volume of the television down. Truly, did the horror show of primetime news never end? She picked up her vibrating phone. "Greetings," she said.

"Hey, are you coming out tonight? Please? I need a wing woman," Denise asked.

"Oh, I guess," Cary said. "I might as well start looking around myself."

"Still disappointed over Doctor Dreamboat?" Denise asked.

"Shut up," Cary said. "I have to do a little bit of work and then I can meet you at Coco Cabana, if you want. We can pregame with some margs and appetizers."

"Work? Ew. I thought you just answer phones and did scheduling anyways."

"Well, I do, but Brad asked me to—"

"Oh so we're calling him Brad now?"

"He asked me to keep some copies of documents safe for him, and I just thought maybe I should review them. Get familiar with them."

"Abandon all hope, ye who enter here," Denise said.

"What?" Cary wasn't sure why, but the words sent a shiver of unease through her.

"You're still trying to suck up to him. You've got it so bad, it's embarrassing."

As Cary listened to Denise continue to tease her, she saw a breaking news alert flash across the screen.

Edom Luxury Cruises Ship, the Minos, has Disappeared in the Pacific Ocean.

"Denise, I have to go," Cary said. She hung up the phone without hearing her friend's response. She grabbed the remote and turned up the volume slowly, as if it would slow down the words coming from the television speakers.

"Experts are currently saying that they believe the cruise liner fell victim to a phenomenon known as a 'rogue hole'—a theoretically possible, but never before witnessed, phenomenon where the ocean unexpectedly forms a deep dip—"

A knock at the door caused Cary to jump clean out of her seat. She then froze, torn between answering the door and processing the shock she was feeling from staring the television. The knocking came again, and in a daze, as if walking through water, Cary walked to the door and opened it without looking through the peephole.

"Hi, are you Cary?" the stranger asked.

"Yes," she said.

"May I come in? I'm an investigative analyst with Edom Technologies. I have a few questions about your work colleague, Bradford."

Cary couldn't help but notice that the man was sweating all over. His skill was dull and gray and wet. He didn't look well, nor did Cary feel so good herself, but she was in such a state of shock that she found herself nodding.

"Yes, come in," she said. "I'm sorry. I've just heard the news and I'm in a bit of a state of shock. Can I get you a glass of water?"

"I bet you are," the man said. "Yes, water would be excellent."

Beauty Shimmers Before Darkness Falls

by Renee S. DeCamillis

Amara, Gianna's best friend since preschool, went missing in May of 2017. Last place seen—boarding the same yacht Gianna and Giuseppe now prepared to board: *Solaris Rising*, owed by business tycoon David Romanov, docked in San Diego Bay at Kona Kai Marina.

Amara's dream of gracing runways in Milan and Paris, posing for covers of *Vogue* and *Vanity Fair*, led her straight into the arms of the world's elite sex trafficking ring. Gianna had warned her. Giuseppe, Amara's ex-fiancé, had also warned her. But Amara thought they were foolish, overly dramatic, maybe even jealous.

Dipping her toes into the cesspool of the modeling world had shown Gianna the dangers of the profession. A job involving her as eye candy for perverted people with no respect for women never sat right with her. She preferred deeper, more intelligent endeavors rather than modeling—the soul-sucking profession of vanity, objectification, and meaningless recognition. This realization led her to become Detective Gianna DiPaolo of the Tucson, Arizona P.D.

Amara had told Giuseppe and Gianna about all the lavish yacht parties and island getaways her "agent" (or, more accurately, her pimp) procured for her. "Lead-ins to big gigs," she had promised Amara. And Amara fell for it hook, line and...

With Giuseppe's lucrative position as a prosecuting attorney, he proved that money and clout truly *can* buy anything. Giuseppe—Joey to friends—secured his and Gianna's roles on the multi-million-dollar yacht and its guest list of politicians, corporate CEOs, Hollywood entertainers, movie and music producers, and "models." The roles he secured for them were not so much for an investigation.

No. Giuseppe and Gianna had other plans in mind.

This missing person case, Amara's case, well, let's just say—no paperwork followed their discoveries.

"Chloe? Is that her name?" From across the expanse of the second lower deck (level two of five to be exact) at the bow of this dick-waving yacht, Joey stared and tipped his wine glass in Gianna's direction, while she lounged across a cushioned bench in a string bikini and a sheer turquoise sarong. The woman with him held a thin black folder in one hand. She stood a couple inches shorter than Joey's six-foot-two bodybuilder frame. She couldn't have weighed more than 130 pounds soaking wet.

Surrounded by four other scantily clad bombshells—each of them desperate, dying to make a name for themselves—Gianna focused all her energy on blending in. A server had started passing out glasses of champagne as soon as they'd left the marina. Gianna hadn't even had time to bring her bag to her cabin before the bean-pole server practically shoved the alcohol at her. No way in hell did she dare take one sip. She saw how only a few small sips turned total strangers into BFFs. All hugging each other and professing their love—having only just met twenty minutes prior. Nope. The hug-drug didn't fit into Gianna's need to stay sharp and focused.

Glass of champagne in hand, she laughed and chatted and pretended to drink, while nonchalantly scoping out the layout of the monstrous vessel and all the party goers in attendance, some of whom she already recognized from the media, as well as from her surveillance of Amara boarding this very yacht—*Solaris Rising*.

James Burros and Clint Williams, corporate CEO and politician respectively, flanked Lakita and Jasmine on the sofa. Each billionaire caressed the model beside them, a lean leg, a rail-thin arm, while whispering in their ears.

David and "philanthropist" George Francis stood shoulder-to-shoulder leaning against the port side, sharing flirtatious glances and hushed conversation.

Ron Trudeau, real-estate tycoon, hovered near Gianna and Lola, reeking of some expensive cologne.

Then, something pulled Gianna's eyes away from the immediate surroundings. On such a large vessel, one could easily forget they're floating on the ocean rather than sitting at a luxury resort on solid ground. She turned around, shifting her body to gaze out beyond the bow and across the cobalt blue expanse of the deepest ocean in the world. White, foamy waves lapped the sides of the yacht, rippling across the massive stretch of open water. Salty ocean breezes swirled her long hair all around her sun-kissed face. With no sign of shore in sight, her heart rate revved up, muscles tensing.

Lovely—no escape.

Lola-with-legs-for-miles, one of the other four eager model guests, bounced up from the bench cushion and stood beside Gianna. Her head bobbed along with the ocean waves. "Breathtaking."

Gianna mumbled, "That's one word for..."

"Hey, look!" Lola shot her skeletal-thin arm out, crossing Gianna's line of sight, pointing to something out in the water.

Gianna noticed a line of fins cresting periodically, one after the other, like undulating waves.

"Oh my god...It's a sea dragon!" Lola yelled.

Gianna turned away, suppressing amusement.

Obnoxious laughter burst from Ron as he squeezed in between the two gazing ladies. He threw an arm around each one's waist.

"Sugar, sea dragons don't *exist*." More laughter. "I'm sure it was just a pod of dolphins."

Gianna focused intently, staring across the rippling water. More fins. At least ten. All in a line. Each taking turns cresting and submerging. Unable to see what lurked beneath did nothing to settle her racing heart. Then she felt it.

A hand squeezed her ass. She turned. Ron had one on hers and one on Lola's.

Gianna stepped away toward the starboard side. She gazed back beyond the stern, where she could still see the shore in the far distance. Her heart rate slowed as a restored a sense of safety blanketed her mind.

She sat, leaned back on a cushioned seat, and reflexively raised her champagne glass to her lips. Just as the crystal grazed her lower lip, her muscles tensed again.

Shit! Nothing about this scene is safe. She lowered the glass and rested it on her bare thigh. She looked back across the deck toward Joey and the woman accompanying him as they approached.

"Names don't matter here, Mr. Valente. Call her what you will. If she's the one you want, she's the one you shall have. Price is the same for all of them, even though she's new." Ms. Mikala Jenner, the madame of this sadistic crew, winked and caressed Joey's shoulder.

They strode arm-in-arm down the short staircase leading from the dining room to the one-of-many sunbathing decks. The sea breeze blew Ms. Mikala's sheer black dress all around her long, lean legs. Gianna internally screamed for Ms. Mikala's dress to tangle around those stick-legs, sending her plummeting to the bottom of the stairs in a bloody puddle. With her arm now around his shoulders, Ms. Mikala led Joey out onto the deck among all the menu items.

"Yeah, she's the one," Joey said. "I'm partial to strong, athletic women, and she looks like she could go quite a few rounds without losing any stamina." A hearty, chest-bouncing laugh followed from both of them.

They now stood mere feet from Gianna, close enough that she could hear their every word, despite the banal chitchat of the vanity crew surrounding her.

From an outsider's perspective, Gianna imagined, *the bikini-clad gals look like pretty little cookies in a display case, all baked golden brown and decorated with designer swimsuits and makeup rather than frosting and fancy confections.*

"Yes, I've been told she can go a few rounds in the ring as well." A come-hither sidelong gaze accompanied by a caress of Joey's heavyweight-boxer-sized bicep accompanied Ms. Mikala's next words. "But you look like you can handle her if you find she likes to play rough." Ms. Mikala passed a black folder to Joey, then looked down at Gianna and reached out her hand, each long finger tipped with a pointy claw-like red-manicured fingernail. Two large diamond rings sparkled in the fiery sunlight.

"Darling Chloe." With her singsong greeting, she grasped Gianna's accommodating hand, leaned down and kissed the back of it, leaving behind a red smear of lipstick, as she simultaneously pulled, guiding Gianna to stand up. "Mr. Valente here is quite intrigued with your portfolio." She glanced to the folder Joey held.

Gianna's old modeling portfolio had finally proved valuable, giving her a legit cover as an aspiring model. Plus, she'd always looked much younger than her age. At thirty-two, she still looked about twenty-two.

"Really?" She donned a starry-eyed, naïve smile and leaned in closer to Joey.

"True story." He winked and held his wine glass out. Gianna returned the wink, and they shared a crystal clink of their wineglasses. Faux sips followed.

"Your acting background and martial arts experience open up many possibilities for a variety of gigs beyond modeling. If your skills are as good in person as on paper," an up-down scan accompanied his words, "you could be seeing your name in lights, on billboards, at red-carpet events, as early as next year if you work with me." Taking a step closer, entering her personal bubble, he leaned down and softly asked, "Shall we find a quiet room where we can discuss the possibilities?"

She took in a deep breath, smile beaming, shoulders hiked up to her ears, and feigned giddy excitement. "Of course. I'd love to, Mr. Valente."

"It's Giuseppe, but you..." he put his arm around her shoulders and turned to guide her toward the stairs leading inside, "you can call me Joey."

"Well, nice to meet you, *Joey Valente*." They shared sidelong smiles as they climbed the stairs arm-in-arm, then strolled down the long portside deck toward the hatch and cabins.

The instant the cabin door shut behind them, Gianna scurried around the room searching for CCTV and any type of bugging devices. She and Joey faked laughter and flirtatious talk the whole time. Once assured they were alone, they sat across from one another, Joey on the mahogany canopy bed and Gianna on the burgundy velvet Chaise Lounge.

"Thanks for doublechecking my room. A second set of eyes is always wise." He flashed his award-winning smile.

"Can't be too careful with the company we now keep."

"Yeah." He chuckled, the room keys on his coiled bracelet jingling as he motioned toward his outfit: board shorts, sleeveless gray muscle shirt, and black and white Vans. "Gotta make it look like I'm ready for fun in the sun with all you ladies, right?"

Gianna let out a tense laugh as she tugged at the sheer turquoise sarong wrapped around her waist like a peekaboo window over her string bikini. "Blending in...this getup doesn't leave room for a concealed weapon."

Joey smirked. "No worries—the evening's festivities still await."

The king-sized bed coupled with Joey's outfit made him look like a muscle-head teenager rather than a professional who'd reached their thirty-fifth year around the sun. "I've been dying to get you away from the others. I took a self-guided tour around the yacht as we left the marina, and let's just say...it's been difficult to refrain from premature violence since my discovery."

"Discovery?" Gianna perked up. "Damn...I haven't been able to go *anywhere* alone, though I've *tried*. And the no cellphones rule is really fucking with me. What'd you find?"

"Yeah, well, the rule only applies to you ladies. The rule for us *buyers*—don't let the ladies see us use them." He shook his head and shrugged. "Anyway, while looking for any sort of sign about Amara—maybe some evidence of what actually happened to her, I discovered..."

"Hey, we already *have* evidence. *Remember?* I have all those pictures from the day she boarded this exact yacht before she went missing. And don't forget all the..."

"Wait. Let me finish." He leaned forward, elbows on his knees, as he continued. "We know she was *onboard*, but we don't have proof she's *dead* and not being held prisoner somewhere...where we could possibly *find*..."

"I *know* she's dead. I know in my *gut* our girl's gone. She never misses our weekly Facetime calls. *Never.* I haven't heard from her since she boarded this dick-on-the-water six weeks ago. You better not be getting cold feet on me *now*."

"I still haven't finished...while searching for some sort of office or room of operations where they might hide photos or keepsakes or some other creeper shit, I started calling Amara's phone. Over and over, I dialed her number and just let it ring until voicemail picked up. Then I heard it."

Face painted in shock, Gianna jumped to her feet. "Someone answered?"

"No, no one answered but..." Joey stood up and grasped her by the shoulders. "I heard it *ring*. While standing outside the door to the pilot house, I heard Amara's *Foxy, Foxy* ringtone." He shook his head, fuming. "Gigi, Amara's phone is still on this fucking ego-trip of a boat." Sweat beaded on his forehead and dripped down his temple.

With a furrowed brow, Gianna cocked her head. "Why would they keep her phone *and* keep it charged?"

"I don't *know*. A trophy? Maybe they collect cells rather than notches on bedposts. Shit, Gigi, I have no idea. But you know as well as I do that Amara never..."

"...went anywhere without her phone. Yeah, I know." A sorrow-filled laugh escaped Gianna. "I always joked with her that she should get that damn thing surgically attached to her palm. And you know what she always said? 'I would but she's not photogenic.'" She looked down at the oak floor and shook her head. Then, cracking her knuckles, she stood tall and looked back up at Joey. That's when she saw it.

He held out his hand, palm up and open. In the center sat Amara's cell with its hot pink metallic cover. "And I just happened to snatch it out of the pilot house when the captain left to use the bathroom." A sly crooked smile emerged. "And it holds our proof." He nodded toward the phone. "Go ahead—remove the case."

She grabbed the phone. While peeling it out of the case, she asked, "Why the hell couldn't I get a trace on this?"

"Just goes to show the extent to the billionaires' reach and power." He snarled.

Then, Gianna noticed it. She lost her breath for a moment, tears welling in her eyes.

Blood. Traces of crusted blood under the grooves of the case's edges, as well as a dried blood smear on the hidden side of the phone. "Now that *circumstantial* has no part in this..." She wiped her eyes, careful not to smear her makeup, then handed it back. "Hide it." She cracked her knuckles again as a look of determination washed away the sorrow. "Let's get this shitshow started already before I burst." Her eyes accidentally looked out one of the portholes, where she saw a long stretch of azure ocean. No more shoreline. "You're *sure* your boat-buddy knows where to meet us?"

As accustomed to undercover work as she was, her usual confidence deflated a bit. It wasn't the strictly-off-the-books-no-paper-trail job they were undertaking. Born and raised in Arizona, boating had never been her thing. Boats always made her feel claustrophobic with no escape route. And though a phenomenal swimmer, ocean travel—with no shore in sight—unsettled her immensely. Who knew what creeped under those deep, dark waters? It's like freaking outer space in those depths. Anything could be lurking nearby, and you'd never know until it's too late.

Joey must've noticed. He reached out and placed a hand on her shoulder. "No worries. Brandon's just awaiting my text to know when to come get us. He took a week off for a 'fishing trip' just to make sure he'd be available for whatever we need him for. You know..." He shrugged. "...just in case things don't go *exactly* as planned."

"Hey," she said, playfully shoving him, "don't go filling your head with self-doubt. As long as we stick to the plan and make sure none of the scum remains when we're done, we'll be fine. *Leave no trace*, remember?"

Joey held his hands out to the sides, puffed out his chest, and laughed in his charming and self-assured way. "Hey, don't forget my profession. The *leave no trace* rule is what I catch criminals fucking up all the time. I got this." He winked and did his signature crooked-mouthed tongue-clicking move, like a true hustler. "We got this. Oh, and from what info I gathered from my self-guided yacht tour as well as a little chitchat with David, there are eight crew members and seven concierge staff aboard. And in his own words, 'They're a trusted crew who've been working for him for many, many years.'"

Gianna smiled and nodded as she grabbed their glasses off the nightstand and dumped the alcohol down the bathroom sink. Then, they made faux sex-capades noises: bounced on the bed, rattled the headboard and the bureau around, ran the shower.

During all their blending-in theatrics, they checked out the furniture and décor to see what felt heavy enough—but small enough for relocation: sinkables. With fifteen people onboard working, four other "buyers," as well as Ms. Mikala and David, that meant they had twenty-one scum to eliminate. With dinner and dancing planned for that evening, the guests would be the easiest. The crew, on the other hand, took some strategic planning.

With his hair all wet and slicked back, Joey left his cabin wearing just his board-shorts.

The very bottom level of the yacht housed the cabins for the crew members as well as the engine room, storage closets, and some large storage rooms for small motorboats and whatnot. Joey wandered around feigning interest in everything involved with owning a yacht, convincing a couple crew members that he was in the market to buy a yacht of his own.

Gianna may have had acting experience, but attorneys—that's a profession full of Oscar-worthy individuals. The only boat Joey had ever been on was his buddy Brandon's boat tour ferry.

Two young male crew members led Joey down the long hallway that housed their sleeping quarters.

"Yeah, I've heard these bad boys have some *serious* engine power."

The heavier-set guy laughed. "Well, with its 450-foot length and five levels, there ain't no other way to haul a vessel like this."

"I imagine it must take a large crew to operate such a big vessel. Or are you two so damn good it only takes two?" Joey flashed that charming smile of his. You know, stroking egos and flashing pearly whites—the manipulator's way.

"Tell that to Mr. Romanov," crew member two chimed in. "Maybe he'll give us our long overdue raise."

"Long overdue?"

Number two flipped his college hair out of his eyes, looked over his shoulder and up at Joey. "It's been three years."

"Damn. Maybe when I get my own yacht, I'll hire you two and give you a 10% raise right off the rip." Joey laughed, knowing damn well he had these two right in his pocket.

"Thanks, man," college boy said.

"Yeah, dude, thanks." The stalky crew member held out his hand, palm up. Joey slapped him five.

"But, no, seriously, normally it takes a crew of about 20 to 25. But on *certain* trips with *certain* guests, Mr. Romanov insists on only having fifteen, including the concierge. Always the same small team, since we're the best, Mr. Romanov always says. Even so, we're not allowed upstairs unless him or Captain Dmitri requests us or if there's an emergency. And when they come down to jump in the ocean, usually skinny-dipping, or to take out a small boat, we're ordered to stay out of sight."

"Doesn't mean we don't sneak peaks at all those rich hotties running around half naked or bare-assed. And all their *shenanigans*..." College boy cleared his throat and nudged his co-worker with his elbow. They shared a sidelong look. Then, they both laughed like they had some inside joke.

Joey laughed along, while imagining stabbing each guy in the face repeatedly. But he contained his rage—for now. Lawyers—so much hidden beneath their depths.

They headed to the engine room to show Joey the superyacht's powerful motor. Once inside, Joey started pointing at everything he could think of, asking a ton of questions. That's when two older gentlemen stepped out from behind some large pipes, carrying their dinner plates covered in half-eaten enchiladas and rice. Joey's joking and ego-stroking got them all excited. They eagerly started showing him all the hard work it takes to keep such a vessel in tiptop shape, especially with such a condensed crew.

While the two mechanics chatted and pointed and showed off their knowledge to David Romanov's wealthy guest, the two younger crew members stepped out and waited for Joey outside the closed engine room door. As soon as the door clicked shut, the shorter dark-haired mechanic sidled up beside Joey. The guy had to look up to speak to him.

"So...which spicy enchilada you hooking up with, tipo?

"Only the spiciest for this dude, amigo." It took all Joey's resolve to keep from smashing the guy's face in after that question, but he let out his chest-bouncing laugh instead.

The redheaded mechanic smiled a laughing-grin. Then, he crouched down to point something out to Joey while his partner stood right behind him. Joey towered over the two men from behind. As nonchalant as fixing a friend's wrinkled collar, Joey reached out his massive mitts, grabbed the enchilada perv by both sides of the head and snapped his neck. The man crumpled to the floor like a bag of oranges. Just as the crouching man turned and gasped, Joey grabbed him by the head and snapped his neck too.

Joey dragged their bodies to a back corner of the room, where he hid them behind some large piping. When he opened the engine room door, two more crew members stood chatting with the others. Joey towered over each one of them as well. Though the two new arrivals had athletic builds, they were nothing compared to Joey's bodybuilder stature. While standing with the door still open behind him, he introduced himself, never taking note of their names. They shared some frivolous banter as they continued the yacht tour. Then, Joey praised them for something he still to this day can't remember, before he snapped each one of their necks. Unfortunately, the last two he took out needed an elbow in the face first to shut them up before they attracted any attention. But their necks snapped "like butta" as Joey liked to tell it in his perfected mob boss impersonation.

Joey dragged the four bodies inside the engine room and hid them with the first two. He cursed under his breath about needing to clean up the blood from elbowing the two guys in the face. Good thing he went shirtless. Using one of the mechanic's bandana-rags from his back pocket, Joey cleaned the blood off himself quickly, eager to move on to the rest of the crew.

Six down. Only fifteen to go.

At the dinner party that evening, Gianna headed straight for the bar first. The panoramic ocean view around the large dining room immediately sent her mind reeling. No shore in sight kept reminding her of *no escape.* Even with the vibrant sunset on its way, she refused to gaze. The blazing beauty shimmers just before darkness falls.

Leaning on the marble top bar, she ordered a sparkling water—in the bottle—and trained her eyes on the mahogany class-front cabinets while she awaited Joey's arrival. Numerous marble statues of mythic deities and demons stared back. They harmonized with the abundant tall marble statues she'd noticed in many other rooms she'd passed on her way there, as well as a few on the other side of the dining room.

Just as the pristinely primped bartender served her drink, Clint Williams slithered up, invading her personal bubble. The strong scent of cologne made her cough. She flashed him a smile, but quickly returned her gaze to all the heavy marble statues, imagining using one to crack his skull.

"Well, I already see what I want for dessert," he breathed into her ear as he slid his hand down the front of her dress and cupped her breast.

Before she had a chance to respond, Joey swooped in on her opposite side. He slid his arm around her waist, pulling her close to his side. Clint's hand got yanked out of her dress with the movement.

Perfect timing. It took all Gianna's self-control *not* to pull out her hidden piece and blow his brains out right then.

"Hey, hey there my pretty lady. I was wondering if you'd show up before me."

"Couldn't wait. I'm *starving*."

Clint leaned in again. His hand rested on Gianna's hip, then quickly shifted to Joey's ass. "I'm so hungry I want *two* desserts tonight. What do you two say? My cabin after dinner?"

A low rumble of laughter rolled out of Joey as he pivoted and removed Clint's hand. "No offense, but I don't roll that way. I've only got my eye on this feisty lady right here."

"No offense taken. Sorry for the intrusion." Clint raised his hands up in surrender.

"Hey, sometimes you don't know if you don't ask. No worries." Joey leaned on the bar, turned to the bartender, and ordered a ginger ale—in the bottle.

Just before Clint walked off toward the large rectangular dining table behind them, he leaned down close to Gianna's ear again. "When he runs out of stamina later, come by my room. Cabin ten." He slapped her ass as he walked away.

Cringing, Gianna gritted her teeth, took a deep breath, and smiled through her boiling rage.

Just then, David Romanov sauntered out of the swinging kitchen doors off to the right behind the bar. His khaki pants and coral button-up shirt appeared neatly pressed with pleats. "Dinner's about to be served. Let's all get seated. Shall we?"

As he walked around the edge of the bar nearest Gianna, he stopped and jutted out his elbow. Gianna glanced up at Joey. He nodded. Smiling, she linked arms with David and walked with him to the dinner table. Joey followed close behind.

As she waited for David to pull the high-backed mahogany chair out for her, she noticed one of the four other models hadn't arrived yet. The observation piqued her curiosity. All the other guests were accounted for.

A petite waitress with long, silky black hair delivered appetizers and salads, placing them in the center of the long table for all to share.

Clint sat on the opposite side of Gianna from Joey. She'd played her part well, since he appeared to have no idea how badly she wanted to slice his throat with her steak knife.

Liquor flowed and silverware clinked as everyone laughed and chatted. Gianna could tell that intoxicants other than alcohol had hit a high, so to speak. Jasmine and Lakita kept tongue-tangling with one another, though they'd just met during boarding earlier that day. James Burros and Ron Trudeau flanked Lola, one with his hand down the front of her dress and the other whispering into her ear with his arm around her shoulders. David and Mikala watched over their guests, smiling and laughing, while they ate and talked with George Francis. David and George kept leaning close, whispering to one another.

"I thought you were starving?" Clint nodded toward Gianna's empty plate.

"Just saving room for the main course. You know, gotta watch my figure."

His eyes steamrolled her body. "I'll watch *that* for you, sweetie."

She leaned forward and spoke to David down at the head of the table. "I notice Naomi isn't here yet. Should we wait for her?"

David and Mikala shared a look she couldn't read. "She'll be along soon. She wanted to take a nap before the evening festivities. Said not to wait for her."

Joey refrained from eating as well. The energy of his eagerness for *different* festivities was palpable.

Fifteen minutes later, the bar tender and the chef burst through the swinging doors of the kitchen with a very long, covered platter.

David pushed his chair back, stood, and clapped his hands together. "Attention, everyone."

Mikala clinked her butterknife against the side of her crystal goblet, shushing the guests. The efficient waitress removed the appetizer dishes, making room for the main dish.

"The main course," David began as the bartender and chef stood beside the table with the large, covered platter, "is now served." They hefted the dish over the heads of the guests across from Joey and Gianna and placed it in the center of the table. It appeared quite heavy by the look of their straining facial expressions. "I hope you all enjoy the *fruits*." David smiled, glanced down at Mikala and George, and reseated himself.

A murmur rose among all the guests as their wide-eyed, eager expressions glommed onto the dish in the center of the table. They weren't the only ones curious about the gourmet delicacy awaiting them.

Joey nudged Gianna with his elbow. He rubbed his eight-pack stomach when she looked over at him. "Gotta fuel up for the night ahead." They both smirked and looked back to the center of the table just as the bartender and chef readied themselves to lift off the lid.

Both chef and bartender looked to David. With a small, smug smile he nodded at them. Then, they lifted the lid.

Joey and Gianna immediately sat up at full attention, staring and silent.

Gasps sounded out from all around. Lola let out a quick, high-pitched yelp.

Spread out in front of them, adorned with orchids and lilies and a rainbow assortment of fresh fruit, lay Naomi. Naked. Unconscious.

Feigning excited amazement, Gianna reached out and gently grasped her hand. "She's *such* a beauty," she gushed as she secretly felt for a pulse. Slight ticking pulsed under her thumb. "Feel how supple her skin is." She held up Naomi's hand for Joey to check, before he prematurely lost his shit. Adrenalin surged through Gianna.

"*So* soft," Joey replied as he gently placed her hand back on the dish beside her bare thigh.

Out of her peripheral Gianna detected questionable movement. Her hand reflexively slid under the table to her inner thigh, reaching into the slit of her long evening gown. She unsnapped the holster, ready.

To her right, near the end of the table, Lola sat shaking her head in a *no, no, no* gesture, eyes wide.

Just as Gianna turned in her direction, Ron grabbed a hold of the back of Lola's neck and shoved her head forward, forcing her face into Naomi's breasts. "Don't be shy. I *know* you want a taste of that. You were ogling her perky tits all afternoon."

Joey and Gianna shared a look.

Then a nod.

In a flash, Joey jumped to his feet and lunged at Ron, as Gianna pulled a gun from her thigh holster and another from inside her knee-high boot.

"Nobody move!" Gianna shouted as she stood, knocking over her chair in the process, aiming a gun toward each end of the table.

Joey grabbed the back of Ron's head and smashed his face against the table. "How's it fucking feel, tough guy?"

Ron's blonde toupee flipped off his head and landed on Naomi's unflinching face.

"What the fu..." Ron growled just before Joey snapped his neck and tossed him to the floor.

Lola screamed, slid out of her chair, and hid under the table, leaving James wide open for Joey.

"Which one of you sleezy motherfuckers is next, huh?" Joey bellowed, spittle spraying out from between his lips. Looking down the table at every face staring in dumbstruck fear, a rumbling baritone laugh erupted from Joey. "Well, looks like the cat's love for tongues makes it my choice."

He elbowed James in the face. James instantly covered his blood-gushing nose. "What the hell is goi..."

Another neck snapping shut the mouth of another rapist. Joey left that one face down on the table.

Mikala shot a suspicious look at David, and then he reached under the table.

"Hands on the table. *Now!*" Gianna stepped back cautiously and stalked toward the head of the table. "Let me see them, *all* of you!"

She stepped up behind David and Mikala and held one gun aimed at them, and the second aimed down the table at the rest of the guests. Everyone slowly rested their hands on the tabletop.

Gianna looked toward the ladies—the *models*. "Jasmine, Lakita...Lola, it's safe to come out from under the table. We're not going to hurt any of *you*. Just move away from the table and go sit by the front window please. And don't even *think* about leaving this room. I don't want to have to hurt any of you."

Jasmine and Lakita immediately scurried to the far end of the room. With a bit of hesitation, Lola eased herself out from under the table—on the opposite side from where Joey dropped the bodies. Streaks of black ran down her cheeks from her frantic sobbing. She passed a sheepish look to Gianna and then Joey, before bolting away from the table and joining the other two ladies by the front window. She ran barefoot, having kicked off her heels under the table.

Just then, Clint—who must've been cocaine-loaded, considering the stupidity of his bravery—jumped to his feet, steak knife in hand, and dove at Joey. With a sidestep-duck, Joey avoided the downswing of the blade. In a crouch beside the table, he pivoted just as Clint jumped him. The serrated blade grazed Joey's shoulder. He grunted and gritted his teeth. Clint dropped the knife and jumped back.

Stupid motherfucker.

"Hey, you ripped my favorite shirt, fuckface!" Joey yelled as he grabbed Lola's stiletto shoe off the floor. Then, he jumped up and buried the heel in Clint's left eye.

Clint released a guttural scream—cut short when Joey snapped his neck and threw him to the floor.

Gianna aimed one of her Ruger .38 Specials at George's right temple. "There's no forgiveness for what you do. Go to hell, hypocrite." She pulled the trigger. Blood sprayed up Gianna's hand, spattered his gray hair crimson, and George dropped off the side of his chair.

Mikala screamed.

"What is this all about?! Who the hell *are* you two?!" Blood spatter shown vibrant on the shoulder of David's coral Armani dress shirt.

Both Rugers were now aimed at the back of David's and Mikala's heads.

Gianna leaned down between her two targets and spoke softly into each of their ears. "We *know* your not-so-secret secret. We *know* you killed our dear friend Amara. We *know* you've killed more and abused *even more*. Who are *we*, you ask?" Sardonic laughter escaped her. "We're your executioners, you evil motherfuckers!"

Two skull-ripping gunshots rang out, one after the other as she shot them each in the temple. Gianna shot Mikala first—just to see the look of shock and disgust on David's blood-drenched face right before she snuffed out his life.

As soon as David's body fell across George's chair, Joey yelled, "Behind you!"

Before Gianna had a chance to turn, she lost her breath and doubled over from a solid kick in the ribs. One of her revolvers slipped from her grasp and slid across the table.

As Joey dashed down the length of the table, Gianna kicked up her heel and caught the bartender in the groin. He bent forward. Then, she spun around, kneed him in the face, and took him to the ground. Stradling him on the floor with a knee holding down each arm, she aimed her second revolver in his face. "And you, you sick fuck, you delivered Naomi all drugged out of it on a *fucking platter*. You are the scum of the Ear..."

Joey's hand landed gently on Gianna's shoulder. "How about we make less of a mess than a face shot?"

Gianna nodded.

Joey moved from the bartender's feet to his head. Gianna shimmied back, still sitting on the bartender's legs to keep him from kicking.

Crouching down, Joey grabbed both sides of the young man's head and quickly twisted, snapping his neck like the others.

As soon as the body went limp, Gianna jumped up and grabbed her revolver off the table. It had slid halfway down, resting beside Naomi's naked hip. When she grabbed the Ruger, Gianna's fingers grazed Naomi's golden-brown skin. Gianna immediately froze.

"Joey?" She reached for Naomi's limp hand, felt for a pulse.

Now at the other end of the room, consoling the three frightened ladies, Joey turned toward Gianna. "Yeah? Need some help, Chloe?"

She placed Naomi's professionally manicured hand gently onto her flower-adorned abdomen and looked at Joey and the models. "Naomi's dead."

Disgusted, Joey shook his head. "Leave her. They'll find her when the abandoned yacht gets found. It'll be better that way."

Gianna nodded.

"Wha...?! She's dead? How...Wha...What the *hell* is going on?!" Lola cried out, sobbing and out of breath. Lakita and Jasmine huddled close to her, also crying.

Leave it to Joey and his lawyer-speak—he explained everything and helped calm them down, while Gianna headed to the kitchen.

On the other side of the food prep counter, in a cabinet underneath, she found the old silver-haired chef and the petite server hiding. They each held out a kitchen knife when she flung open the double doors.

"So, you two like serving up dead runway models for dinner, huh?"

Bang!

Bang!

Two face shots, each right through the eye. Both bodies tumbled out of the cabinet as both meat cleavers clattered to the floor.

Five bullets down. Five to go.

Shuffling sounds leaked out of a pantry in the back of the kitchen. Gianna slowly made her way to the closed door. When she eased it open and peered inside, she noticed a middle-aged food prep worker cowering behind a stack of fruit crates. On the floor beside his black nonskid shoes, he had dropped a handful of orchid blossoms.

Resisting the urge to berate him as she had the others, she simply stepped up to him as he cowered and whimpered and tried to turn away, and she put a bullet straight through his temple. He crumpled in the back corner of the pantry as blood spatter ran down the white wall.

Six bullets down. Four to go.

The last purple and pink sunset streaks across the sky had disappeared. The full moon shined down on *Rising Solaris*. Starlight peppered the night sky's canvas. Illumination from the yacht's blue running lights around the hull shimmered on the rippling waves of the ocean.

Out on the lower deck, the ten dead bodies from dinner lay in a pile on the starboard side close to the bow. Beside the pile of death sat a collection of marble statues Joey had lugged from various entertainment rooms throughout the yacht. Many long pieces of heavy-duty rope lay coiled like serpents around the art collection.

Lola sat curled up in the fetal position on a cushioned loveseat, sobbing. She kept rocking and repeatedly mumbling, "I can't believe Naomi's dead. I can't believe what they were going to do to us."

Gianna heard those words. Her stomach knotted, remembering Amara.

Just then, thudding footfalls quickly descended the steps leading from the second level deck near the dining room.

Gianna spun around, gun aimed.

"Whoa..." Hands up, palms out, Joey halted. "It's only me. Crew's all taken care of." He wiped his hands together as though brushing unwanted filth from his palms.

"What about the captain and the first mate?"

"Done deal. Even the three remaining Concierge. Gone. *And* disposed of."

"What? All on your own?"

"No problem. I just hauled each one like a sack of potatoes over my shoulder. Plus, the stern was closer, and lower—easier for dumping. But I will confess..." He shook his head and wiped sweat off his brow. "I wasted a hell of a lot of time lugging those statues and tying 'em up."

"What do you mean? What happened?"

"I don't know what, but a shark or a whale or something chomped 'em all to shit. The ocean now runs red at the stern."

"Holy shit! Really? Fucking sweet! At least we know *those* bodies will never be found."

Lakita laughed, her wavy black hair blowing across her flawless face in the ocean breeze. "Never thought I'd be an accomplice to murder when I packed for this ocean voyage. And here I thought I'd be signing a modeling contract by the end of this trip, not trying to find an alibi when the cops come knocking."

Donning a courtroom-serious expression, Joey stepped up beside Lakita. "You were never here. *None* of us were. Remember that. Stick to it. Smash your cell phone. Get new service. We'll clean up. No problem."

He walked over to the statues and rope, where Gianna was already tying a body to one. "I texted Brandon. He's on his way."

A sigh of relief blew from between Gianna's tense lips.

Lakita and Jasmine watched as every dead body, followed by a marble statue, went overboard. Peering over the edge of the gunwale, each time a body sunk they both let out a cheerful, "Woo-hoo!" It sounded like the party was just starting. Until the nineth body—Ms. Mikala's—hit the water.

"What the fuck was that?" Jasmine yelled, terror painting her face.

"Holy shit! I don't know." Lakita jumped back from the edge, hands shaking.

"What? Did another shark come and clean up our mess?" Joey grunted as he lugged David Romanov's body to the gunwale and glanced over the edge. Blood dripped from the gunshot wound in David's head.

"Does a shark have five fins and a long spikey tail?" Deadpan, Lakita stared Joey square in the eyes as he looked at her with confusion.

He shrugged his shoulders and glanced back over the edge. "Maybe it brought some friends for dinner?" A chuckle accompanied his weak words as he hurled David's body overboard. The rope whizzed past him, halting when it stretched taught between statue and body. David's corpse dangled from the bow, slightly swaying in the ocean breeze, dripping blood while awaiting its submergence.

Just before Joey turned around to heave the statue overboard to sink the body, an enormous serpent—with a mouth wider than a blue whale's and rows of teeth longer than any known sea creature—jumped up out of the water and snatched the body out of the air.

A torrent of salty sea water surged up, drenching Joey. He fell to the side, jumping out of the way of the marble statue as it whizzed past him and Jasmine. It crashed into the side of the boat, then flipped up over the edge as though merely a cat toy.

Gianna gasped. "What the..."

Another huge gush of water shot up onto the deck as the creature splashed back down into the ocean.

For the first time since boarding, Gianna felt the yacht rock.

Jasmine fell to her knees on the deck, screaming and crying.

Lola, still curled in the fetal position on the loveseat, sobbed louder as she covered her head.

Lakita, spewing obscenities as she fled, had already reached the top of the stairs, running toward the doors to the dining room.

At the base of the stairs with one foot on the first step, Gianna looked across the deck in shock. "What the fuck are you three waiting for? Let's get the hell inside before it resurfaces. Let's *go. Now!*"

All hiding out in the pilot house with Joey at the helm and their luggage stacked and ready by the door, they eagerly awaited Brandon's arrival.

Joey's eyes never turned away from the ocean ahead.

Gianna stepped up beside him. "You got this alright?"

He shrugged. "Just like driving a car."

"Any sign of his light yet?"

"Nothing." He didn't turn to look at her.

Brandon's last text chimed-in an hour ago. *Only an hour away.*

She stared ahead with him, searching for any sign of Brandon's spotlight.

The yacht moved through the water at a starfish's pace. Waves rippled all around under the hull's line of blue lights.

A trail of fins followed along the starboard side about thirty feet away. Joey insisted the fins belonged to a dolphin pod protecting them. Gianna couldn't imagine dolphins surviving with that giant *other thing* lurking.

"What if it comes back?" Lakita asked.

"How are we supposed to get on the other boat?" Jasmine said.

"What if it never left?" Lola chimed in.

All five survivors exchanged worried looks. No one had an answer.

Summoner

by Franklin Ard

I haven't seen the crustacean yet, but I have faith it will appear. The seagulls make aching sounds, and my stomach tenses. The bay water glistens with the colored lights of The Crimson Claw, a restaurant that serves greasy seafood with gimmicky names. Beside it is a hotel with a giant crab on the roof. The crab's claw repeatedly snaps a plaster man in two. This stretch of beach doesn't have any expensive places, no twenty-story condominiums. The crustacean keeps the high-dollar tourists away and draws only weirdos, monster hunters, cryptozoologists, X-Files fanatics. These people have been visiting this beach for ten years, waiting for the creature to reemerge.

Many people don't believe in the crustacean, but it isn't a myth. Ten years ago, the thing took my boyfriend. I was pregnant then, and I thought I'd reached the very bottom. Until now. I feel dizzy thinking about all the ways things could have gone differently. If I hadn't taken my daughter swimming, if I'd gotten in the pool with her, if I'd paid more attention. I'm nauseated and shaking and I can't hold it together. The monster enthusiasts swivel their video cameras on tripods, record me screaming for the creature. A man with a shy voice cautions me not to step in the water. I don't listen.

I'm not frightened. Not anymore.

Yesterday, I took Jewel to swim. The Renaissance Hotel where I work has a nice indoor pool, and my boss lets employees use it on our off days. We just can't wear our uniforms or name tags. Jewel begged me all week, giving me those sad looks with her blue eyes, and I gave in. We had breakfast at Waffle House before heading downtown, then we took the interstate and rolled the windows down. Her hair needed cutting, and it blew wild. She made faces into the wind. Looking at Jewel right then, I thought she resembled Clyde, her father. I remembered his way of apologizing. He would get down on one knee, hold my hand as if he was going to propose, and then he'd say that he never meant to hurt me. I still hated myself for believing him.

The hotel pool was crowded, and my instinct was to turn around and leave. I feel that way when I walk into a crowded room. But I knew it would disappoint Jewel, so I let her jump in while I waited for a chair to open up. Hotel guests drank and laughed and whistled at each other. Leaning against the wall, I tried and failed to read a James Patterson novel while Jewel paddled around. I glanced at her over the top of the pages, making sure the bigger kids didn't get too rowdy. It's frustrating that I still can't remember how many times Jewel came out of the water to rest. Twice? The doctors and nurses wanted to know. Did she inhale any water? I told them I didn't think so. They acted like they didn't believe me.

Before having Jewel, Clyde and I lived in a rental house in Mobile, Alabama. It was off Dauphin Island Parkway, which was not nearly as glamorous as it sounds. The windows were busted out and covered in dry-rotted plastic. Mosquitoes got in at night. I had bites up and down my legs, so I never wore shorts. The entire time I was with Clyde, I had this sense in my gut that I was in the wrong place and time, that I'd found myself in a parallel universe in which everything was messed up. I'd met Clyde in high school, when I was trying to get away from my mom. He was older than me by three years, was good at cooking but not at cooking food. He said his name with this thick Southern drawl, like he was saying *collide*.

At the time of my pregnancy, I had pretty blond hair that I didn't brush often. I wore loose-fit jeans with triangles cut out of the ankles and this one R.E.M. t-shirt that I washed every few days. I worked for this place that paid me to make fishing lures from home. They provided all the materials. I spent whole days winding green wire around mass-produced lure bodies. Then I'd glue the tiny fins in place. I got twenty-five dollars for each box that contained five hundred lures, so I made about five cents per lure. Clyde and I used some of the money to buy bourbon in plastic bottles. We drank until we couldn't stand the sight of each other.

Jewel fell asleep on the way home from swimming. She looked cold, still in her bathing suit, a hotel towel wrapped around her like a robe. I drove slowly because I don't see well at night. The other cars streamed by, some of them honking at me. The road crawled along, and the air carried a brine scent. Seagulls clustered on the bridge's halogen lights. I stared at Mobile's two tallest buildings, the Renaissance Hotel and the RSA Tower, both lit up in Mardi Gras colors. I couldn't believe another year had passed already, and here I was still thinking about Clyde. My stomach dropped with a familiar fear. I sensed him lurking in the backseat, even though I knew he was dead. I remembered the look in his eye when I told him I was pregnant. The look told me that he'd decided to drown me with his bare hands.

For weeks, I'd debated telling Clyde. I had this hope that something would change inside of him when I revealed being pregnant, that it would command his attention, cause him to become a different person. Jewel was an accident, but sometimes accidents can change the entire direction of a person's life. Any direction would be better than the one we were headed in. At the time, I hadn't decided on a name for Jewel. I had this belief that once the child had a name, it would become real, and I wasn't sure either of us were ready.

I decided to test the waters. "Friday I'm in Love" played on the radio as I drove to the animal shelter. I found this wiener dog puppy that was going to be put down. The puppy's ears were too big for its body. It had black fur with brown paws and was underfed, rib bones showing. I named the puppy Charles, because it kind of reminded me of Prince Charles, distinguished yet gangly. I carried it around all day while Clyde was out roofing a house. He'd gone to work with one of his buddies, but it wouldn't last long. None of his jobs did. It was the heat of summer, but the puppy was shaking, so I wrapped it in a one of my old shirts. It drank a gallon of water.

Clyde finally came home, and I hugged him like we'd just met. When he saw the Charles yawning on the couch, Clyde dropped his lunchbox, snatched the pup by the neck fur, held it like it had a disease. Clyde said that he couldn't afford another freeloader. Then he strangled the puppy.

I haven't eaten since yesterday. The cafeteria food at the hospital was rubbery and I only picked at it, thinking about what the doctor said. I didn't know that a person could drown on dry land, hours after swimming. He referred to it as a rare phenomenon. I should have realized something was wrong when I'd carried Jewel from the car to her bedroom. She had dark rings under her eyes, and her words slurred when she asked if we were home. The house was quiet, and she was curled up in my arms, like a doll with glassy eyes. I laid her down on the bed, and she blinked, said goodnight, fell back asleep. I pulled the covers over her, then went to the kitchen, poured a glass of wine, and another. And another. I drank most of the bottle of Cabernet, lay awake on the couch, the TV glaring at me. I watched the door, thinking I heard someone on the porch, that Clyde would kick it open. I didn't sleep much, and I woke up late with a hangover. I found Jewel still face-up, her hair matted against her cheek. White foam leaked from her mouth. I remember calling 911, almost dropping the phone. One EMT pumped Jewel's chest with clasped hands while the other patted her face. Her skin was a light purple color, like lavender.

I hadn't meant to tell Clyde about being pregnant. I was still frightened after what had happened a few weeks before. He'd given me a concussion because of the puppy. The nurses at the emergency room had whispered to each other about him. He kept sniffing, couldn't keep his hands in one place. One of the nurses made some notes about it.

When I let it slip, we were on the beach by Mobile Bay, and he'd taken hold of my neck. He was going to throw me down on the sand, maybe kick me. He worked himself into these paranoid, manic episodes after using. My toes dug into the sand. The words just blurted out of my mouth: "We're going to have a baby."

Clyde pulled me into the surf and I screamed, kicked my feet. The water was lukewarm, the air stifling with the smell of dead fish. There had been a jubilee a few days ago, and fish carcasses lined the shore, some of them pulled apart by crabs. I cried for help. Please, someone. I said a lot of things that came out like some kind of incantation, a jumbled mantra, a plea to the universe to set things back on the correct axis. Clyde pushed my head under, and I opened my eyes.

Through the murky water, I saw something rise. Clyde let me go, and as I got my head above water, he was cursing, sloshing backward. Some people had gathered on the shore, and one of them held up a Polaroid camera, the kind that spits the picture out on the spot. I coughed, took heaving breaths as Clyde splashed, fell down, trying to run.

A giant crustacean lifted above the surface, its major claw at least three stories high, the carapace outlined by the setting sun, purple and blue and white. The creature was the size of a dump truck. Its mouth hinged open and shut like a mythical grasshopper's, and I felt that it was trying to communicate with me. I trembled as I vocalized the words in my head—a request.

Take him under.

Exhausted, I wipe water from my eyes. Monster hunters have lined up along the shore, many more than when I first arrived. Amateur photographers take hundreds of pictures, while onlookers point and shout in my direction. The people wait, soundless, as if they know the power that I wield. But how could they?

It doesn't matter. I ignore them and say the words, a domino of utterances, the psalm or mantra that worked ten years ago.

The dark outline of the crustacean rises up and overshadows me. Its claws clap shut, sounding like a wine bottle hitting a wood floor. I hear music playing at the restaurant, a vocalist singing falsetto, something that I know but can't recall. Customers climb the deck rail for a better view.

My toes just touch the slimy bottom. I've waded farther out than last time. I'm not afraid of anything now. The creature watches me with elongated, alien eyes. Its spiny mouth-parts collapse, extend, collapse again. Its shell has jagged grooves, crisscrossing battle scars. For a long time, the crustacean has been deep beneath the surface. I have summoned it from a place where night lasts forever.

Till Human Voices Wake Us

by Rachel Halpern

I was one of four who made it back to land, crawled up spitting brine onto the gritty shore. I'd forgotten the sheer unclean foulness of sand on my skin with nothing to wash it away, the way saltwater tasted to my human mouth, the slowly building stickiness of drying hair. Someone had called the police, out of concern or out of fear; I thought the latter, perhaps, more likely, here on a beach where mermaids sang, and the police carried earplugs with their nightsticks.

The police kept tugging at something in our hands, and I looked down to see a long string of pearls spilling through my fingers. I remembered thin cold hands, not human, pressing the pearls on us. Then even that memory faded, lost in dark confusion. When the officer finally got them free, the pearls collapsed, wet sand crumbling in his fist. He made a noise of disgust and stripped his sand-packed glove into an evidence bag. I doubted he would find anything there but sand, in the end.

They wrapped me in a blanket, eventually. It seemed like a long time later that they took us to the hospital. Doctors pricked our fingers for blood, poked and prodded, but the room was full of cops with wary eyes. The others were still unconscious, another man and two women, and I imagined I must look the same as they did, damp-skinned with seaweed still tangled in their hair, eyes heavy-shadowed under fallen lids.

As we awoke, the police asked us, *What do you remember?* and the memories slipped away as they asked, like the last traces of a dream. They left behind only faint, distorted impressions: fear, hunger, loss. The memory of pushing slowly, blindly through dark waters, the merfolk around us effortless and graceful among the shadows. They had traded us among themselves, for pearls and stones and shark teeth, and hurt us sometimes for their own amusement. Even as I tried to grasp the memories, they melted away, leaving only traces of beauty and terror.

When the doctors released us they took us back to the station. We waited in stiff, uncomfortable chairs as they searched databases for us, missing persons files going back for years. When they found us, they looked between our faces and the photographs with slowly dawning horror.

"Computer says that's you," the nearest officer told me, her voice sick. I only half-recognized the man who stared back at me from the screen, his skin the brown of wet sand, his face unfamiliar, strangely alive even as he smiled the awkward smile of the DMV.

The others were looking at their screens, I thought, with much the same weary blankness I felt, as though they had shown us a picture of a long-dead pet and expected us to run calling its name. Names, I thought, yes, and tried to read the words on the screen. The letters seemed to shift and twist, and it took long moments before I could resolve them into words. *Geoffrey*—I could make out that much, though the last name was only a distantly familiar set of scribbles. The line for age I couldn't even find.

"Geoffrey," the officer said, and I tore my eyes away from the screen, thinking that she must have read my mind until I realized she meant me, was calling me by a name I was supposed to recognize. "It says you've been missing three years, the others more or less."

Three years made as much sense as anything, I supposed, and I tried to blink acknowledgement so I wouldn't have to find the words to speak. My throat felt choked by dry air and the look of pity and horror on her face.

"What I don't get," said another officer, leaning on the desk across the aisle and staring at me with cold eyes – not as cold as the merfolk's, but cold enough, and wary. "What makes you so special? The sea takes a person or two every year; it doesn't give them back."

I tried to smile at him, but it was hard to remember the sequence of muscles, and I wasn't sure what my face looked like. No one smiled back.

"They grow tired easily," I said, and this time the words came out properly, like I had a voice again, though the sound to my ears was uncomfortably solid, so rough it hurt. "They must have gotten bored."

Hotel beds were a mystery, unyielding, unlike the constant shifting of water. The hospital at least had been brutally clean, but they sent us away after our examination, as if we might be a threat to the other patients. The hotel smelled of cigarette smoke and dust, the opposite of water, and I breathed it in and tried not to miss the sea.

They'd put us all in one room, for the first night, which was wise and foolish of them. We were lost and waterlogged. We hated the sea but we understood it. In the sea we could be sure of our humanity, if nothing else, but here we felt as much like merfolk as humans. We had dreamed in the depths of coming home, but now it seemed we had no home, and in the night our despair fed each other's.

We all knew who would be the first to try. He didn't even get the sheets around his neck before we came and carried him to the bath. He went still in the water, rigid and afraid. He relaxed slowly as we washed his hair and spoke to him, human voices with the cadence of the ocean, and eventually, he sank back into sleep.

We dried him, returned to our beds, and waited for the second of us to fall. I barely remember my time in the tub; that night, we all did our parts, and we all feared.

When morning came they found us huddled in our beds, dreaming, and one of us woke screaming at the sound of human voices and the sight of ordinary daylight. I don't think it was me.

The officer who had brought us to the hotel watched in grim silence as we crawled from our beds and took our turns in the bathroom. None of us, I knew, looked at the tub as we dressed.

She didn't say, "Are you ready?" until we were, and then just led us away. I was wearily grateful for that, that she ignored how lost we were but still gave us someone to follow.

There was talk at the station about returning us to our families, about whether they should keep us to identify danger in the water, and we shuffled our feet and tried not to look as if all the things they described were beyond our comprehension.

Our officer said the name she had told me was mine, and after a moment I recognized it and looked up from my contemplation of feet and carpets and all the things that had not been real only a day ago. She said my name again, *Geoffrey*, and I made eye contact and half-nodded.

"Can you live on your own, do you think?" she asked, a little slowly, like she might have asked it before. I shrugged uncomfortably and glanced around at my fellows, who avoided the officers' eyes with the same unease I felt.

"Can they at least go back to their families?" an officer toward the back asked, and I shrugged again, miserably, into the silence.

"They could work at the aquarium," another man suggested, and the rest snickered.

A desk phone rang sharply into the fading laughter, and we flinched as one. Our officer, who had brought us from the hotel, reached out to lift the nearest headset. I had trouble understanding – hard enough to follow any conversation, let alone one with only one side.

Mermaids at least were easy to understand, singing truth at each other through the water.

She put the phone to her shoulder, perhaps to muffle the sound, though I knew the voice from the other end would hum into her chest, spread to fill the air in her lungs, the reverberations echoing through her bones like ripples, like waves.

"They've found another body," she said. "Not clear if it's alive. I know you're not really up for much yet, but do you know if there was another of you? Could you try to ID it?"

That she called the body an "it" might have been a bad sign, but the mermaids called us all *it*, us humans. I looked at the others, and we nodded reluctantly, eager and frightened to return so close to the sea.

The body, when we found it, was pale all over, like waterlogged parchment, almost translucent, with long black hair spilling in all directions. The hand was the giveaway, seven thin broken fingers pointing toward us like a crooked accusation. That it had legs, half-covered in kelp, was meaningless; that part could even be glamour still clinging, to fall away with a touch like the pearls had crumbled into sand. But we all knew what seven broken fingers meant, and we recoiled, stumbled back up the beach.

They saw us move and drew back further, hands reaching for radios and nightsticks, and the officer in charge turned to us and growled something I didn't catch. One of us shook her head, long black hair swaying with the motion, but that one had yet to start following the conversation, and shook her head at every question, so I doubted it was an answer. I turned to look at our officer in the hope that she would translate.

She argued with the man in charge, and he returned and spoke more slowly. "You all backed off fast when you saw it," he said. "What is it? What does it mean?"

I did not want to bring bad news, did not even want to say the words aloud in human speech and make them true when their watery unreality was frightening enough.

It was another of us who spoke, smaller than me, and paler, with fragile blue-veined hands, her voice shaking almost as much as mine would have.

"You have not found a human," she said. I saw recognition and fear in their faces, like a superstition coming true. They had kept their distance from the body, but I saw them shift further away at her words. Perhaps they could not see the added fingers, the strangeness of the body; perhaps only we who had been there could see it. Still, even before we drowned, we had known better than to touch what the tide brought. "This is an execution."

"Being—" the man broke off, then shook himself. "Being beached like this, that's a punishment? What could be bad enough that they'd do this to their own?"

The woman who had spoken before had worn herself out of words, and bowed her head, silver curls sliding down to shield her face.

I said, "Murder," and when the police turned to face me, I added, "grievous insult." The other woman among us, the one who had shaken her head, said, "Freeing prisoners, or poisoning the waters."

"All right," our officer interrupted. "But what did this one do? Do you know?"

"Theft," we said in ragged chorus. "Release of precious property."

"We were not set free," said the first to speak, who had had hope.

"We were not sent as bait," said the second, who had had none.

"We were stolen," said the last of us, his voice frail and sick. "We were stolen, and they will want us back."

No one knew how the merfolk might try to draw us back into the sea. No one even knew how people were taken, why some disappeared and not others, whether we had been lured or forcibly dragged into the water. And we still didn't quite know why we had returned. I remembered the thin cold hands, broken now, draping my wrists in pearls. Perhaps our owners were meant to think we had taken their riches and swum for shore. Mermaid politics were complex, but escaped property would be shameful to anyone.

They had punished the transgressor, though, and now it only remained to see if they would feel the need to pull us back – whether there was any point in our returning to human life when we might vanish again any day. The police asked us question after question, but we hid even from the few memories we

had. There was music all through those memories, and the swallowing dark of
the sea, and we avoided the thoughts at all costs.

Days passed, though, and we were not pulled back into the water. There was no
reason to think we were safer at the precinct than home with our families, no
reason to hide our names for fear of giving false hope.

I had had, they told me, some family; we all had families, demanding our
release. Mine wasn't much of one – a sister, and a sister-in-law, an uncle who
lived far away. My sister and I were estranged, they said, and I rolled the word
on my tongue to feel the sound it made. *Estranged*, I had known that word, but
it had never before seemed to fit me so precisely.

We may have been estranged, but my sister and her wife came anyway. I
supposed that was what you did, for family. I had to meet with them alone –
the others had their own families to contend with.

As I waited in one of the interrogation rooms, our officer came by to remind
me again what their names were. "Marian," she said, "and Simone." She must
have seen the blankness in my face, because she added, "Marian is your sister."

I nodded shakily, and she left, returned with two women following. Marian
was my sister, I thought, I could remember that. If only I could tell which one
she was.

Once we were seated, the woman on the left said, "Geoffrey," staring like she
barely knew me. It took me a moment, caught as I was in remembering her
name, to realize that this was mine.

I said, "Marian," because I remembered it first, and then "Simone," dragged
awkwardly out of memory, but they only stared at me in disbelief. I glanced at
the officer, but her expression told me nothing except that I had probably not
switched their names.

"We just heard," the one who was probably my sister said, and I envied her
that *we*, trapped as I was in a room like a terrarium with none of the others.

She hadn't asked me a question, so I didn't answer, and I saw them both relax as if they had expected a fight. The other woman, the one who was probably Simone, said, "We would have come sooner, if we'd known."

They both looked expectant, now, so I said, "Yes."

"What *happened* to you?" Marian asked. I flinched at the rise in her voice and caught the table to stay in my seat. "You're not..." She turned to the officer. "Are you sure that's even him?"

"It'll be another day or so before the DNA results come back," the officer told her, "but yes, we believe so." I had seen what I used to look like, and how I looked now, painfully thin, my hair grown long. Most of all, I suspected, it was the lack of life they saw. Even as a photograph, my image had looked more alive than I did, its eyes alert and watching where mine seemed fish-dull and blank.

Simone touched Marian's hand, obviously reassuring, and then turned to me. "This must be as strange for you as it is for us."

I thought about it. "They tell me it's been three years since I last breathed air," I said, and somehow that surprised a laugh out of her.

"All right, you win," she said, smiling at me. "It's got to be a lot weirder for you."

When our families finally left us to regroup, we were all shaken. Marian had vibrated with relief and frustration, exhausting to be around. One of us, the silver-haired woman – her name might have been Claire – had settled on the narrow lobby couch with a hand on another of our shoulders. Daniel—David?—trembled under her grasp. He was younger than the rest of us, I thought, and his father had come to see him.

I sat beside Claire as we waited for the fourth of us to return. She set a hand on my shoulder, gently, as she had on David's, but removed it when I twisted away. A door across the room opened, and the last of us came out, Padma, from a meeting with almost a dozen relatives and a young man who stood apart and watched her family with blank eyes.

She sat on the lounge chair next to us and watched them go, then murmured, "Our parents were hoping we would get engaged." She nodded toward the young man. "That's what they tell me." She didn't seem happy or sad. She added, in a reluctant, baffled voice, "I had thought... I thought I liked..."

I looked up at her, saw remembered fear in her distant gaze, and offered, "Women?" so she wouldn't have to say it.

She shook her head—tilted it side to side, really—in lieu of answering. I decided, after a moment, that she probably meant yes.

A few days later, they sent us home, assuming if we had not been dragged back into the water yet, we were safe enough for now. No one said that if the merfolk came, the police might be helpless against them in any case. They had been taking one or two of us a year for as long as we could remember – and from other coastal towns – and no one knew exactly how they did it. Scientific missions here came back without data, their recordings static, their memories blurred. The few photographs that survived were as convincing as the Loch Ness monster to anyone who lived inland: enough to bring us plenty of tourists, but telling us nothing new. On land, mermaids seemed not to exist, beyond a few haunting notes when they sang, beautiful and inhuman as whale song.

Given that we were the first to return, no one knew quite what would happen to us – whether we would survive on land, whether we would return to the sea. With nothing more the police could do, our families made arrangements to bring us together again at the end of two weeks, as a sort of support group. When they were all ready, the officers drove us home.

The trip to the house was brutal, cramped in hard bucket seats in the back of a police car. David sat beside me, anxious and strained, hands curled helplessly in his lap. We huddled closer together when we reached his house until his father came to draw him from the car. We would see each other soon, but it still felt like being torn from my last mooring. The rest of the ride was a blur, alone and dislocated without the others.

Marian and Simone showed me their home – I couldn't tell whether we had been so estranged that I had never been there before, or if this was only another thing I had forgotten. It had wooden floors and warm colors on the walls, welcoming and unfamiliar after the sea and the station. They had made up the guestroom, and though neither of them seemed especially happy to see me, there was no mention of my being left to live on my own. If there had been any hesitation, it vanished, I thought, when they saw the way I touched the oven with hesitating fingers, only half-remembering how it worked.

Both of them had jobs to go to, during the day, as I gradually discovered. I realized that they were taking it in turns to stay home and watch me, try to talk to me, put a book in my lap or play me a song they thought I should remember.

Simone did this with care, as if I might break, but Marian shifted between fondness and impatience so quickly I found it hard to follow, resentment just beneath the surface. I wondered what we had done to each other, or if this was only the way she reacted to three years of grief come suddenly to an end, too much emotion finding only anger as an outlet, and me unable to respond in kind.

By the weekend I could make myself a sandwich, and turn on the radio. I had always been a little backward on technology, I thought, and now I had lost three years. Their computer was thinner than any I had ever seen, and they carried whole libraries in a single book. I stayed away from the electronics.

It had been nine days since the hotel room, fewer since the police station, but when David next tried to kill himself, none of us was there to stop him. We got the call from the hospital, and I sat in the dim living room wondering how we could have missed it. Somehow I had thought – surely we should have known?

I had heard no singing in the night, felt no urge to return to the water, but something had taken David and sent him bullet-wounded to the secure ward of the hospital.

"What was that about?" Simone asked, coming in, and her voice, careless and friendly, turned serious at my expression. "Hey," she said, softening, "tell me what's wrong. What happened?"

"David," I said carefully, and it occurred to me that she might not know who that was. "He came up with us," I ended up saying, and it sounded like a question.

"Sure," she said. "Asian? Wears sweater vests?"

I had noticed neither of these things, but I nodded. "He's at the hospital," I said. And, realizing it was too far to walk and I didn't know the way, "Do you think you could drive me?"

She grabbed her keys immediately, which was why Simone was my favorite. She waited until we were in the car and already moving to ask me what had happened. That was another reason.

"I don't know," I admitted as we drove. "I think—they said something about a gun." I didn't tell her he'd shot himself; I could hardly believe it myself. I no longer wanted to die, quite, but if I had, I knew down deep that I would have wanted to drown.

I froze at the thought, suddenly too stiff to move. I would have wanted to drown. I would have wanted... I had wanted... There was surf roaring in my ears, and an echo of singing, and my hands reached for the door as if it would open to the spill of water.

"*Geoffrey*," Simone said, and hit the brakes, and I didn't know if it was the no-longer-quite-mine name or the jolt of the car stopping that shook me out of it, but I clenched my hands into fists to stop the tremors and took deep, gasping breaths.

"Everything is fine," I said to her, and then couldn't stop saying it. "Everything is fine."

Simone drove to the hospital even faster after that. Because she thought seeing David would help, or just to get me out of the car, I didn't know. I stared at the signs by the side of the road, and the crooked trails of tar running along the asphalt. I could trace them with my eyes, watch the idle branching of them, and breathe, and think about nothing. Beside me Simone turned up the radio without seeming to think about it, the music entirely unlike siren song, and I remembered distantly what that had been like, when I was younger and happier, and adjusting the radio had been enough to make the singing fade unnoticed.

The hospital lobby was oddly elegant—it even had a fountain, and I was proud of myself for following Simone past it without a second glance. She knew David's last name, which was more than I did, and it was a relief to get into the elevator, just us and no sound of water.

Simone pushed the button, and I stared blankly at the elevator doors and tried not to think about anything, which worked fairly well until Simone spoke.

"They said he's on a secure floor," she said, and her voice was careful. I looked sideways at her, not sure what she meant, and she said, "Suicide risk."

"Oh," I said. "Yes." Her mouth tightened, which I suspected was disapproval, and I muttered, "Sorry, I should have said."

"You told me you didn't know what happened," she said, and there was something—resigned, maybe even familiar, in her tone. I had only been frightened of the word—suicide—couldn't bear to say it aloud. I had been asking myself the same question—what happened, what had made him do this. But it was possible that I—that Geoffrey—that I had often left things out.

"I meant," I began, and hurried on at the impatience on her face. "I meant I didn't know why he did it." I tried to think of a peace offering, and said, "The gun part was true." I was enough myself, now, to be distantly horrified by how small my voice sounded.

We rode the rest of the way in silence, but it wasn't an entirely unfriendly silence, and I had to hope that meant I'd been forgiven.

The visiting area was nice, soft couches and thick rugs on the floor. The nurses standing guard stayed out of our way, mostly, quiet against the wall. David was curled up in a yellow sofa, one with deep enough pillows that he seemed to sink into it completely. His head was bandaged, but that was all. I had to assume he hadn't been motivated enough, or steady-handed enough, to do himself much real damage. The singing in my head rose at the thought—perhaps he had heard the same music, and his hands had been clumsy with the call of the sea.

I refocused, and saw Padma sitting on the opposite couch, watching him. She wasn't moving, or speaking, and her fiancé and parents and a cousin or an aunt were all sitting around her talking softly between themselves, a little too animated, as if to make up for her silence.

Claire was in one of the chairs, and she looked up as we came in. I realized as she did that she'd been the only one in the room actually looking at David.

"Geoffrey," she said warmly. "And…"

"I'm Simone, Geoff's sister-in-law," Simone told her. "Claire, isn't it?"

Claire offered her a distant smile, already turning back to me, perhaps with the same feeling I had, that all other humans were too real, and only among ourselves could we speak comfortably. Perhaps she only had a purpose, one I served better than Simone. "He hasn't spoken yet," she said. "You should talk to him."

I nodded reluctantly, made myself approach, moving slowly so Simone could stay with me, the only person in the room who made me feel human.

"Hi, David," I said, and his eyes slid over to me and away, glazed and uninterested. "You want to talk about it?"

He looked at me again, this time incredulous, and I thought of how we had felt, coming out of the water, voiceless and strange. It seemed we had not all been getting our words back at the same rate. At home, Marian and Simone kept expecting me to talk back, to argue with them, like we must have fought before the water. Somehow that expectation pushed at my throat and my tongue. I remembered the way David's father had looked, possessive, protective, and wondered if his family avoided pressing him, if his house had been silent.

I reached out, moving slowly so he could dodge me, and touched his throat, remembering how my own throat had choked against speech. "Why did you do it this time?" I asked, and was horrified at myself even as it turned out to be the right question, as he finally focused with recognition and grief.

"Nobody understood me, before," he said softly, and I felt sick with bitter knowledge. I remembered that, what it had been to be young and not know what to do next; I could feel the family pressure that, even unspoken, must have pressed on every choice he made. "Now I don't even understand myself."

Back home, I wondered—would it happen to the rest of us? Had David been caught by the song of the merfolk trying to bring us back, or only lost in his own despair? I tried to remember my own fall into the sea, the singing that had drawn me in. But my thoughts grew hazy when I thought back, the beach, the pull into the water, all running together like water smearing the ink on a page.

I remembered that I had been miserable, and angry, but those seemed like such distant feelings compared to the numb isolation I felt now. Trying to bring it back made it hard to inhale, my ribs too tight, like I once might have thought it would feel to breathe underwater.

Underwater, breathing had been easy, though speaking was largely impossible. We fought, at first, but the mermaids couldn't seem to understand us as we shouted bubbles through the water, and they hurt us if we struggled when they used us as game pieces or toys. When they grew bored, they left us alone, so we drifted in the dark water. Somehow, however long I swam, I never reached the air, and the mermaids always found me. It was cold and suffocating and frightening, but there had been some relief in giving up, in the loss of control, in letting myself become a thing instead of a person. I had wanted that escape, before I entered the water. It had been the only relief in drowning – the only part that had turned out as I expected.

Looking back to that day, to my last time on land, I knew I had walked the shore several times before, trying to commit—even that last moment, I had not been sure. Had it been the same for the others? Looking for release, and finding the sea? Each time I visited the beach, the rhythm of the waves seemed closer to matching my heartbeat, the soft roll of water and harsh screams of the gulls a little more like someone calling my name.

There was music, though, that last time, sweet and achingly sincere, like a child making a solemn promise. I could feel the music as much as hear it, smooth, consuming, like water closing over my head. There was a rightness in the way the foam washed against my leg, in the solid weight of soaked jeans. I breathed in the smell of brine and safety.

Everything would be all right, in the water. If only my hands were steadier on the doorknob, the water rising against my legs as the music soaked into my skin.

"Geoff?"

I was standing in front of the screen door, looking through it at my sister. Marian was watching me like she had never seen me before—she seemed to wear that look constantly, though by now she had been seeing me for weeks.

At the moment, though, even I didn't quite know what was happening, except that it seemed even the memory of siren song could be enough to pull me in.

The reason the merfolk had never come to fetch us, I realized. It was all a game to them. They knew they would not have to leave the water. They knew that we would be hungry to return. They could wait, and sing, and laugh at our efforts to stay on land and make a life with the water always pulling us back.

Better not to think about it. And, better, perhaps, to forget the way the world had seemed before the beach, the gray indifference and bleakness of everything, the way I could hear the water calling because I had no energy to keep from listening.

"Hi," I said, and saw her shoulders relax, though she still watched me like I might slip past her into the night. Padma stood behind her, and it was a surprising relief to see someone like me. I focused on her and said, "Welcome," and felt some of my tension ease.

"Geoff," Marian said, and I watched her decide not to interrogate me in front of company. "It's...good to see you. Look, Simone told me about your friend, and I thought you might like to have one of the others over, support each other."

I didn't say that Claire was the one who actually managed to support any of us, that she would have been a much better choice. It seemed like something I might have said, once. Now it took too much effort, and, thinking it through, I realized Marian had understood more than anyone else, to guess that spending time with another of us would help rather than hurt.

"Hi, Padma," I said dutifully, and thought how much better I felt just seeing someone I knew was like me, and I asked, "Marian, when does Simone get home?"

We ended up all having dinner together, and watching Padma watch my sister and her wife was a surprisingly effective antidote to the siren song still fading from my mind.

Padma talked about her family during dessert, and Marian, with what I was beginning to recognize as a familiar lack of tact, responded with something snide about arranged marriages.

"It isn't exactly arranged," Padma argued, soft-voiced but silencing them with the sheer fact that she was arguing. We didn't like conflict, coming out of the sea, where we had never dared express our will. "It could be, that's, you know, that's a little old-fashioned, but I wanted help finding someone. If I said no, not this man, they would find another."

Marian took a breath to say something, and I saw Simone shift in her seat, just slightly. Marian sank back quietly into her chair, as if this were a well-known signal, and Simone said, "It's lovely that your family cares so much about you."

Padma nodded, although she didn't seem entirely happy, and Simone asked her, gentle the way she sounded when she spoke to me, "Did you have someone else in mind?"

After a moment, Padma said, "Not exactly." She trailed off, looking hopefully between Marian and Simone.

Marian still looked blank, but I saw Simone's whole posture change, softening into understanding. "Have you told your parents?" she asked. Marian started as she got it, something in the way Simone moved or spoke making it obvious to her as Padma's body language had not. She threw me a startled look, as if wondering whether I had understood, and I hunched into my chair, not sure how I had surprised her.

When I came back into the conversation, Padma and Simone were talking about how to tell her mother, and I saw something between hope and resignation in Padma's face, at least an acknowledgement that hiding hadn't worked either. I wondered whether hiding had helped push her to sea, whether part of her had chosen the ocean over facing the truth.

"Make sure," Simone told her, "that they know this isn't just since the mermaids. But maybe they'll be relieved that it's only this. You know they've been worried sick."

Padma's smile was crooked, like she knew it wouldn't be that easy, but it was a smile, and when Simone offered to help her, she seemed sure she could do it alone. As she left, I told her, "We would come with you, any of us."

She blinked at me, then nodded. "I'll call you," she said, and ducked out the door.

"You knew," Marian said, when Padma was gone. "That's why you asked her to stay."

I shrugged, not sure whether her stare was an accusation. I knew Marian was still angry with me for things I could barely remember—things I was only beginning to guess. When we fought, I could hear the echoes of earlier conversations sometimes, that I was selfish, that I was manipulative, though I seemed to have too little voice or sense of self, these days, to manage either. In arranging dinner, though, I must have been falling into old patterns.

I took a breath to apologize, and as I did, I saw Simone about to speak, trying to head my sister off, perhaps. But Marian pushed on. "You—before you—before. You never approved."

I blinked at her, trying to remember. What I knew of my sister came mostly from now, through the waterlogged haze of drowning, but I pushed back into the half-remembered past before the ocean. Simone had been a matter of indifference, I thought, because I had not got on with my sister. It had never been the other way around.

"Well," I said cautiously, and neither of them interrupted me. "I don't... I don't think so, actually." I let myself drift back to the beach, and saw my own anger and my own loneliness, Marian only a distant figure failing to save me.

It must have looked like I had deserted her, turned on her when she came out, and I didn't quite know how to tell her I had only been too self-centered, too lost in my own unhappiness. "I don't remember anything like that."

Simone put a hand on Marian's shoulder, and I saw my sister's mouth twist like she was fighting not to cry.

"We just didn't get on, maybe," I offered, and that wasn't all of it, but it was a start. "And then we weren't there for each other." That had been the worst of it, I thought—how desperately we had needed each other, and how little we had done, how little we had understood each other. "I never cared who you dated."

I thought back to our high school days, and remembered a tall boy with greasy green-streaked blond hair and a glossy band T-shirt. I couldn't find his real name, but I remembered I had nicknamed him after whatever I'd been reading at the time, and said, "No, wait, there was the Jabberwocky. I hated the Jabberwocky."

Marian laughed, a startled, broken sound, and reached out to hug me, too rough and too hard. I leaned in anyway, pressed my face down into her hair. Simone put an arm lightly around us, and we stood there, one or all of us shaking, in the warm-lit hall of my sister's house.

It was a long drive to any of the beaches, and even then the road kept its distance from the water. The nearest access point was a cliff overlooking the sea, the edge only about twenty yards from the street. That was near enough that, as we pulled up in a soft crunching of gravel, I could see Claire sitting at the edge, staring down into the waves, just as the police had said when they asked us to talk her down. For anything less, I doubted Marian would have driven me so near the sea.

I crept closer, so as not to surprise Claire into a fall, but she turned and smiled at my approach.

"Of course they would call you when my daughter saw I was missing," she said, which explained the woman waiting in a dark blue car as we drove up. "I'm sorry. I just wanted to see."

"To see what, exactly?" I asked, sitting beside her. This close, the sound and smell of the ocean was almost overpowering. I didn't dare look down. Instead I focused on her face, watching me with the quiet confidence I remembered.

"I was happy enough before the call," she told me. "Not like you. But when I heard it, I thought that God was finally calling me back to him." She smiled, a little. "But we all came out again, so I must have been wrong, and it wasn't our time. We all have a new chance at life. Today, though, I just had to be sure that I was committed to a new beginning."

I stared at her, awkward. I said uncertainly, "You came here just to test yourself?"

Her smile widened. "I'm fine," she said proudly. "I don't even hear them anymore."

Behind us, someone approached and stopped a few yards away. I turned to see David waiting, swaying, ever so slightly, like the wind might blow him over.

Or like he was standing in a tide, I thought, moving with the waves, and I rose to set my hand on his shoulder. He stopped swaying at my touch, and refocused from the sea to my face.

"Rock music," I told him. He looked blank, but I went on determinedly. "Or pop, or opera, whatever you like. When you get home. Listen to something that isn't them."

Padma joined us, and I remembered that Claire wasn't the only one who had been worrying me. "What did your mother say?" I asked her, and she smiled, not entirely happily.

"She asked me if all of you were gay now," she admitted, faint laughter in her voice, and I tried to smile back. "She said she wants to find me a nice Indian girl like they found my brother, but she hasn't told my father, or my aunts and uncles, so... anything can happen."

Claire said, "Anything *can* happen." Padma shrugged, but her smile grew steadier.

"I'm going back to school," David told us, and we all turned, words spilling out of him as if he'd been storing them for weeks. "Community college, close to home. They've got counselors and I'm starting with just math and art – I would never have taken art before." He glanced up to see us watching, and looked quickly back down. "You guys could come over sometime if you want. My mom's family doesn't know what to do, so they keep sending movies to watch while I get better." His voice was strained with the effort of optimism.

"That sounds like fun," Claire told him. "My daughter, she went there, when she was your age. We could go talk to her sometime if you wanted."

David nodded hesitantly, and she set her hand on his shoulder. For a while we stood in familiar silence, just staring into the waves as if we might see our faces reflected in the water.

There was a flicker, the tip of a tail breaching the water, and the sun turned the gray fin brilliant with color, like light on a film of oil. The singing rose in my ears, and I breathed in the smell of the sea, and I could almost forget the fear and the pain, and Marian waiting in the car. Beside me, David stiffened, and I had to resist the music enough to grab his arm and keep him there, and that anchored me, somehow. On my other side, Padma leaned in, and Claire's hand brushed me as she put an arm around David's shoulders, and together we were enough to brace ourselves against the pull of the tide.

Eventually we left, returning to our cars, Padma detaching herself first to go back to her family. I turned to watch the others leave, the smell of the ocean still pulling at me, and I wished it could be easy to return.

I finally got in next to my sister. She grabbed my arm, briefly, hard, before returning her hand to the gear shift. I turned up the radio as we went home, Padma's car ahead of us and David and Claire following behind, and let the last traces of singing fade with the drumbeat. We pulled back onto the road, all of us, and headed together back toward home.

About the Authors

Franklin Ard is the Editor-in-Chief and publisher of Rogue Owl Press. He is a graduate of Clarion West Writers Workshop and the University of Southern Maine's Stonecoast MFA program. Prior to founding Rogue Owl Press, he served as Fiction Editor and Editor-in-Chief of *Oracle Fine Arts Review* and Managing Editor of *Stonecoast Review*. Franklin's fiction and poetry blurs many genres, from science fiction, fantasy, and mystery to magical realism and Southern gothic. Over the years, his writing has appeared in numerous venues, such as *Nightmare Magazine*, *Sherlock Holmes Mystery Magazine*, *Suspense Magazine*, and *Deep Magic*. He resides in Mobile, Alabama with his wife and son, where they enjoy the humid frog weather. Find him online at www.franklinard.com.

Elizabeth Beechwood is your typical scarf-knitting, bird-feeding tree hugger who lives on the fringes of Portland, Oregon. Her Pushcart-nominated fiction has been published in Nightscape Press's award-winning anthology *Nox Pareidolia*, Third Flatiron's *Hidden Histories*, Not a Pipe Publishing's *The Year of Publishing Women's Short Stories* series, and others. She earned her MFA in Popular Fiction at the University of Southern Maine's Stonecoast program, is an associate member of SFWA, and doesn't think that talking mountains are strange at all. Visit her at www.elizabethbeechwood.com .

Joseph Carro holds an MFA from Stonecoast at the University of Southern Maine. He coauthored the *Little Coffee Shop of Horrors* anthology and serves as Community Manager for Headless Hydra Press, a publisher of tabletop roleplaying game supplements. Most recently, he co-edited *After the Burn*, an anthology of post-apocalyptic short stories (Rogue Owl Press). Additionally, he has served as an editor and proofreader for the *Glyphs Productions* line of comic books since 2015 and has written for *itcherMag*. When not writing or editing, he can generally be found engaging in some sort of geeky/nerdy activity throughout the day. Oh, and he was also in a movie with Kelsey Grammer (and will say that every chance he gets). He currently resides in Woodford, Vermont inside the infamous Bennington Triangle, although he'll always be a Mainer at heart. Find him online at https://www.josephcarro.com.

Paul Carro was born and raised in Maine, where he was published at an early age in an anthology of Maine authors alongside one of his horror icons. After college, he left the lakes of Maine for the oceans of California, where he toiled for years in the film/TV industry before recently returning to his literary roots. A longtime comic book and horror nerd, he now writes novels featuring both his passions. When not writing, he can be found hiking all over California.

Shane R. Collins is the owner of Headless Hydra Press, a tabletop gaming company that creates accessories and supplements for roleplaying games. His work has appeared in *The Master's Review* in an issue that won the INDIE FAB Silver Medal for Best Short Story Collection. Shane lives in rural Vermont with his wife and their assorted pets and children.

Renee S. DeCamillis is a dark fiction/horror author and editor and the author of the psychological thriller/horror novella The Bone Cutters. She is currently a novel editor for Wicked House Publishing and is a former editorial intern for Crystal Lake Publishing. Her short fiction appears in *After the Burn* (Rogue Owl Press), *Wicked Women* (NEHW Press), *Northern Frights: The Journal of Horror Writers of Maine*, *Deadman's Tome*, *Siren's Call eZine*, and *The Other Stories Podcast*. Her poetry appears in *The Horror Writers Association Poetry Showcase* Volume IV, and she has a comic book forthcoming through Phi 3 Comics. She is also a former gravedigger; she can get rid of a body fast without leaving a trace, and she is not afraid of getting her hands dirty. Renee lives in the woods of southern Maine with her husband, their son, and a house full of ghosts. Visit her online at reneesdecamillis.com, as well as on Facebook (Renee S. DeCamillis Author), Instagram (@renee_s._decamillis), and Twitter (@ReneeDeCamillis).

Devin Gaither lives on the Mar-Lu Ridge of the Blue Ridge Mountains in Jefferson, MD with her dog, Pippa. She is a Business Analyst by trade and is also the Aerial Arts Program Director for Luna Aerial Dance & Performing Arts in Frederick, MD. Additionally, she enjoys making time for creating stained glass artwork (Mar-Lu Glassworks) and laboring over math puzzles. Devin earned her MFA in Creative Writing from Stonecoast at the University of Southern Maine. In 2022, she was selected as one of the Top 50 Young Professionals Under 40 by the Frederick County Office of Economic Development.

Rachel Halpern is a graduate of the Alpha Workshop for Young Writers and the Stonecoast MFA program. At her day job, she writes and edits children's books, from original picture books like *Unicorns Have Bad Manners* to licensed books for Disney, Marvel, Sesame Street, and more. Her short fiction for adults has appeared in *Beneath Ceaseless Skies*, *Daily Science Fiction*, and *Liminal Stories*. She also helps administer the Alpha Young Writers Workshop. Rachel lives in the Chicago area with her parents and a cuddly, slightly evil dog named Grendel. In her free time, she enjoys doodling, watching home renovation shows, sharing octopus facts, and taking pictures of interesting clouds.

Derek B. Hoffman is a graduate of the Stonecoast MFA program at the University of Southern Maine. He is a freelance author, editor, and tutor. For over thirty years, he's authored works ranging from slipstream poetry, to stories supporting abused children, to inspiring young adult and transmedia odysseys. He also leverages his writing skills as CEO of Veracity by Design, LLC, where he composes, edits, and designs award-winning websites, translates technology into understandable user tutorials, and publishes in peer-reviewed medical journals as part of research projects performed at leading universities. During the day, he resides with his wife and three boys in Austin, TX. At night, he ventures into the fifth corner of his mind, crafting an ever-growing collection of multiverse tales and adventures. Find him online soon at www.derekbhoffman.com.

Rebecca McKenna teaches English literature and writing to high school students, whom she finds quite interesting and engaging. She has been a professional mapmaker for almost two decades and has spent a lifetime loving maps and creating them for her enjoyment. A graduate of the Stonecoast MFA Program at the University of Southern Maine and a charter member of the Tiny Chair Writing Cooperative, she lives in eastern Maine with her husband and misses her kids, who have grown up.

Karen Menzel (née Bovenmyer) earned an MFA in Creative Writing: Popular Fiction from the University of Southern Maine. She teaches and mentors students at Iowa State University. She has served as the Assistant Editor of the *Pseudopod Horror Podcast Magazine*. She is the 2016 recipient of the Horror Writers Association Mary Wollstonecraft Shelley Scholarship. Her poems, short stories, and novellas appear in more than 40 publications and her first novel, *Swift for the Sun*, debuted from Dreamspinner Press in 2017. Visit her online at http://karenbovenmyer.com

John Christopher Nelson's youth was split between ninety-four acres of chaparral in East County San Diego and a mining town in the Nevada high desert. He lives with his cat, Proulx. He earned his BA in American Literature from UCLA and is a graduate of the Stonecoast MFA in Creative Writing. His work can be found in *DUM DUM Zine*, *The Real Story*, *The New Guard*, *Chiron Review*, *Able Muse*, *Indicia*, *The Matador Review*, *BE ABOUT IT Zine*, and elsewhere.

Sarah Parke holds an MFA in Popular Fiction from the University of Southern Maine's Stonecoast MFA Program. She has been published in *The Writer* and *Speculative City*, and her fiction plays with alternate historic timelines and magical circumstances. Earlier in her own timeline, she spent six years helping authors polish their prose as an acquiring editor at a regional trade publisher. She currently works at Wesleyan University where she writes stories about the campus community for the magazine and newsletter. A New England native, Sarah lives in Connecticut with her husband, Sean.

Cristina Perachio's stories have appeared in *Narrative*, *EPOCH*, *Zyzzyva*, and more. In 2013, she was named a finalist in *Narrative's* 30 Below Contest. *Narrative* also named her story "Nightstands" a Top 5 Story of the Year in 2014. She received an MFA from the University of Southern Maine's Stonecoast program. Perachio lives in South Philadelphia with her husband and three-year-old daughter.

Richard Squires is a writer, editor, and musician living in New Jersey. His fiction has appeared in *North American Review*, *The MacGuffin*, *Jewish Literary Journal*, *BigCityLit*, Rogue Owl Press's post-apocalyptic anthology *After the Burn*, and other places, and he has book reviews forthcoming in *American Book Review*. Richard is the owner of LifeStory (www.LifeStoryMemoir.com), a company that writes people's memoirs for them, creating legacies their families cherish for generations. A proud member of the Tiny Chair Writing Cooperative, Richard earned his MFA from Stonecoast at the University of Southern Maine.

Genevieve Williams's work has appeared in *Asimov's, Strange Horizons,* and several anthologies. She lives in Seattle.

Acknowledgements

The editors and writers wish to extend our sincerest thanks the following backers for their support of the initial Kickstarter campaign, which made possible the production of this book:

A. B. Archambault, Aaron Foster, Aarron Kemp, Ace, Adam "Chili" Stevens, Adam Pierzchala, Alexis Hilgert, Andrea Tatjana, Ann Choate, Arnar Benjamín Kristjánsson, Ashleigh F., Bess Turner, Brandy Pastore, Brian Hadley, Cameron Jones, Carla Saint-Paul, Carolyn Poncelow, Cathy Green, Cerulean Grey, Chad Bowden, Chelsea Persen, Chester Bomont, Christopher L Corbett, Colleen Feeney, Conor Neilson, Courtney Behrens, Daniel McCullough, Dave Holets, David Earl Collins, Deborah Moylan, Devin Gaither, Diego Hernandez, Donald A. Brennan, Dylan Humphreys, E. A. Gerber, Ed Matuskey, Eduardo Angel Rodriguez, Edward P. Abbott, Eileen Gettle, Emily Ahl, Emily Mohler, Emily Rousell, Emmy Teague, Ernie, Esapekka Eriksson, Finley Ymir, Hatteras Mange, Howard Blakeslee, Jace Chretin, James Barron, Jan Rasch, Jay Bower, Jessica and Joshua Hengel, Jim and Rhonda Lancaster, Joey Oconnor, Joey Scotch, John Howie Jr., John Liang, Johnny B., Joshua Hair, Joshua Krzych, Kaitlin Henry, Kayla O'Hare, Kenneth and Kathi Dodd, Killer Kev's From Outer Space, Kimberly Wescott, Lauren Weston, Lisa M. Gargano, Laurie LaDuke, Lou Tambone, Lynn Miner Carroll, M.G. Davis, Malfor, Mark DePreta, Martin B., Mary Ellen Durkin, Mary Gaitan, Matt Cowan, Melanie B., Michael Axe, Michael Nachtigal, Michael Whitmer, Mindy Geres, MLtheimpossible, Marshall D.M. Dillon, Nicholas Stephenson, Nijeara "Ny" Buie, Niki Coppola, Nova C., Olivia Havens, Paul and Laura Trinies, Paul Hoffman, Pyndan and Roxy Wulffe, Randy P. Belanger, Rebecca Howard, Rob McNeil, Rob Russell, Ronald H. Miller, Ronald Olaf, Rune, Ruth Lucas, Ruth Ireland, Ryan Meyer, Ryan Scott James, Sabine Blanchette, Samantha Landström, Scott Casey, Scott Chisholm, Scott Shields, Sylvia Rogers, Takeo Endo, Thomas Scholtes, Tiffany Smith, Tiffany VanWagenen, Tony Pisculli, Travis Keller, Tyler "Mr.Muliverse" Shepard, WarOrdos, William Botta, Windi LaBounta, Yancey Drake, Mandi Armstrong, Zack Fissel

Rogue Owl Press wishes to thank:

The authors for their creativity, inspiration, hard work, time, and belief in the potential of this project.

Stephanie Evers Ard for her love, encouragement, and guidance throughout this project.

Rebecca McKenna for her feedback and steadfast support throughout the entire book production.

Tiny Chair Writing Cooperative for the motivation, humor, and incredible friendship.

Hanscom Construction for generously allowing the use of their large-scale printing facilities.

About the Publisher

Rogue Owl Press is an independent publisher specializing in *startling stories*. We're drawn to writing that is entertaining, exciting, and captivating, while simultaneously powerful, complex, and genre-bending.

Writing may be considered startling for many reasons. While dark fiction such as horror comes to mind as indicative of the most viscerally startling of all fiction, writing may be equally startling in its raw honesty about the human condition.

Startling stories may also take the form of a thrilling tale that leaves the reader breathless by the finale, or a story that contemplates existential reckoning. Likewise, a poem may startle the reader with its aesthetic beauty and poignancy. A story may be startling in its fantastical worldbuilding or the vividness of its characters and their own emotional lives. A work may even startle the reader through the avenue of absurd humor.

In short, we publish writing that stops us, as readers, in our tracks—that jolts us in astonishing ways. We seek creative work that makes us ponder the universe from a new angle and provides an opening to fall into another reality. In the words of Jack Kerouac, we want to feel everything all at once.

Startling stories transcend any one genre, style, or storytelling philosophy. A startling work of art may color within the lines of genre conventions, or it may blur those lines—or defy expectations altogether. But such works all have one thing in common: their beating hearts. Startling stories are alive.

Find Rogue Owl Press online at www.rogueowlpress.com.